THE CIRCUS

THE CIRCUS

DREW SMITH

HUTCHINSON
LONDON

© Drew Smith 1997

The right of Drew Smith to be identified as the author
of this work has been asserted by Drew Smith in accordance with
the Copyright, Designs and Patents Act 1988
All rights reserved

1 3 5 7 9 10 8 6 4 2

This edition first published in 1997 by Hutchinson

Random House (UK) Limited
20 Vauxhall Bridge Road, London SW1V 2SA

Random House Australia (Pty) Limited
20 Alfred Street, Milsons Point, Sydney,
New South Wales 2061, Australia

Random House New Zealand Limited
1 Poland Road, Glenfield, Auckland 10, New Zealand

Random House South Africa (Pty) Limited
Endulini, 5A Jubilee Road, Parktown 2193, South Africa

A CIP record for this book is available from the British Library

Papers used by Random House UK Limited are natural,
recyclable products made from wood grown in sustainable forests.
The manufacturing processes conform to the environmental
regulations of the country of origin.

ISBN: 0 09 180221 0

Typeset in Great Britain by Deltatype Ltd

Printed and bound in Great Britain by
Creative Print and Design (Wales) Ebbw Vale

To Sue, Oliver and Grace

AUTHOR'S NOTE

Long ago I decided I would only write a novel if I had something to say. I wanted to write a work of pure fiction. The Hôtel Martinez is real enough, as are many of the background details, but even if the characters share the passions and enthusiasms of many people involved in the London restaurant kitchen renaissance of the last ten years, they are not real.

Eating and cooking are so intensely personal that I needed a structure that was not prejudicial. Hence the fairy story. And with the fairy story the darker side of some of the characters came out as a way of expressing the very intimacy of our relationship with food, land and the way we live.

Let the Circus begin.

Drew Smith
Foxley, August 1996

I

THE BEAUTIFUL BOOKKEEPER'S
FIRST SOUP

JOJO COLTRANE WAS rich, elegant, quick . . . and cursed. Even in this town where most of the women were good looking, the waiter's eyes lingered admiringly for a few moments longer than they should have, taking in the sassy, coltish hips, the swell of the slightly overlarge breasts, the tumble of curled, groomed auburn hair, the cut of the worn, dusty Versace jacket, with a thumbed copy of the poems of Jules Supervieilles in the side pocket. She ordered for one. Women like her were never alone for long in this town.

Jojo was not alone. The spell was with her. It always was. Not in any obvious way, but there right enough, even in this anonymous train station of a brasserie, a presence around her, like a handkerchief overlooked in the pocket from the last time she wore the jacket.

The spell toyed with her. It put up walls. It shoved her through doors. It demanded things. It was insistent about the geometry of her life. It was there all the time, like the taste of too much rosemary in a sauce.

A spat of a storm snuck grimly over the beach, hurling stair-rods down on the groomed sands. The tall palms trembled. The heavy leaves swirled, then the hail smashed loudly on to the tin roof above Jojo's head. A gush of water burst through the ceiling cornicing and spurted on to a corner table.

'*Attention!*' the waiter cried, grabbing a silver ice bucket from the next table and positioning it under the spouting torrent.

Sears of blue lightning flashed down the Croisette. Jojo watched two boys on a moped drive up on to the pavement and park under the awning of the next café to get out of the rampant downpour. She sipped her coffee calmly. She could wait. She had time.

The spell cast at her christening had been incubating all those years. It was subtle. This storm was not its style. It was not showy or apocalyptic like that. It was devious, more like the seemingly innocuous first bite of the mosquito that brought malaria, or the sweet drunken coupling with a syphilitic boy.

'It will pass,' the waiter said, returning with a smile. She could hardly hear him against the crashing of the storm.

He laid a wicker basket of crescent-shaped croissants, the oblong *pains au chocolat* and long halves of baguette on the table in front of her. Jojo dipped the bread into the coffee and sucked, then went back to flicking through the hieroglyphics of the fat red guide book in search of a room.

Now she could be what she pleased. And it pleased her to take a new name to fit her exile. Little personal pleasures mattered now. They were all that was left.

In English Jojo had always sounded a bit plump and bouncy, but the French shortened it into a couple of warm, urgent rhymes. She liked that. Changing her name felt like restyling her hair. Josephine seemed so long and Napoleonic and old-fashioned. It took an age to be introduced to anyone as they stuttered over the syllables as if they were three names: Jo-Geoff-Jean.

She scrolled through the grey and pink listings and chose the hotel with the most pink castles next to its name.

'*C'est bien, mademoiselle? Ça vous plait?*' the waiter asked. He spun out the syllables – ma-dum-oie-zelle. His eyes were on her.

The storm was letting up. Big blotches of blue were reappearing in the sky, and the long, thin puddles on the road were stilling.

She could still feel the crease of that dune along her back from where she had slept on the beach. She needed to shower and clean up. She nodded and asked for the bill.

On the Croisette, the late morning sun was hurrying back through the clouds, casting its yellow light on the clean wet greys of the road. Its gentle, early summer heat evaporated the running water in the gutters, sending up small clouds of mist.

The Hôtel Martinez was grand in the way that nothing seemed to have happened to it, or, if it had, it had all been a long time ago and all that was left were its balustrades and good manners. There was a flurry of activity outside, as Jojo walked up. Two men in green uniforms with gold braid were using brooms to divert the streams of water away from the hotel's circular porch, back on to the side street.

She booked the suite for a month, and paid cash, passing a thick wodge of francs on to the counter.

'There is no need, mademoiselle,' the concierge said, eyeing the dirty notes, unused to seeing anything so brash.

'I prefer it. This way you know I am serious.'

'Where are your bags?'

She shrugged. She would have to get some.

The suite was large without being ostentatious. In her mind, Jojo hung the spell up in the empty wardrobe and allowed herself a few days to sprawl out on her large bed between trawls of the cafés and swims in the sea and the hotel pool. In the late afternoon she flirted with the men behind the market stalls; bought some new clothes, and ate formal, solitary dinners in the hotel restaurant. Finally, she judged herself acclimatised enough to make an approach.

She knew his name from the gawky fat type on his lapel badge. Christian was a sweet, middle-aged, moustached mouse of a man who scampered around the hotel looking for crumbs to tidy. He took a pride in the trifles of life. No whim was too much trouble for him.

'What can you do?' he asked, unsure of how to respond to a guest looking for work. Perhaps she had run out of money? No, she had paid in advance. She still had three weeks of credit. Jojo was pleased she had so obviously rattled his sang-froid.

'I can do the books. I am good with money. But what I want to do is to learn about *la cuisine*.'

He studied her carefully. She was such an unusual guest. Young, clever, beautiful, sophisticated, alone.

'Are you sure there is nothing wrong?' he enquired.

'No. I just want to learn to cook.'

'This is not a school, mademoiselle.'

'That is why I want to work.'

He was reluctant to refuse. He could let her do the books. They were always a chore. She would tire of it quickly. Hesitatingly, he offered her the accountant's booth by the kitchen. It was a tall, three-sided wooden box with a worn desk top and a stool. The open side looked out on the kitchen, which whirred like a machine in front of her, hissing and bubbling, rattling and steaming, in need of constant attention.

'I'm not sure it is you,' said Christian.

'It will be.'

'Mademoiselle, if you don't like, you can always stop.'

'I will like.'

The books were a mess. In fact she had never seen accounts in quite such disarray. She was ruthless. Christian was impressed. She went back one year, two years, three years to compare prices. She tidied each page. It was easy, unstressful work. She made little savings, which pleased him.

She was used to handling money. The spell had made her rich. Well, it would have, wouldn't it. That was the sort of thing it liked to do – to make her life different from anyone else's. Her father had left her the estate, or rather his lawyers had, when he had reached the point where he was no longer deemed responsible. She had invested the legacy. It had grown quickly into a lot of money. The stockbroker said she had been unusually fortunate. Luck, of course, had had nothing to do with it.

Getting into the kitchen was more difficult. She pressed Christian. She nagged.

'Really, to do this properly, I would have to do the shopping. How else can I tell if the prices are right? Won't you ask Marcel for me?'

Marcel, the head chef, was less used to dealing with guests.

'Why do I want a woman in my kitchen? There has never been a woman in this kitchen.'

'She wants to learn,' Christian replied. 'Her books are first class. She knows the menu. She has eaten every dish you have cooked.'

'Because she is a good guest does not mean she is a good cook.'

'Humour her. Give her a trial, and when she fails, then it will be all right, you can say she does not have the talent. She will get bored, she will give up.'

Jojo could overhear them talking about her from where she sat. Christian, small, dapper and suited,

5

Marcel, a bull of a man in his whites and looming toque. The stool was puritanically French and erect and made her back ache. Her French was good enough to pick up the gist. They thought she didn't understand.

'She will be upset. It is man's work.'

'Tell her then. Ask her. Be nice to her. If she wants to do it. Talk to her at least.'

Marcel peered round towards her through the glass and waved at her to come over. He opened a bottle of Bandol and offered her a glass:

'Why do you want to do this cooking?'

'I could save you more money if I understood better what you do.'

'It is for men, French men, at that.'

'There have been great women cooks.'

'Who?'

'There must have been.'

'Can you cook?'

'Yes.'

'What do you cook? Yorkshire pudding?' he mocked.

'Yes.'

'I never had one I liked.' He stared at the floor in mid sentence, gazing at her new turquoise shoes. He shrugged.

'If you insist, I will give you a trial. One day only. It will be hard. You must do what I say. You will not like parts of it. But that is what it is. If you don't like it, you don't like it and we can forget the whole thing, and you can go back to the books or to being our most valued and charming guest.'

The whole idea was both charming and ridiculous, but he might condescend to spend a little time to amuse her.

'I will like it,' Jojo said.

Perhaps the spell had also made her beautiful. Or, more

likely, it had picked on her because she was good-looking. In its conniving way it needed someone who would have an easy effect on other people, drawing them to it and to its power.

Perhaps, if only to spite it, the humbleness of the kitchen appealed to Jojo – to be a part of that machine, to know what was inside those pots and cauldrons, what the heat was doing to those ingredients as they cooked, and where the machine needed oil and tending to make it work. And more than that, more than being a woman among these men, being English among these French, was the sense of renewal, of touching and feeling those things that had so recently shared the same earth. To make something out of nothing. She was walking through the gates of a new world, to a place where she had no memories, no baggage, no guilt, a world where perhaps even the spell might forget her, for a while.

She slipped quietly into the little booth with her receipts and her pencils, and waited to present herself, until the afternoon, when the other chefs had gone.

'You need some clothes. You are too smart. Get a tunic and a hat. Your hair must not get in the way. Show me your hands.'

Marcell grasped her by the wrists. Her hands were slender in his fat palms.

'Keep them clean. Wash them before we start and after each job. I do not want them to smell of fish when we start to make the soup.'

She nodded dutifully. The induction was intoxicating. She didn't notice him as a man, only as a symbol of the religion of cuisine. He was her front door. In the same way, she didn't notice the other chefs as boys, or men. They were fellow initiates.

She went to wash and dress. When she returned, Marcel had humped two huge nets, one full of onions and one full of shallots, on to the preparation table. He had a knife in his hand.

'I will show you how to do this, then you can practise. You can have the whole bag. First you do the onions. Then you do the shallots.'

She nodded. The onion was as big again as his hand. The knife flashed in the air.

'You take the top and the bottom off, you stripe the side so the skin peels away – and be sure not to waste anything here, just take the skin off. Then you cut across in half and – be careful here you do not cut yourself – then . . . you save the skins in one pile, to colour the stock. Nothing is wasted, you understand me. Nothing.'

The knife became a machine in his hand as it diced the onion lengthways and then sideways.

'You understand, I want very neat little square dice. Pretty squares.'

In five seconds he had reduced the handsome brown globe to a glittering heap of white shards.

'Take your time. There is only you and me for the next couple of hours. No one will see you. Do not be embarrassed. When you have done that, call me and we will cook something for the chefs' dinner. They can be your judges.'

He smiled and walked away, leaving her alone with her onions. She grasped the knife and felt the silkiness of the brown skin of the onion. Close up it looked so beautiful.

She began clumsily.

The smell was hot and invasive. Tears poured down her cheeks. She could taste the salt on her lips. The insides of her nostrils were inflamed, a bush fire through salt marshes. Her sense of smell was being assaulted. He wouldn't beat her like this. Jojo stopped and washed her face, then went back to her task. Three onions. Four onions. Five onions. The tears started again, but this time not so badly. She was drying up. Six onions. Seven

8

onions. She had walked into a cloud of hotness. Eight onions. She stopped again and dried her face, then restarted. She was in a trance. The heat of the onions destabilised her. The concentration of mind over hands was like a mantra. Twenty-eight onions. Chop. Chop. Forty-two onions. Her movements were robotic.

When she reached the last, she was almost sad they were all gone. She moved quickly over to the shallots, intent on keeping the trance going. There was healing in this heat. The onions seemed old and primitive compared to these silverine purple-fleshed aristocrats. Their smell was different, more perfumed. She had to concentrate harder because they were smaller. The incisions had to be more accurate. She was glad there was nobody to see her cry, but if there had been, it would not have mattered. She had been enjoined in another world, a world of her own hands and fingers, the gleaming knife, the lines and curves and shades of blues and browns like a sunset on the surface of the shallot.

He startled her.

'Let us see what you have done. You can stop now.'

Her senses were rimmed in red, around the eyeball, down into her throat, as if she had become an etching in red. She no longer responded like a woman. She was a cook. She was proud of her tears.

'You have not done much of this before, have you? Do you want to stop now?'

She shook her head.

He pointed to the onions in their raggle-baggle, luminescent, worm-like heap.

'You can put those away. I never use them except in soup.'

'Why did you make me peel them, then?'

'To see.'

'To show me how tough it is?'

'No. We waste nothing here. And to show you the difference. The shallot is beautiful. It is to my cooking what garlic is to peasant cooking – much gentler, more charisma, more difficult to handle, more difficult to cook, you understand? If you cook it too much it becomes bitter. You will see.'

He was placatory now, not judgemental. His big, booming voice had a gentle lilt to it she hadn't noticed before. He was trying to put her off, but she wasn't going to let him. Whatever he said, she would do.

'Do you know how to make soup?'

'Everyone knows how to make soup.'

'Then you will make a soup. But I will help you. You can use the chicken stock. There will be four stages, so you cannot go too far wrong. Remember, cooking is just a lot of very simple jobs done one after the other. If you do them properly then you achieve a magical transformation. If you get one of them wrong . . . disaster.'

He moved to the stove.

'First we braise the shallots in some oil. Be careful they do not catch in the pan. Go on, take the pan. We have not got all day. We learn as we go.'

She heaved up the heavy pan and slid it over the gas. The shallots tumbled in, spitting as they hit the puddle of golden oil.

'Take a wooden spoon and mix them well. Keep the heat down. Keep watching while we do the vegetables. You have done enough chopping. I will do the carrots, the turnips, the celery, the white of the leek.'

As he recited the list his hands worked over each vegetable in turn and passed it across, ready to go into the pan.

'The shallots should have just started to give up their juices by now.'

He peered into the pan to check.

'Put the chicken stock in first.'

She looked at the huge vat of stock alongside her pan. There was no way she could lift it when it was full. It was another test. She reached for a small pan and ladled out the juices.

'Pour it in slowly and turn up the heat so it is simmering. As soon as it simmers put the vegetables in – but not before it is simmering, or the vitamins will be lost. Use the *haricots* from lunch. They are cooked. They can go in now. There is no harm in a soup for them to break up a little.'

They waited until the bubbles appeared.

'Now we prepare the more delicate vegetables. You can do these while the others cook a little more. Quarter the mushrooms. Check the watercress over and wash it. Peel the tomato.'

She looked up quizzically

'Put it in the soup for ten seconds and then scoop out again. The skin will come off easily. The lettuce wants to be washed and chopped. The cucumber must be peeled and diced. And the beans must be topped and tailed. Make them pretty or the boys will give you a horrible time. They do not like ugly lumps of vegetable in their soup. They can be more fussy than the customers. They like them as small jewels.'

'In the restaurant you purée this soup.'

'Not for the boys. They prefer the vegetables whole. So do I. There are so many interesting flavours. I like to see what I am eating. For the restaurant the cinema is not to know. Here it is to understand.

'Lastly you make a *pistou*. You do know how to make a *pistou*, don't you?'

Marcel disappeared and she was alone again, tending her saucepan. Handling the gentler vegetables and smelling them revived her senses. The warm smell of the chicken stock gave her confidence.

She went over to the spice section to get herbs. She gathered her garlic cloves and a handful of basil. There was chilli in the drawer. Small spindly red pods. She took one.

In the mortar she pummelled the garlic on the cold, hard marble, and battered and tore the leaves of basil and then bathed them in the burnt-grassy yellow oil as though she was applying a soothing balm.

She could hear men's voices gathering in the dining room. She turned the heat down, gathered the plates and spoons and knocked on the door.

Five chefs were seated at the table. She put a bowl in front of each of them in turn, and a spoon.

'The beautiful bookkeeper's first soup,' Marcel announced proudly.

Jojo came back bearing her soup in a tureen. She put it on the table. Marcel grabbed the ladle and helped everyone. The men shared round the grated Parmesan, greedily scattering the cheese over the green surface.

'Jojo, you have not laid a place for yourself,' Marcel said. 'Get yourself a plate and sit down. Today you are a chef. You eat with us. You have worked hard. You deserve to eat well. And if it is no good then you will have to eat it as well as us.'

By the time she returned, they were all quiet. They had been talking about her.

'What did you put in here, Jojo?'

Jean François, Marcel's number two, was fishing in his bowl with the end of his spoon.

'There is something here, a little unusual.'

'Unusual?'

'A little fire in here. Perhaps life in England is a little too cold for you and you wanted to warm us up a little?'

'The chilli?'

The men erupted in laughter.

'You don't like it?'

'It's different.'

'In England, Indian restaurants use it a lot.'

Marcel intervened.

'It is not bad. It is not too much.'

'You could cut the vegetables a little more prettily,' said Jean François.

'It is not a bad soup,' said Marcel.

'For a bookkeeper it is a very good soup,' said Jean François, breaking himself a chunk of bread off the communal loaf.

She had never had such a compliment. They all bent their heads over the soup and ate.

Jojo had not arrived at the kitchens of the great Hôtel Martinez completely unprepared for a career as a cook. Her mother had not been good with children. The young Josephine had spent much of her pre-school years sitting in the basement kitchen listening to their cook, Ellie, chatting away about this, that and anything else that came into her head. Her early years had been filled with the smells of cooking. Ellie would find jobs for her to do. Mixing the butter and cocoa, rolling out the pastry, cutting out the tart shapes.

Most of all Josephine liked to help with the bread. The last job of the day was always to mix the yeast and flour for tomorrow. The first job, which Ellie usually kept back for her, to her delight, was to knock this bulbous, wheaty, yeasty-smelling living animal back into manageable shape for mixing and kneading.

Bread was Ellie's litany. She baked a different loaf every day of the week – a milk loaf on Monday, a malt loaf on Tuesday, her special bloomer on Wednesday, wholemeal on Thursday, Frenchie on Friday, farmhouse on Saturday, cottage on Sunday. She kept a different tin for each one. They hung like the calendar from the shelf. Beside each one was a tubby paper bag filled with different flours. Ellie arranged her cooking and most of her life around making bread.

'Flour is the stuff of life, nature's miracle,' she would say, letting the dry grains run through her hands. She would then scoop out a pile for Josephine to make into shapes down the other end of the long wooden table that dominated the kitchen. Josephine's early perceptions were moulded as surely as the dough that the old Cockney woman pummelled and stretched into shape. Along with this came a sense of comfort in making things and the companionship of working closely with someone else. Once Josephine put her whole face right into the mound of soft flour and sneezed so it went everywhere. The old woman just laughed and wiped her clean.

'You're a one, you are, Josephine, a real one, that's for sure.'

Josephine was nearly seven before these contented interludes were discovered. Her mother descended unexpectedly into the kitchen. She rarely ventured downstairs. The basement was for servants. Ellie and Josephine were up to their elbows in dough. Her mother thought Josephine was having lessons with the nanny. But the nanny had got fed up trying to coax Jojo out of the warmth of the kitchen and was liable to skip off in the afternoons, leaving Ellie in charge. Josephine's mother exploded.

'Stop this at once, Mrs P. You are teaching this girl to be a servant.'

'We are only making bread, ma'am, if you please.'

'Bread!'

'Bread is important, ma'am.'

'Perhaps to you, Mrs Parsons, but not to my daughter, and definitely not more important than reading and writing. My daughter, Mrs Parsons, will have other people to make bread for her.'

'With respect, ma'am, if she can make her own bread she'll never be beholden to others.'

Ellie Parsons was known to speak her mind, especially if she was in her kitchen and especially if she was on her favourite subject.

'This conversation is finished, Mrs P. And, if you are not very careful, so will you be. Josephine' – she shouted so that every cadence echoed through the length of her name – 'come with me.'

At dinner that night, Josephine's mother ceremonially sent back all her food without touching it by way of rebuke to Mrs Parsons. Josephine was not about to let this huge black cloud settle over her happy afternoons with Ellie. But Mother's moods were famously difficult to shift.

For a time, a compromise was reached. Josephine was allowed to go back downstairs with Mrs Parsons and everything seemed all right again. The condition was that she had to do her writing and Mrs Parsons had to supervise.

'Definitely no bread-making. You can only watch. You were born to eat, not to cook, and best you remember that.'

Ellie laid a clean place at the far end of the table to set out the books and crayons, but somehow Jojo could not sit on her chair for very long and would find herself wandering up the other end. Then she discovered Ellie's old cookbook. She would rifle through the illustrations and ask: 'Can you cook this, Ellie?' And of course Ellie could. And of course they had to try it. They baked gâteaux and rolls and pies and anything else they could find. Josephine learned to spell using that book. Ellie would pull something new and strange out of her bag and pronounce:

'See what the book says about beetroot, Josephine. B-E-E-T-R-O-O-T.' And even if she could not read all the recipe she could give enough of it to get Ellie started.

'Oh, I hate that. They would be better in cream. Isn't there a recipe somewhere there for grated beetroot?'

All of this came to a rude halt when Josephine was packed off to boarding school, with the promise that her old friend and mentor would send her a cake every week so they could stay in touch.

Jojo started going in early to get her books done so she was free in the afternoon to cook. Marcel was there on his own, doing his orders. She kept asking to do little jobs. Would he mind if she practised a little more cutting the carrots? Could she do the soup again? Could she do the run to market to pick up the herbs? How does this recipe work? Slowly Marcel caved in and let her buy the vegetables and the fish. She seemed to understand the difference between fresh and yesterday's.

'You know something, Jojo. You have a very good sense of smell. It is quite a gift,' he said to her one afternoon. She beamed back with pride that he had noticed such a trivial thing. Dutifully each day she checked the prices in the covered market against the prices in the books from the year before.

She loved the market. She loved just being there in the half, almost violet, light out of the sun, wandering between the shadows and the rows of trellises covered with pregnant bundles of spinach, the emissions of sorrel and the spiky, unkempt endive, the swathes of fennel fronds, the neat bundles of asparagus sprue, the boxes of tiny turnips with their imperial bands of purple, the gleaming fish. She got bolder and brought back things that were not on the list.

'I found this. I didn't know what it was. It looked so beautiful.'

Marcel enjoyed these surprises as much as her.

'It is a morel. I hope you lost that in the books. I don't want Christian to notice how much you spent,' he chastised happily.

The boys in the kitchen found ways of bringing her into the cooking. She was their sister in arms. They would beckon her over suddenly from her booth to taste something. Somehow they seemed to trust her tongue.

Eventually, one afternoon after she had audited the entire year's accounts, Christian took her to one side and spoke to her solemnly:

'Mademoiselle Jojo, we cannot go on like this. There is a little flat on the ninth floor which is rarely used. Why don't you take it? You can pay us a little rent and we will pay you a little wages. I cannot go on charging you for the suite as if you were a guest. You are one of us now. It is not as luxurious, I know, but it is the busy season and you would be helping me, if you wouldn't mind, for a few months at least.'

She felt as if she had found a new family.

It was Marcel's mother who really taught Jojo to understand cooking. She lived in a little village above Cannes. Every Sunday evening, Marcel's only night off, Jojo would go up to the hills to see her, with Marcel, his wife, Brigitte, and their two boys, and eat this amazing bouillabaisse. Her food was an act of love. It spoke of family and friends and somehow it seemed to taste even better than the impersonal, formal dishes at the restaurant.

Marcel's mother bickered about food with her son.

'You can't do that in the restaurant, Maman. The clients want it more sophisticated.'

'Bah, if they do not know how to taste a proper *rouille* they should not be so silly as to spend so much money on chi-chi food.'

She didn't like chi-chi food. She thought Marcel was robbing the guests. She made a wonderful fish soup.

On Fridays, Marcel let Jojo take the fish up to his mother in the hotel van. She would pick over each one, staring into its eyes and running her thumb along the scales, to see that she had selected good fish. She would get out the plates and lay the fish on them one by one, cover them with olive oil, wine and herbs from her garden. Sometimes she would send Jojo out to pick some more thyme from the veranda. Then she would nod her approval. Once Jojo brought her a crawfish.

'Ah, you are so clever, Jojo, this will be fantastic. You really understand the flavours, my little bird. My poor Marcel. He looks such a strong man, but since he was a little boy he has fallen ill with this and with that. It is only my soup that keeps him going. This crawfish will make him strong.'

Then they would have a glass of wine together on the terrace. The two of them would gossip about recipes.

'Oh, that one, that is not really Marcel's. That is an old trick from Dijon, the Hôtel de la Gare, I think. They used to do it there, I'm sure. People don't really invent, you know, my little bird. They just borrow a little.'

She was a wonderful woman. Jojo loved her a lot.

2

THE CURSE

THE CALMNESS OF the Martinez was regal compared to the sticky clatter of the side streets. The rays of the afternoon sun dripped like glue on its balustrades. The leather steering wheel stuck in Jojo's hands. The smell of litter from the street and fish from the back of the van clung to the chiffon of her dress. And the noise: klaxon, klaxon. Clusters of cars huddled around the lights. Engines revved. Tyres squealed. Drivers leaned out of their cabins and swore and leered.

'Hey gam-eeen. Cum t'ait belle. Ca schauuffe. Tu viengs boire un potte ensamble avek MOI!' a Savanna driver yelled at her in the local patois.

'Désolée.' She smiled and pointed north towards the hills where Marcel's mother lived. As the car choked up the steep incline, the stickiness evaporated into a dry, burning heat. Jojo moved her elbow off the window rim where the sun was scorching her skin.

A goose announced her arrival, flapping and clacking in its wired pen. Marcel's mother stood, hands on hips in her customary black, just inside the line of shade on the veranda, without venturing forward. Instead she shouted:

'Alors, la pêcheuse, qu'est-ce que tu as pour moi?'

'Des jolies sardines,' Jojo replied, getting out of the van.

'*J'ai horreur de ça. Je t'ai dit je n'aime pas les sardines. C'est uniquement pour les Portugais, les sardines.*'

She too spoke in the southern patois, spitting out the last word as *sar-dee-nez*.

Inside, in the cool, the two women sorted through the fish. Jojo moved around in the semi-darkness, guided as much by smell and touch, reaching for the herbs from the far shelf, picking a chilli off the bunch on the wall.

'You can't be such a snob about fish, Maman,' she chided.

'Better to be a snob about fish than people, *n'est-ce pas?*'

'Shall I take the sardines back?'

'No. No. You can't let Marcel serve these at the Martinez. I will keep them here, so he doesn't find out about your little folly. He does not need to know.'

'You can't waste them.'

'The cats keep me company. They deserve a treat.'

'Are they Portuguese?'

'Vagabonds. Same thing.'

'Maman!'

'You English, you are the ones who are supposed to be so good at all this *snobisme*. You don't begrudge me a little, do you?'

'I don't begrudge you anything, Maman.'

'Come. These will keep in the oil,' the old woman said, wiping her hands of the herbs on an old cloth and shoving the dish into a dark recess under the shelf.

'We will have a glass of wine. Or maybe two. I feel like a chat.'

From the terrace, the hills split like a pair of scrubby-haired legs dangling into the blue of the sea. They could see tiny white specks of yachts on the water.

'So tell me, my little one, why is it you are so unhappy?'

'Just because I am quiet does not mean I am sad.'

'I know you better than that.'

Jojo decided to confide in this benign old woman.

'Everything about the old country was bad. It was ruined. It was suffering. It was run by madmen. There was no hope for it. Or so Mother said. We could never go back. "You can never go back," she used to tell me. She never, directly, not in so many words, talked about the curse, or not until it was too late, but there was always this presumption that everything to do with the old country was full of evil, of bad omens.

'We had left. That was it. We had been lucky. Lucky to get away. I don't remember anything about it, although I was born and christened there. I had no first-hand experience of the great sadness that had consumed the country. As far as I was concerned I was a Londoner. My early memories were mostly centred around Ellie's basement kitchen. And it was happy there.

'Mother lived in the past, haunted by this great nightmare which had changed her life. The house was filled with these old Russian artefacts and provided ammunition for her memories. Sometimes my parents would argue about selling another painting or a piece of silver to raise some cash. Mother always fought to keep them. Father was always after the money and wanted to sell. He used to call them bad talismans. I thought the house looked much better without these relics, but nobody asked me. We were well off, but Mother thought we were poor.

' "You will not have to worry about money, my child, but you will never be rich like you should have been."

'On Fridays Mother entertained. The long lacquered table in the dining room was extended with two shiny wooden leaves and set with the old silver. The candlesticks were taken out of the safe. Ellie would lay up the table with bowls of stewed cherries, chicken livers mashed with eggs, mounds of pike that she had mixed with herbs and bread, delicate little pastry tartlets, thick red sauces with the meats. I was not allowed to stay up. I would be presented to the guests and have to curtsey, say hello, then be dispatched to my bedroom. The next day I would slip down to the kitchen early and nibble the leftovers, wondering what these strange combinations were.

'You see the kind of house I came back to. I was sixteen. I had been locked away in a Sussex boarding school for ten years.'

'Have another glass of wine, my child,' the old woman said, leaning forward and pouring the rosé into her glass.

'Then it all happened so quickly. I had no idea. The love and the luck, they were entwined. That was the curse. The first time I saw Didier was at one of Mother's grand dinners. She had invited him to placate me. I don't blame her. The adults were all sunk on their sofas. It was not so much a seduction as a mutual agreement to plunge into being grown-ups together. If only we had known. The following day we went to the park together. We sat chastely, chatting, plotting as the watery sun went down behind the lonely black trees. I can still remember my knees trembling when he kissed me.

'I lied to my mother. I said I was staying with a girlfriend. We were obsessed. I do not even remember losing my virginity. I remember four days of crumpled sheets, wavy blankets, sweat, snatches of sleep without dreams. I remember his soft hair sweeping across my stomach. I remember licking the beads of sweat off the hairs in his armpits. I remember forcing him underneath me so I could ride off the last vestiges of my innocence. I remember the sense of triumph.

'Eventually we had to stop. He had a fencing tournament. I washed him in the shower. I took him to the Brasserie du Nord. We had scrambled eggs on toast and coffee. Black for me. White with sugar for him. He smoked a cigarette. I didn't like that. It masked his smell.'

Jojo paused for a moment, tracking the olive groves across the valley.

'We have all loved and lost, my dear,' ventured the old woman.

'I have not finished. It is not that simple,' Jojo answered sharply.

'Mother was horrified. "My child," she said, "you are just sixteen. Tell me it is not so." I told her it was love and not to worry. She should have shared my happiness. I had dreamed of falling in love, of making love, of having a baby. In less than a week I had all three. I was no longer a child. I felt so free. Then Mother surprised me:

' "You do not know about these things," she said sternly. I didn't know what she meant. There was a look of terror on her face. I remember it now even.

' "I am a woman now," I said.

' "You are cursed, my darling," she said.

' "Don't be so silly, Mother."

' "You will see . . ."

' "What do you mean?"

' "I cannot believe what I am hearing. All this was foretold."

' "So what?"

' "So it is the start of a great unhappiness."

' "Mother, you are barmy," I said. But she was not barmy. That same night Father had a stroke. The ambulance came. And amid all my joy the house was filled with my mother's wailing and sobbing.'

'You cannot blame yourself for that,' the old woman consoled.

'If that was all, then I would not have believed my mother's ramblings. The next day, on his way back from a tournament, Didier's car went off the road in some awful village in Hampshire. I saw him in the hospital. I didn't know whether he died in front of me or if he was already dead. At the funeral, I lost his baby.'

'My poor child.' The old woman reached out a hand to stroke her arm. 'And what of your mother?'

'Her grief is for Father, not for me. She says it was all preordained.'

'Do not be so hard on her.'

'I am not. She has gone to sleep. It has all been too much for her to bear. She is ashamed.'

'How can she be ashamed? It is only love . . .'

'She is ashamed of what has become of her life looking after an old man in a coma.'

'It is over now,' said the old woman.

'No, it is not,' Jojo retorted. 'Mother was right. I am cursed.'

'You cannot believe such things.'

'I do.'

'You are unhappy, it will pass.'

'There is a spell on me. I have lived my life and now my feelings are asleep. Like my mother's.'

'You will wake up.'

'Not for a long time, I fear.'

The old lady nodded quietly, not trying to test the depth of her feelings.

With some urging from his mother over dinner on Sunday, Marcel agreed to allow Jojo to take over the sauces. This was a big concession.

'How do you expect the poor girl to learn if all she has to do is chop vegetables all day?' she admonished him. 'She cannot learn to cook if she does not cook. Give her a chance.'

Back in the kitchen, he said:

'Cooking, Jojo, is like magic, you understand? It is magic because it is what we make of what this planet gives us. We take what some people might throw away. And we change it into something beautiful. But the magic is very simple. All you have to know is what . . . goes . . . with . . . what . . . and when . . .'

He showed her how to make stock. It was Jojo's first job after lunch. The bones from the fish she had bought in the market that morning and from which the lunchtime fillets had been taken were set aside in a pot. Jojo crushed them with her cleaver on the chopping board. She diced her shallots and sweated them in the olive oil. Marcel was particular about his basics. She threw in a few tiny branches of thyme, and the leaves from the celery. And then the bones. She brought up the heat, stirring all the while to release the sugars, and then drowned the pan in a bottle of Mâcon. She simmered it for ten minutes, flicked the heat off and left it to cool. She would finish it later.

Jojo knew the full repertoire of the menu by heart. As it hardly changed from day to day she became accomplished in all its conceits.

The other part of Jojo's culinary education came from restaurants. Since the funeral, since the curse had done its evil worst (she prayed), she had hardly eaten anywhere else. This part she chose not to tell Marcel's mother.

For a while she had been insane. She had lived through too much in too short a time. Sex was the only reality she could find. The only good fairy left in the boarded-up and otherwise deserted house of her emotions was the physical action of sex. It was sport. She had lost track of how many men she had had. She had even taken money once or twice.

It became a ritual. She starved herself. Usually for four or five days. Then she went out as a predator. She made it a condition, before or after, that they eat with her. And she ate not just any foods but things she had never tasted Oysters, samphire, *pied de mouton*, white truffles, *foie gras*, whelks, sashimi, miso, shark's fin dumplings, quinces, sorrel, sweetbreads, partridges. Being half starved heightened her pleasure. With a stranger in a restaurant, drinking new wines and eating new foods, she could, if only for a few moments, even if it was part delusion, access her feelings again, out of sight of the spell before it would avalanche all around her again and clasp her to its body, holding her feelings tightly, frozen and immobile.

One Friday at the end of winter, Jojo and Marcel's mother were drinking a glass of rosé on the terrace, just the two of them.

'You are not looking your best, little one. You should take a lover. It would improve your complexion. You cannot hide yourself away. A woman needs attention. Besides, summer is coming and the heat will dry out your skin.'

'Maman, really. In England we don't talk of such things.'

'Well, in France we do.'

The old woman was silent for a few moments and then returned to her subject.

'Sometimes an older man is good for a young woman. An older man knows things.'

'I don't mind older men,' Jojo replied idly.

'I wish you would take Marcel as a lover. He is so unhappy.'

'Maman!'

26

'Why not? He deserves some pleasure.'

'What about Brigitte?'

'Brigitte is not interested in such things. She is a good mother but she does not give him pleasure like that. She has what she wants. She has the boys, the house, the car. She has her girlfriends. She is content. My Marcel has given her everything. They sleep in separate rooms. I do not think she likes sex with men. Besides, sometimes it is better for a man to take a mistress than to force himself on his wife.'

'Maman, you are a wicked woman.'

'No, I am not. The family is my jurisdiction. He is my son and I am allowed to want for him to enjoy a young woman once again in his life after so many years of celibacy.'

'What makes you think he would find me attractive?'

'Bah! You have forgotten what sort of woman you are. You need a man, my little one. All this cooking the two of you are doing is making you both go crazy.'

For the evening service, Jojo now occupied her own place at the far corner of the range. As the orders came in, Marcel shouted:

'*Sauce, Jojo, rouget.*'

She varied the ingredients according to the centre-piece – cream for turbot, livers for the red mullet, red wine for strong fish, the good Riesling for sole, crayfish for the chicken. She made each sauce individually. It took her six minutes precisely.

In a small pan she reduced the stock she had made in the afternoon. When the call came she added shallots, red or white wine, sometimes lemon or wine vinegar, and let it bubble over the flame. She carved her butter into sections and as the mix thickened, she dropped the first cube down the side of the copper pan and began to flick with her whisk. When it had melted and been absorbed, she dropped the second, then the third, flicking the sauce around the pan so fats crashed against the walls and absorbed the liquids, until she had a sauce as thick as velvet. The sous-chef, Jean François, would then arrive with his dish and she ladled the sauce over it or to the side.

'To go!' he would shout. In English.

For an hour in the afternoon Marcel and Jojo were the only ones in the kitchen. Marcel worked in his cubicle checking the orders and talking to other chefs on the phone. Then he would disappear for an hour or so, either to sleep or to have a Pastis in a nearby café. From where she sat, Jojo could watch him intently across the kitchen as his hands worked over a carcass, judging its quality; or as he slipped the knife under the skin of a fish; or as he lifted his gaze to redirect one of the boys. She had come also to notice the way the dark hairs sprang out of his olive skin.

She had chosen her moment two or three times before, but this time she found the courage to walk into his cubicle when he put the phone down.

He looked up at her.

'Yes, my little bird?'

'I'm not a bird, Marcel. I am a woman. Sometimes you might prefer to remember that.'

'You are also a guest.'

'And a chef.'

'A commis chef, my pupil.' He raised a cautionary finger.

'And you are a man.'

'So?'

He stared at her, suddenly struck by what she was saying, if she was saying it, like a bull in the ring that suddenly realises he is facing an adversary.

'A married man.'

'Should I care?'

'I am your chef. Your teacher.'

'Not in all things.'

'You should not talk so.'

'Why so prudish? I thought all you Frenchmen thought of yourselves as great lovers. Are you frightened? Am I not desirable? Even bookkeepers have needs.'

'It is bad enough that you want to cook. This is too dangerous.'

'I could give you pleasure.'

'You give me pleasure now.'

'Not that kind of pleasure.'

'You are a hard woman.'

'I have to be to work with you lot.'

'I mean, emotionally.'

'My feelings are locked up safely, thank you very much. Besides, what would you want with some airheaded bimbo spilling her feelings all over you?'

'I find you a little unnerving.'

'You're just not used to women. I am rushing you.' She was standing next to him and brushed his cheek lightly with the back of her hand.

'Yes.'

'Do you want me to stop? Do you want me to go back to my books?'

'No.'

His reticence surprised her. She was so accustomed to him giving orders. For a second he looked like a little boy who had been found out, as he looked up at her through flat, unblinking black eyes. She reached her hand down into his trousers.

'You want me. I can feel you.'

'Any man would.'

Before he said any more, she straddled her leg over him. She grabbed his hair and cradled him to her breasts. She sank deeply on to him. Before he realised, he was inside her. He was not making love, she was taking him. She had taken him. She hugged his big black head like a trophy.

Jojo heard the footsteps on the wooden stairs below. Marcel was always punctual. It was 3.38. He would have finished in the kitchen at 3.15. He had showered, shaved, put on his day clothes. He was a man of ritual. The kitchen would be deserted but, even so, he would have walked out of the side door as if he was going into town. He would check no one was watching him before turning back and starting the climb up the back stairs. He would take the lift on the second floor to the penthouse. And then through the service door to the final flight. She could hear him now.

He didn't knock. The door just opened. He stood there smiling. His bulk filled the frame. The garret was almost too small for both of them. He stooped his head to avoid hitting the open beams.

He was her only visitor. He came every Tuesday and every Friday afternoon. Regular as the postman, she thought.

'*Alors*, my leetel bird?'

It was the only English phrase he ever used, and even then, she noted, it was just a literal Gallic translation with no meaning, one he had borrowed from his mother at that.

Jojo thought of him in terms of food. His torso was a flank of beef; the black hair as soft as rabbit fur; the profile as proud as a partridge; his buttocks had the complexion of fattened lobes of goose liver. His breath always smelled of Beaujolais. He still needed a little extra courage to come up to see her. She likened it to one of his sauces, an intense seasoning that he would drift across her nakedness, like a dusting of wet pepper.

Of course it was not love. Love was taboo. Down-stairs he was her mentor. He guided her through the cooking. She was avid to learn. Upstairs, he had that boyish expression again. She had to lead him. It stopped her sliding over the edge into an abyss of treacherous emotions. With him as her lover she could ignore the yachts, the racy cars, the young boys, the cafés, the markets, the palm trees and all the other postcard trappings, and concentrate on her mission. Her world was distilled into a microcosm in the Martinez basement surrounded by gleaming silver and hot steam.

For him the intensity of her nudity, the frankness of her body, her scent were an intoxication beyond which he could not and dared not look. He took mental snapshots as he roamed over her body, against the day she would not be there. He sniffed her armpits in search of souvenirs.

Their mood on these afternoons was invariably set within the first few minutes. Sometimes he would crush her with his huge biceps and they would make love thirstily, immediately, guiltily and quickly. Then they would talk. When he was ready she would make love to him again more slowly. Other times they would just talk, lying on the bed, a hand outstretched to caress the nakedness, a tongue licking skin. Sometimes it was just too hot. The sun bore down on the rafters of the old building and, if there was no breeze, the garret became unbearably hot, too hot to move. They lay, she thought, like loaves baking in an oven.

Marcel sat down on the corner of the bed. His fingers unpicked the buttons of his shirt. The hairs sprang out from under the cotton. The other hand stroked her leg. He bent down and kissed the exposed thigh in greeting. He was in one of his contemplative moods. She sat up in the bed. Her shirt fell open, showing him her breasts. She wanted him to see her, to want her. She stroked his

31

black hair with the back of her hand. It was still damp and cool.

'Jean François is leaving. He has a posting at the Hôtel de Ville in Toulouse. It is a good job for him. He will do well.'

'Hurrah for him. Perhaps hurrah for me too – now you will have to make me sous-chef.'

'I cannot do that, Jojo. You know that. The boys would be furious.'

'You cannot bring anybody else in.'

They both stopped. Almost at the same moment. They had seen into the future and held back. The comfort of their afternoon tryst was too fragile. She sensed the spell was working again. Was she even to be denied her middle-aged lover? Could it be that jealous?

'Poor Jean François. If only he knew what his departure could mean for us.' Her voice sounded weak and reedy.

'He would not want to make us both unhappy.'

She leant forward and parted the hairs on his chest with two fingers and then circled his nipple. She blew lightly on the dark, pimpled skin, and licked the tip. His smell comforted her.

'You smell of coriander.'

'Yes, I was making the *pistou* with coriander today. You are always so sensitive to smells.'

The closeness was reassuring.

Outside, the saturated sexual heat of the coast butted in through the window. It was like having another person in the room with them. In the distance the taxis whined along the promenade. There was a faint recurring echo of the tiny waves slapping the beach.

She sucked the nipple. The heat drew a huge, hot, wet blanket around them, weighing them down, so intense it was like sex itself, the ghost of their coupling. She licked the newly burst beads of sweat off his breast.

She looked for a distraction to ward off the impending calamity.

'You are just a conjuror. Conjure something up to make it possible for us to be together. Make me sous-chef.'

'You are asking for something that cannot be.'

'I do not ask you to leave your wife . . . I do not ask you to give me children . . . I keep your secret . . . I give you pleasure . . . Other men would kill to have a mistress like me, half your age. I work for nothing. Why is it so much to ask you for something that should be mine?'

'It is not mine to give. It is not your inheritance. You have not trained properly. You are not French. You are not a man. You are an outsider. It would not be fair on the others. They have worked too hard.'

'I am as good as they are. I have a calling. Other women want to be wives. I want to be a chef. Anyway, I would not be the first. What about La Mère Guy at Lyons? She was Scottish.'

'That was a hundred years ago.'

'I will buy the hotel.'

'It is not for sale.'

'Everything has a price.'

'Not here. Not this. Not what you want. Besides, you are a beautiful woman. You do not want to be locked away, out of sight, in service to rich people. You are one of them, not one of us. You cannot hide yourself away from what you are. You cannot force me to give you something I do not own just because I make love with you. Nor can I pretend to you that you might succeed just because I am so selfishly in love with you.'

He looked at her dispassionately. She was expected to accept, without argument, like a nun. Only she had made no vows, not to him at least.

His expression was of surprised, sad complicity. They

had shared this illicit journey together and now the price being asked was too high. Perhaps if she had just wanted ordinary things like other women, a lover, even a child, or for him to leave his wife, then maybe it could have been all right. But not his vocation too. Not everything. She seemed to want his very manliness. Had she just wanted ordinary things he would not have loved her so much to allow them to have got this far. Because he loved her, like a father he knew, he would let her go. He could not keep her.

He pressed his face into her breasts to hide his sadness. He could feel from her body that she had already left. Before, she had been like the sea, wrapping around his every muscle inflexion, but now she was a rock, solid and ungiving. She stroked his head. But it was a polite, familial caress. The formality hurt. Each touch seemed to cause a deeper ache. Suddenly he felt very selfish, mourning for the passion he would go on feeling, but she would not reciprocate. He wanted to force himself on her one last time. He wanted to rape her. He felt her lips on his hair and her soft cheeks by his ear.

She was whispering a promise.

'You can make love to me one more time, Marcel. Just once. You choose when . . .'

Lying alone in her little garret, Jojo had often pondered on what was the right word for someone who had been cursed. Victim implied finality, which was always possible, but as yet nothing had really ended. She was still the prey, and the spell stalked her.

She felt as if she was in a state of grace. There was a presumption that one day, like virginity, she would have to give it up, or have it taken from her, but for the moment she was its agent, or perhaps its manifestation?

Jean François's departure unravelled them. Quickly, and with some relish, the spell untied the knot that had wrapped Marcel and Jojo together. They were not, Jojo realised, one piece of string after all, but two strands held together by a clumsy loop.

Marcel was kind. He persuaded her gently. She was only adopted, a stepchild, a mistress. He need not have been so gentle, but it was in his manners and his upbringing to be so. She had never confided in him the emptiness he was returning her to.

His mother looked at her with those soft, wrinkly eyes that seemed to say, child, we all feel sorrow, but there is worse sorrow in this world, do not drown in it, rest, sleep, it will pass. When she told her she was leaving, she said simply:

'*Evidemment!* I will miss you, my little bird. But you will come back.'

'How do you know?'

'I will make sure. You will see.'

For all London's reputation, Jojo had never seen fog like this. The car headlights peered yellow out of the mist. The reds and ambers of the traffic lights seemed suspended in mid air. The grey outline of the tall trees waved in the wind. London, she noted coming back to it, was a city of tall old trees. They loomed like memories, even larger in the mist as it swept around the window frames and roof edges. Her disappointments seemed to attach themselves to these tugging wisps. It was cleansing fog, like egg whites clarifying soup.

Not being able to see very far was reassuring. Jojo recalled how, when she was an infant, Ellie had pushed her pram round the parks. All the little details were shrouded from view now in this thick grey overcoat framing her life. She was glad. She did not want to see all those things that had caused her to leave.

She missed the routine of the Martinez kitchen, of being a part of that infernal machine. She missed the heat of it. She realised her life had all been lived in the single dimensions of family, of school, of love, of the kitchen. These had all disappeared. She had always been a private person who liked her solitude, but this was starker.

The fog trailed her down to Brighton. She had a need to see her parents. The nursing home was depressing and the news was bad. The doctor was punctilious and businesslike. Her father did not recognise her. He lay in bed gazing vacantly at the ceiling.

The ward sister had warned her:

'I am afraid looking after your father has not helped your mother's own health. She has deteriorated rapidly since you were last here.'

Even so, Jojo wasn't ready for the woman who confronted her. She was sitting in a chair. She could talk but she seemed intent on thinking Jojo was another nurse.

'Mother, it's me, your daughter.'

'Don't be silly. Just get me a nice cup of tea, thank you, dear.'

'No, it really is.'

'Jojo is in France. We are all proud of how clever she has been.'

'At least they are together. We keep them both very comfortable.'

The sister was sympathetic, but was also anxious to ensure that Jojo sign the standing order payments.

'Can I at least send them some new nightclothes?'

'By all means, though I don't know that they will notice much, I'm afraid.'

Jojo took a taxi to the town centre. She bought a suitcase and filled it with the warmest, softest pyjamas she could find. And a dressing gown each. And slippers. And two shawls. She came back along the seafront and left the case at reception.

Stripped of friends through her exile and of her parents through illness, Jojo resolved to populate her life with anonymous, unthreatening business contacts. She scavenged the billboards on the streets. Meticulously she scanned the lists from estate agents in search of a restaurant of her own. She befriended the agents as they tried to sell her a basement or a failed car showroom or a pub that was more down and out than its locals.

She appointed the grand-sounding Jack Cartier Associates International to handle the marketing of her dream. Signing (quite large) cheques to him was reassuring. It lent a credibility to her actions to have an official agent appointed to her cause. She could buy this dream. For every proposition a broker gave her, a fax would come back to her hotel on JCA paper saying tersely:

'Bad area.'

Or: 'Don't like basements.'

Or: 'Gone bust too many times.'

Or: 'Too close to Triad territory.'

She did not meet Mr Cartier himself. She was not important enough. It was like carrying out business by karaoke. His representative, a svelte, lanky blonde called Lydia, relayed the wisdom. Jack says this. Jack says that. Jack says, have you thought about Oxford? The advice seemed sensible enough. Only the invoice and the faxes carried his signature, scrawled in old-fashioned, often blotchy ink.

Jack Cartier had something of a reputation, she was to learn afterwards. Most people had a story about him. Lunch with him was a coveted invitation and notoriously lasted the whole afternoon. The most often repeated tale was how the success of the XYZ bar near Piccadilly was due to his dealing cocaine in the toilets. When Jojo heard it, she panicked and faxed him:

'Is it true about the XYZ?'

That night she returned to her hotel to find a reply:

'No, but it packs them in all the same. The police have not been able to find anything either!!'

She felt reassured but nervous about the murkiness of the waters she was starting to swim in.

At night she cruised the city and the home counties. She dined wherever she could, sometimes at two or three restaurants in the same evening, not eating much, just picking and drinking and looking, counting tables, numbers of waiters, where the dishes came from, who was eating what, how the walls had been decorated. Fed up with eating alone, she recruited a waiter in a Thai restaurant to become her driver and companion. Usually this meant she ended up drinking the whole bottle herself. By the end of the evening, when he dropped her back at the hotel, she was usually quite merry.

The restaurants were a comfort zone. She loved the way dining rooms were decorated, a mix of kitsch and elegance, over the top in a way you could not contemplate at home. The staff were solicitous without being threatening. The impersonality suited her. She wanted this paid-for propriety without strings.

In the car one evening, her driver, Mr Lee, said:

'There's story here about Jack Cartier.'

'Don't tell me you've got one too.'

'No, it in the paper.'

He passed the diary page over his shoulder. Jojo read it quickly. It seemed like an ordinary business tiff.

Restaurant Svengali Jack Cartier is in hot water with one of his flamboyant clients, former deb of the year and now Marchioness of Twerby, Alison Gooding.

The Marchioness's restaurant, Growls, in Chelsea, has just closed with debts of more than £100,000. She blames Cartier. 'He just didn't do what he promised,' a crestfallen Marchioness confided in me.

Carter is having nothing of it. 'It was just a bloody awful restaurant,' he says.

Jojo laughed aloud.

'Well, he speaks his mind,' she said.

'Sounds like tough cookie OK,' said Mr Lee.

'All the same, I think I might prefer an agent who didn't appear in the gossip columns so much . . .'

'Sometimes, like oysters, you need some grit to get things going,' said Mr Lee.

3

THE DEBAUCHING OF THE VICARAGE

THESE WERE THE great days. The oxygen of money filled the air. Tourists flowed. Washington camped in Mayfair for the summer and patrolled the Cotswolds in Mercedes in search of a piece of history. The French came to check out their bizarre, headstrong neighbour at long last, to play *le golf*, to buy *les tartans*. The English had decided that to eat out was not such a sin after all. The portents were good.

Jojo got a fax from Jack Cartier Associates suggesting she have a look at a site off the M40.

Strictly, the Vicarage was not historic. The brochure eloquently described its history as Tudor and alluded at random to the historic events of the Cotswolds over the last four hundred years to caption the pictures of the stonework and the comfortable beds. The foundations were Tudor, sure enough. They were buried deep in the ground and had not been seen by anyone, apart from the occasional plasterer, for decades. There was the dovecote, of course. Possibly Elizabethan, rebuilt Georgian. It featured prominently in the brochure, which had won an award.

As a building, the Vicarage itself had not won any award. Not even a Grade II listing. The estate agent said this was because the previous owners were anxious not to incur the kind of liability that might attach to such a soubriquet. He was a man well briefed in the language of soubriquets and liabilities and had been rather off-hand at first, thinking Jojo looked a bit young for this sort of thing.

'The Vicarage,' he confided, 'was reconstructed after a fire around eighteen-seventy.'

A few gnarled beams and scorched bits of stone survived to lend credence to his theory.

'There has been history here, but whether it was vicarage, nunerage, puberage, farmerage, I am not completely clear, I'm afraid.'

It was not a house prepared to disclose its distant past too readily. The cold, aristocratic catacombs were without heating or decoration. They had been lived in by the last heirs to the family. Uniform cream walls were splashed, desperately, with enormous oils of mendacious-looking women; pompous colonels; and hunting dogs of nobler demeanour than their human custodians. Where the house had suffered, the garden survived gloriously, obviously preened daily by genera-tions of gardeners. Each prunus was pruned, the box hedges trimmed, there were more than two hundred varieties of rose, seventeen types of apple tree, twenty-six different clematis. The oak at the front might have been Tudor. It said Tudor in the brochure. It was big enough.

The last three members of the family had died *in situ*. They had been cared for by a procession of companions, nursers and carers. The doctors knew the grooves on the gravel drive. The first time Jojo saw the first floor, it resembled a hospice.

'Do you think you might be interested?' asked the agent.

'I'll discuss it with my associates at JCA,' Jojo replied cautiously.

'Ahh. The famous Jack Cartier,' intoned the agent.

'Don't tell me you have a story about Mr Cartier too. It seems everyone does.'

'I like the one about the Duchess and the Italian restaurant . . .'

'Which is?'

'Apparently, Mr Cartier made some impromptu advances on the Duchess's table at San Lorenzo. Unfortunately her bodyguard misread his intentions and karate-chopped him to the floor.'

'Poor chap.'

'The Duchess was apparently so upset, she chauffeured him to the hospital . . .'

'He seems to ride his luck.'

She wanted to be able to do to a house what she had not been able to do with her life. She wanted to change it, to transform it, to bring it happiness. She wanted the Vicarage, not because she was in love with it, but because she was in love with what she could do with it. She set about her task with gusto. On the day she signed, four lorries arrived from the district auction house and stripped the house of everything.

Each of the fifteen bedrooms was to be decorated differently. Each named after a flower. The beds were copious. The linen was sleek. The baths had jacuzzis. The shower heads were imported from Chicago. Jojo made a note to instruct the kitchen to hide little caches of madeleines in secret places where people would least expect them. She left lines of perfumes. Tables had heaps of fruit. Beautifully printed boxes contained freshly baked sugared biscuits. There were chocolates in the ashtrays. Pistachio nuts from Turkey and candied fruit in the bathroom. Each room had a decanter of Amontillado and of Madeira. The fridge contained only Mumm champagne in half-bottles. And fresh orange juice.

The dining room she rag-rolled. The menacing

portraits were replaced by Dutch still lives of food. The drawing room became a palace of cushions, sofas, books, games, and more flowers. As Marcel had predicted, Jojo found she enjoyed shopping for all the pieces. She enjoyed spending the money.

The Vicarage became Jojo's seraglio. Her guests were to be her concubines. She was to be the indolent potentate.

She interviewed six chefs. The most interesting was Vincent Victor. He shuffled around in the sparse and undecorated expanse of the drawing room, looking very unsure of himself, his goatee beard directing his gaze down, over the rim of his round little belly, to the floor.

'Do you think you might feel uncomfortable working for a woman?'

'I, I, I have never worked with one,' he stuttered.

'You seem very nervous.'

'I am, I am, I am a little uncomfortable.'

'Do you always repeat yourself?'

'When, when I am agitated, I do, I think.'

'Why?'

'It's a habit.'

'I meant, why are you agitated?'

'It is my situation.'

'And what is your situation?'

'May I confide?'

It was hardly a question.

'This Aids thing has been very bad news. My partner is, or I should say was, very well known in the area. And it seems people are frightened. Our bookings are down. He is, he has, left. I fear I have to sell . . .'

'Do you have Aids?'

'No. We have been, sorry, we were, together for a long time. Long before all this started, but people are so unfair.'

'I see. Where is he now?'

'He has gone back to South Africa.'

'I see.'

'I am a good chef but all I am doing now is grilling steaks.'

'I will come and eat and see for myself.'

Vincent had worked in some of the best London hotels. His own restaurant had some minor listings in two or three guides. He was not quite what she had expected, but then what exactly did she expect? She needed someone who knew the county and all the kitchen basics. His restaurant was small, too small, the bookkeeper in her said, and cottagey, with beams and pink shades on the lamps. Technically the cooking was OK, if a bit dull and provincial. The stocks were clean. The pastry work just about good enough. She agreed to buy him out. The restaurant would be useful for staff quarters. It was too small to make money. In return she offered him a small share in the Vicarage.

He surprised her, pleasantly, at first. His hobby, it turned out, was entering catering competitions. He liked to sculpt flower arrangements out of sugar and to carve nudes out of fat. The results were ridiculous but fun. She decided to give him a space in an alcove at the entrance to show his bizarre works.

The village marvelled. They had only ever been allowed into the Vicarage once a year, on a Sunday afternoon in July from two to four in aid of the church roof which for thirty years, or for as long as anyone could remember, had been in need of repair. And then they were only allowed into the garden, never the house. Postmen and milkmen left their letters and bottles at the stone gate by the single road that was the village's only artery to the outside world.

The prices were the talking point of the high street.

She tells me she is going to charge twenty pounds for a piece of chicken. You can't charge that for a chicken. Nobody'll pay that for a chicken. It's not natural. Mrs Hemmings told me that you only get a breast for twenty pounds. She saw the chef cutting up the chicken into five different dishes and that means that that chicken costs about a hundred pounds. A hundred pounds! And there's nothing special about it. It is just a chicken from Henry Ross's farm. It runs about a bit, but it is still a chicken. He says she told him to feed it on corn, but the chickens didn't like it.

Everyone became involved in the transformation. The allotments were commissioned to grow more flowers to feed Jojo's vision of the bedrooms. Then carpenters were wanted. And joiners. And a night watchman. And lodgings for the sous-chef arriving next week from France. And then cleaners.

Even Albert Hemmings at the post office, known for his prowess at the annual garden show, had been enlisted to grow those funny long, thin, waxy French potatoes and to give over his cabbage patch in favour of rocket and purslane. His greenhouse was taken over by red basil. Mrs Hemmings had insisted. She, who was known to cook some of the best cakes for the Women's Institute, had been dragooned to help in the kitchen.

Miss Coltrane and Mr Victor had some very interesting ideas about food, she reported. If a mother who knew so much about cakes said so, it had to be true. It has taken twenty years off me, she told friends. Mrs Hemmings was put in charge of breakfasts and the baking of small keepsakes for the rooms. She got her son Alastair the job as night porter and was hoping he might pick up the cooking.

Mrs Hemmings relayed all this enthusiasm to Mr Hemmings, who passed it on faithfully to everyone who came into the shop. After the first week, Mr Hemmings was reassured with the new order for twenty-five more papers a day, and forty-six glossy magazines a month. It was the first time he had ever ordered foreign magazines.

By the time the Vicarage threw its opening night party, it had in some way touched the lives of every household in the village of nine hundred people. The vicar's son poached pike and perch and left them at the kitchen door. The taxi driver took to carrying his shotgun in the boot in case he came across a pheasant in an isolated spot. There were enough of them these days, strutting the lanes like country vicars, fattened in the pens down by the copse for the shooters up from London. Most people had decided that chicken at twenty pounds a portion sounded like a good business all round; that Jojo must be pretty clever after all; and that Vincent must be a genius in the kitchen.

The only person who missed the launch party was Jack Cartier. Jojo asked Lydia where he was.

'He's been unavoidably detained,' she replied.

'You mean he's drunk?'

'Probably.'

'Pity, I was looking forward to meeting him.'

Nancy, filling in on the reception desk for the summer holidays before going to college, alerted everyone to what was to be the first and most glorious coup in the career of the Vicarage. She had been idling through the bookings for the evening to see if there was anyone she might recognise. She came across the name of Tetris, with a London coding. She wondered if this was the same man who wrote about restaurants on the page opposite the college vacancies that she had been screening so diligently for the last few weeks. She rang the number. No, Mr Tetris is on assignment. In the Cotswolds. She waited until she was going off shift before mentioning it.

'I wondered, Miss Jojo, if I should have written VIP next to Mr Tetris here. I think he writes for the *Guardian*.'

'Did he say he was?'

'No, but I did ring the number he left. It was the *Guardian*.'

'Brilliant, Nancy. Quite brilliant.' Jojo beamed with admiration. 'You are going to go a long way in this world. Take a bottle of champagne out of the fridge in my room and take it home with you. Make sure you drink it yourself, mind.'

Nancy curtseyed in surprise.

The Vicarage was destined to undergo the most severe scrutiny. Hannibal Tetris could recommend it to millions of readers. His column was syndicated to America. His anonymous face peered out from behind fat sunglasses on the bleached-out woodblock of his column like some culinary terrorist. Not for nothing was he also called Cannibal.

In France such assessments had been dignified and calming. Jojo had been through them with Marcel. Ten or eleven visits through the year from different experts, long discussions afterwards, clear pointers on policy, suggestions for improvements, and finally more of an agreement to a standard than a judgement.

In England, Jojo knew, it was do or die at the hands of someone like Hannibal Tetris. And three hours was all the time it took. Uncivilised, but necessary. She steeled herself. The trouble with these English writers was you could never be sure what their mothers had fed them. Or worse, their schools.

In a crisis an icy calm descended on her. She knew what she wanted and what had to be done. She called Vincent.

Vincent was well aware of who Mr Tetris was, a sarcastic intellectual yob who made his living being rude about honest working people. Mr Tetris was a point of conversation on the four o'clock ring-round of other chefs. The consensus was that he wrote well and knew little. Vincent begrudged the idea of taking Mr Tetris seriously at all. But he knew the game. He could send the Vicarage a few customers who might order £300 bottles of claret.

Mr Tetris had cannibalised Vincent's last restaurant. The remark about the saltiness of the duck still rankled. 'What do you expect from a duck that has been salted?' he lamented. 'Does he know no Welsh tradition? And the "menu's manic monotony for *magret*". What does that mean, anyway?' But after he had recovered, he noticed that despite the negatives tones, new customers started to arrive. And good ones too. Payers. Apprecia-tors. Not the nervous, frigid couples who made up so many of his regulars. Nor the uncaring, we-are-just-out-for-a-good-time, please-see-to-it-waiter types. Serious people. With a serious interest in food.

'I will cook tonight,' Jojo said.

It was a declaration. Hardly one he had been expecting.

'I am the chef.'

'But I am better than you. You can look after everyone else, but Hannibal the Cannibal is mine. We must have offal. He likes offal. He always orders offal. What else have we got? Take that farmed salmon off the menu for tonight. It is too fatty. Only use the wild from the Tay. Those soufflés Pascal has been doing are excellent. We'll give him one as a surprise anyway. Do the raspberry with the eau-de-vie poured in, unless he orders it, in which case the gratin of fruits with the sorbet. The boys are doing those well too. Is there anything at the kitchen door?'

'No – there was a pike yesterday that I have made into quenelles.'

'Put it on as well as the salmon. Do a Nantua sauce with those crayfish. Local pike, local crayfish, that would be a good joke . . . if he spots it.'

Her eyes glittered. She hardly noticed the look of malicious disappointment that had settled across Vincent's face. He sat down slowly like a deflating balloon in his little cabin, surrounded by order tickets, receipts, invoices, each carefully allotted their own hook space. How could anyone, let alone Jojo, whom he adored from a distance, walk into his kingdom and so consummately pull rank on him?

'No one screws up tonight, Vincent. No detail is overlooked. You must oversee everything. And no drinking.'

He wanted to respond. But she was gone. She might as well have taken his trousers and underpants with her.

She was gone to deliver a similarly vigorous speech to housekeeping.

'Give him room nine. Double up the flowers. More fruit and check the magazines. Make sure they are the ones he writes for. And there must be Italian *Vogue*. Hoover it again yourself. Renew the chocolates. And the cakes. Upgrade the sherry. A new bottle. I'll send one up. Neaten the bed. HE MUST NOT KNOW. Understand?'

The chambermaid, Sandy, aged sixteen, the new receptionist, Mary, aged nineteen, and the porter-cum-gardener-cum-anything-else, Alastair Hemmings, aged seventeen, nodded obediently like schoolchildren.

'Anything he wants. Anything at all. And quickly. Except sex, of course, girls. I don't want you to give him sex. You understand me? This is not the sixteenth century.'

The two girls nodded some more, wondering nervously what on earth this man *might* ask for. And if Mr Tetris was not quite important enough to be allowed sex, did that mean that one day there might be someone who was so important they might be instructed to give everything for the great cause of the Vicarage? They intoned dutifully, yes, ma'am, yes, ma'am, as the instructions poured over them. They had not seen her like this before. She had always been so nice. Alastair shifted uncomfortably. He was not used to people talking about sex. It was rarely mentioned in the post office.

Jojo stared hard at them and tried to reassure herself. They were not as bright as Nancy (one morning Mary had distinguished herself by forgetting to put the tea in the pot for breakfast in room nine; the next day she had gone one better and forgotten the cups), but they were diligent, committed and had good eyes for cleanliness, which was the important thing. If only they could be persuaded to smile.

'I will take room six as my headquarters for tonight. I do not want to be disturbed for an hour. Then I will inspect his room. Let me know the moment he arrives.'

Having disturbed the calm of the Vicarage, Jojo needed her own space to prepare.

Mary broke the news of the arrival. Infected by the energy and excitement that surrounded this strange visitor, she would not have been overly surprised to have opened the door to the Pope. She had been looking out for a BMW. Or possibly an Audi. She imagined pinstripes; silk shirt; matching cases; Italian shoes; some exotic aftershave she had never smelled before, manicured fingers, a deity who would walk in and bless this extraordinary venture and all who worked there, herself included.

What she saw was this battered old Peugeot, the wheels having sprung their hub caps and the sides streaked in grime, scrunch up the gravel. Out stepped a holdall and a pair of Doc Martens. This did not accord with the sense of importance Mistress Jojo had attached. A white cane tapped into the hallway and this huge figure loomed over her at the desk, wearing sunglasses despite the drizzle outside. His breath smelled of Murraymints. She checked the name. The American Express card was not even gold. Mystified, she led the man and his waif-like companion safely up the stairs to the sanctity of room nine. As she closed the door she breathed a sigh of relief that her brief tenure of responsibility had passed. She skipped down to the kitchen.

'You won't believe him. He is enormous. Huge. Must be twenty-five stone. He could hardly get through the door. And you wait till you see the girl who's with him. She's a sparrow. She could almost fit in his pocket. There ain't nothing to her at all.'

Her brain was awash with visions of this corpulent giant copulating with this petite raven, on the sheets she had so carefully ironed. She felt an impulse to rush upstairs and offer the girl twin beds. Perhaps that was why Jojo had mentioned the sex. Perhaps she knew that the girl was physically too small and that Hannibal Tetris might be in need of a surrogate? She comforted herself with the thought that at least she had the hips for him.

'Call Jojo, Mary.' Vincent was in control. And Mary did as she was told.

Jojo strode into the kitchen. She was wearing a headscarf and a modest black dress with pockets into which her hands were sunk. Deliberately she toured each station. She tasted the veal stock. She tasted the fish stock. She opened the chill drawers to examine the pre-cut vegetables.

'Cut some more vegetables. These are going stale.'

She opened the fridge and stared into it. She said nothing. She glanced over the orders for the other tables. She moved to the stool behind the pastry. She waited. Like a fisherwoman.

Quietly the kitchen worked its ritual, punctuated by the waiters, Henry and Gaston, exploding out of the revolving doors and Vincent shouting orders.

'Table four, fish soup, chicken with vinegar; table seven, tartar of salmon, Châteaubriand with oysters.'

Jojo waited, listening, calculating.

Mr Lee bustled through the doors. He posted the order on the hook above the chef's head.

'Table six. They are go.' Vincent's voice rang out. 'One soup, one salmon, one kidneys, one brill.'

Jojo was her off her stool and behind him.

'What is he having?'

'The soup, the kidneys.'

'Typical. Vincent, you look after the starters and the fish. But don't overcook it, he is not a farmer. Pascal and I will do the main course. Gaston, get me a bottle of Yquem.' She moved round next to the range by Pascal. He was young but obedient. He was French, he understood. She stood straight behind him so she could whisper in his ear as he worked. He was her instrument.

'We are doing the kidneys. We will make two dishes. One for the sauce. One for the meat. We will garnish it with lentils. First we will do the stock.'

Her voice was serene. Her eyes closed. He nodded without looking behind. He could feel her breath on his neck. He could still smell her soapiness above the smells of the kitchen. He was her violin. She was the bow. Had he looked, he would have seen Jojo's intent etched on her face; as it was he could feel its powerful epicentre behind him. The instructions rippled out of her, like a mantra, or some old white witch unburdening her spell.

'Slice the kidney. Thinner. Warm the butter. Not that one. Use the Echire. Warm it gently just till it foams. The kidney must surf on it. Wipe it across the pan. Sear it. Now, turn it over . . . Now, little stock, just wash it, let it bubble down. Don't be impatient.'

Her hand stroked his arm to restrain him.

'Do that again, with the stock. Where is the Yquem? Pour me two glasses. I will have one.'

In the pan the juices were vanishing like an ebb tide under the meat.

'Put the wine in, half a glass. Let it go down.'

They watched the golden liquid disappear in a mist of bubbles and steam.

'Turn it again. Now put all the rest of the wine in, and pour it over there where it is not too hot. It will be fine there. There. Now the lentils. Did you pick them over?'

'Yes, Chef.'

'Do it again. Be sure. No grit. No little pebbles.'

Jojo sipped from her glass. She was glad Pascal had called her Chef, not *madame*. She was painting. The rest of the kitchen bustled on, watching them out of the corners of their eyes, in awe. No one dared interfere or do anything that might upset the balance. Not even Vincent. He had buried his honour and, to his annoyance, found himself acquiescing. He took her over a ladle of soup in a clean pot.

'Do you want to taste?'

'Have you put anything in it?'

'No.'

'Then slice the scallops and an oyster finely, as we discussed, and make a little clump in the bottom of the bowl. You will need the thyme. But it is a good soup. Let us risk it with a little star anise to surprise him, not a teaspoon, just a soupçon.'

Vincent backed away, a monk retreating from the altar. He didn't like the way Jojo changed recipes as she went. It offended his sense of security. This was not football after all, but cuisine. He had come to trust her intuition, even though it alarmed him.

Jojo to Pascal:

'Cook the lentils in the Yquem.'

'*Vous êtes sûre, Madame Chef?*'

'*Sûre*. Put in an anchovy and two cloves of garlic.'

'*Un anchois, madame?*'

'*Pascal, t'inquiète pas.*'

She took another sip of the wine. She had bought it for £21 a bottle, ten times what she had paid for the whole bag of lentils. Still, that was cinema.

'Now for the other kidney. Straight in the oven, just as they are, no tricks. Then make a salad of mache and rocket, and wipe it in the olive oil with the hazelnut oil, and three turns of salt.'

Pascal obeyed, a blind man being led out of the tunnel.

'Now I want a new pan. Dice some *foie gras*. Warm it down, so the juices run. Not too hot. Strain the lentils. Keep the Sauterne *jus*. Put the lentils with the *foie gras*. Put the garlic on top to brown and put it in the oven with the other kidney. Now, let me taste the sauce.'

She pushed him to one side. She took a spoon and plunged it into the white wine and kidneys. She hesitated as she swallowed.

'OK.'

Jojo walked back to her stool and waited, still as a kingfisher on a telegraph wire watching for fish to glint in the river.

'Table six ready.'

Out of her dress pocket she took a neat miniature bottle. She walked across to the stove again. Pascal pulled the plate down from the microwave, where it had been heated.

'The salad first. The lentils on top. One tablespoon of the Sauterne *jus*. The garlic on top.'

She watched his fingers intently as they played with the greens, greys and beiges.

'Now the roast kidney. Carve it lengthwise, three times.'

The inside still bore a rose blush.

'OK, now the juice of the kidneys, one spoon of Sauterne *jus*, and two drops of this.'

She poured the black, viscous liquid out of the bottle in her hand. It bubbled in the hot pan.

'Quickly, a little butter.'

The butter collapsed on the black surface.

'Stir. Taste.'

His turn now. He lifted the spoon to his mouth.

'Good, *n'est-ce pas?*'

'*Magique*. What did you put in there?'

'Later. Serve it now quickly, while it is warm. Spread it over the kidneys. Old-fashioned style. *Vite. Vite. Allez. Allez.*'

She moved away. She crossed to the sink, turned on the tap. She washed her face and hands of the sweat that had built up around the stove. Vincent sidled up beside her.

'Was it OK? Will he like it?'

'He will like it.'

'You are not staying to see?'

As she walked out, Jojo was conscious of the tension siphoning out of the kitchen with her. She retired to room six and opened a bottle of champagne. She showered again, lathering the kitchen out of her thick locks. Even the bandanna she wore could not keep out the stain of the cooking. She put on a silk emerald wrap and tied it tightly round the waist like a toga. She made some calls to distract herself. There was a knock. It was Vincent.

'He ate it. Everything. She didn't finish hers, but she is so small I am not surprised. He ate some of hers too. She does not look as if she has ever eaten more than a sandwich all her life. They are on dessert now. He ordered everything as an *assiette*. One of us should go and talk to him.'

'I'll go.'

Jojo swung off the bed, shook out her hair, glanced critically in the mirror, smoothing her dress over her hips, and walked out, an admiral in search of her fleet for inspection. Vincent remained marooned in room six, unsure of what to do next. It was his kitchen. That was supposed to have been his cooking. He poured himself a glass of port from the decanter.

He drank swiftly and absent-mindedly, like someone who was used to having drinks around. His thoughts were elsewhere. And the madness started to envelop him as it always did these days when he drank. It began as a brooding moodiness. Then it would swell up into a clear anger. Reason deserted him but he felt like he was an evangelist with a message to deliver. Sometimes he remained quite jolly, at least on the inside. And then he would begin the descent into a ragbag of emotions that were so intense they made him cry. Eventually sleep would snatch him.

Everyone in the kitchen had become familiar with these moods and accepted them as part of the job. Chefs were expected to be mad. No one in food was quite a hundred per cent.

Vincent consumed half the decanter in about five minutes. When he reappeared in the kitchen, glaring around his kingdom, he focused on Alastair, who was taking a dustbin outside.

'You, boy. Are you the one who wants to cook?'

'Yes, Chef, yes, Chef.'

Alastair always said that. It was safer than saying anything else. He had never had any real ambition to be a cook. His mother had thought it would be a good thing. That was not the type of honest job application chef Vincent Victor was ready to hear from anyone who might be so privileged as to have the chance to work in his domain. Alastair looked up at the swaying figure, trying to assume the impossible stance of the servile and the savant.

'This place,' Vincent declared, everyone looking now, 'is full of moles, is it not?'

'Yes, Chef.'

'How many moles?'

'I've got six traps down to save the front lawn. I caught three last week, Chef.'

Vincent edged closer, his port breath fanning Alastair's cheek.

'Bring me a pair.'

'Of moles?'

'Of moles.'

'I'll see if we have caught any.'

Alastair disappeared. Vincent slumped in his office and rummaged in the bottom drawer for a bottle of Madeira. He slugged it back from the neck. The rest of the kitchen turned back to their duties. They were nearly finished and mostly were tidying their stations. Then Alastair returned, triumphant, with two moles held aloft.

'I got 'em, Chef.'

The size of Mr Tetris made Jojo fearful for her chairs. She had not realised he was blind. She felt the little girl beside him watching her. Self-consciously she toured the other tables first. She took with her a bottle of Armagnac and spare glasses and headed for table six.

'Did you enjoy?'

'Remarkable,' he grunted. The sparrow smiled up at her. She seemed to be checking her dress for splashes of food. Leaning across to her companion, she whispered:

'Miss Coltrane herself, the *patronne*.'

Between the pair of them on the table were spools of tapes. Jojo wondered what was on them.

'Jackie is my eyes and my driver. She tells me the colours of the curtains and about the oil paintings. It must be lovely. I wish I could see it, but at least I have had the compensation of eating some superb food.'

'You are very kind.'

'No, it is not kindness. I know about these things, and I always tell the truth, which is why I have so many readers.'

They accepted the offer of the Armagnac. Jojo filled the glasses high.

'*Santé*,' said Jojo.

'*Santé*,' he said as the girl guided his hand to the glass. 'Ah, the sixty-eight. A great year.'

Backstage, Vincent raised himself up, unsteadily, belly first, from the swivel chair. He stood uncomfortably close to Alastair and ran his thumb over the moles' soft fur.

'How many do I need for a jacket?' he whispered in Alastair's ear.

'A jacket?'

'A moleskin jacket.'

'About forty. I'm not sure, Chef. I can ask my mum.'

Vincent's tone was soothing.

'Well, my young Alastair who wants to be a chef. You do want to be a chef, don't you?'

'Yes, Chef.'

'I have a proposition.'

'Yes, Chef.'

'You will make me a moleskin waistcoat. Can you do that?'

'Yes, Chef, I'm sure I can.'

'And in return I will teach you to cook. For each of the moles you skin, we will cook together and carve and sauce and we will discover whether or not you have any talent.'

'I'm not sure I want to eat moles, Chef.'

'You are not sure. Well, I am not sure I want anyone in my kitchen who would begrudge me a moleskin waistcoat. If you want to be a binman all your life, that can be arranged. No. It is being arranged. But I have always wanted a moleskin waistcoat. And it is only a fair trade that if you want to learn my secrets you offer me something of value in return.'

'But why do we have to eat them, Chef? They can't taste very good. They are worthless.'

'No more worthless than you at this minute. What right have you got to waste a life like that? If you kill something, you are responsible. You have to make full use of what you have done to justify yourself. My vanity for a waistcoat is not enough. You cannot throw it away afterwards. You are beholden to find a use that is at least as important as the life that went before it. So we will not kill like savages. We will have a purpose. Your education. And when they snuffle up in the dark into the heavy metal coils of your traps, they will die in the hope that they will make something better of you.'

'But they don't think, Chef.'

'But you do, little boy, you do.'

Alastair faced the abyss. On one side stood the dole queue and his mother's disappointment, on the other an apprenticeship to this madness. His happy days tending the garden, he knew, were numbered. He pondered silently on the nature of ambition as Vincent's big pockmarked face breathed hot Madeira down the side of his neck.

'We will start with these. You will skin them both – that one will be made into a ham and we will eat it at the end of your initiation. This other one we will roast with a little butter. Pascal will show you how. You will then carve it and plate it and bring it to me, and we will find out whether mole and Madeira go well together . . .'

The glorious début of the Vicarage climaxed in a series of separate emotions.

Hannibal Tetris was inspired by eating one of the great meals of his professional life. He shambled slowly up the stairs on the arm of his petite companion, agog with his discovery. Her pleasure had been vicarious.

Vincent wrought his revenge for being substituted by making the poor Alastair cook something as miserable as a mole. Alastair carved the tiny creature with the dexterity of a blacksmith doing needlework.

Pascal, the true hero of the moment, saved the young man from further humiliation by extracting him from the kitchen at the critical moment with the news that the last bus was about to leave, and smuggling him out before the drunken Vincent could pronounce sentence on his feeble pupil.

Jojo felt vindicated that Hannibal Tetris had enough nous to recognise her gifts.

On the way out, Pascal found her perched among the cushions in the lounge.

'*Madame. Madame*, I wanted to ask. What was that you put in the sauce? It was marvellous.'

'Ha ha. That, my dear Pascal, was the balsamic vinegar of Modena. The real one. Would you like another taste?'

She poured a few inky-black oily drops into the proffered glass.

'Drink.'

He smelled and let his tongue dip into the darkness.

'It is heaven. We must have some more. I will order it tomorrow.'

'Pascal, some things you cannot buy. This is seventy-five years old and was given to me by a dear friend whose family make it. I am glad you have tasted it. You did well tonight. Go now, do not miss your bus.'

Deserted in the kitchen, Vincent wandered into the safety of the garden, where no guests would find him. He stumbled by the rosemary bed, fell and curled up around a rose bush, cuddling the thorns as sleep swept over him.

Ten feet above him, Hannibal Tetris squirmed himself into position for his last pleasure of the evening.

The Vicarage was oustanding, Hannibal Tetris informed his readers. The sauce for the kidneys, he wrote, was 'an intense inheritor of rampant indolence'. The soufflé was to 'suffer and to supplicate at the same time'. He filled three and a half columns with adjectives and adverbs. One sentence famously (among the subeditors at least) ran for ninety-five words on a single verb. Jojo liked his use of alliteration.

Mary made the bed the next morning with continued concern for the fate of the girl who had shared it with such a hippopotamus. The flecks of light bleeding on the sheets were to trouble her for many years to come.

Following Hannibal's fulsome prose, Vincent assumed the credit. Other guides and writers and Hangers-on arrived. He came out of the kitchen after meals and shook hands all round, accepted plaudits like a ballerina, and blessed the rich with his presence and a glass of bubbles, as he referred to the Krug. Then he retired backstage to terrorise Alastair with another lesson in gastronomy.

The Vicarage was adopted by émigré Londoners and food amateurs from Friday to Sunday. In the week, there were business lunches and locals curious to discover for themselves the delights of their amazing new neighbour.

Heady from her early success, Jojo ordered flowers mercilessly. The garden could not keep up with her. She transferred her affection from the kitchen to the house. When they were unlikely to be full, she would take one of her own rooms and lie naked, watching Japanese TV and drinking Montrachet. The Vicarage became a dream. She would return to London armed with new ideas on how to make the rooms more sensual. An antique lion head there. An oil of a naked man there.

Every week, the lithe Lydia from JCA would arrive armed with three or four men, and would sign for the bill in the name of a well-known company, magazine or newspaper. At the end of the month, along with an invoice, arrived a stack of press cuttings, and an itemised list of the people they had brought to the Vicarage and how they had spread the word. The service was as impersonal as a railway.

Jojo's extravagance attracted a new kind of guest, women executives who liked the jacuzzis and the fact that they could order a salad and a bottle of Glenlivet water in the increasingly famous dining room and unwittingly imitate its founder. It became quite a cult.

Vincent was aggrieved that they had not come to enjoy the cooking. His notes in the newspapers and the guides justified his vision of himself as the purveyor of dishes like salmon with a crust of red pesto (using opal basil, not tomato, at Jojo's insistence) and a sauce of crayfish. He felt sad at these urban refugees passing up the opportunity to understand his work.

Jojo told him not to be so silly. They all paid the same. Nevertheless the experience bred in him a bitterness, as if Jojo had conjured up this injustice that he should have to serve undiscerning people. He became immune to praise, almost indifferent. He expected it and began to find anyone not completely uplifted as behaving rather oddly.

For fifteen months, everything seemed, and was, wonderfully, extravagantly, indulgently, scrupulously successful.

As if Saturn rising in the heavens had begun to exert a retrograde pull, the tide of events began to turn. The blessings of good fortune fell from the Vicarage one by one. It was not the stars or astrology or anything so vague, of course. Jojo half expected it. The spell could not allow her too much good fortune in so short a time.

Winter moved in not with a violent gale but with a sudden overnight deep frost. The last petals fell from the roses. The clumps of chives that had stood militarily upright slumped into a squidgy splatter. The leaves of the sage shrivelled. The lemon balm disappeared. The last green leaves froze prettily, then drooped in the watery morning sun.

Jojo was sitting in the drawing room, poring over the big red booking book and the blue book of forecasts, with a small espresso, the *Financial Times* and the phone to hand. She had taken over the drawing room as her headquarters early in the week when they were not overly busy and it was not wanted for a private function or to take the spillover of guests from the main lounge. Idly she flicked back through the books to check when the last midweek booking had been. Surprisingly it was four weeks ago. She looked forward to find the next booking. Nothing next week. Or the week after.

She looked again at the main bookings for the hotel. Surely last year rooms had been booked four months ahead, especially around Christmas, Valentine's Day and Easter? The forward booking pages were blotchy. The open expanses of white space were worrying.

She checked the restaurant. At least that was full. She had seen it full. She thumbed back a few months. There was no doubt about it. The forward bookings were well down. Something was wrong. The spell was out of its box. People were booking on the day, or a day ahead, not the week or two weeks that had been normal since the Vicarage opened. Where had everyone gone? Where were they going?

She surveyed the impending damage with growing trepidation. The City pages spoke of a downturn in the economy. Was this what they meant?

Her eye caught a small piece at the corner of the page. *'KY To Move to City.'* Didn't she know it already? The chemical company sales team used the Vicarage to entertain doctors and persuade them to use their products. The company was retrenching, closing its local office, and all expenses had been stopped. Poor old doctors.

The recession seemed to Jojo to be uncomfortably democratic. It affected everyone and for the most part Jojo regarded it impersonally. However, there were mischievous details, tiny embellishments that were more personal, more familiar.

Vincent felt it most poignantly. The public standing of the Vicarage still surged forward, with mentions in the papers and magazines, as they all hurried to catch up with the news of this amazing venue. There were rosettes in this guide and knives and forks in that. But in the dining room, for the first time, there were empty tables. A crevasse was opening up ready to swallow them all.

Small things started to go wrong. Mary left. She found the whole place too rarified and had come to see it as having a corrupting influence.

Alastair had made two moleskin waistcoats. He had cooked mole with chilli, with Madeira, with chocolate, with tomatoes, with just about everything in the larder, and was in cahoots with a local girl who wanted him to get a proper job with proper people at the car factory.

64

The hours at the Vicarage were unreasonable, he said she said.

Then came the first Lloyd's casualties. They had always liked the Vicarage and held up the trade in the week. Jojo was surprised just how many members there had been in the area. They all disappeared within a few weeks of each other. One Saturday they were full as usual. The next they were a quarter full. Two even planned to set up nearby as bed and breakfasts and asked for jobs in the kitchen so they could learn a bit about the trade. They would leach business.

The tone of the London booking agents changed. Last summer they had been pestering Jojo for block bookings with promises of putting the Vicarage on grand tours of Stratford and Oxford. When Jojo phoned them back now, some of the phone lines had been disconnected. America had done little old England. Perhaps things might improve later and there would be a few late bookings. But don't expect a rush. And then there was the nervousness about hijacks. Americans were thinking twice about getting on any kind of plane at all.

The French – well, they had their own problems, and most of those curious to see their odd neighbour had probably done so. It was not, as one agent put it, understating the case, going to be a great year. Jojo began to feel a very long way up the M40 and a long way from the heart-throb of City money.

Recession was a pack of wolves howling at the gates, savaging her plans and good fortune, embedding their teeth in the balance sheet and shredding it with great angry sweeps of their jaws.

And then Vincent went berserk.

The last guests were on their desserts and coffee. Most of them at this time of night were staying. Jojo had been in the drawing room and had just slipped out into the hall to get a bottle of burgundy. She was looking forward to settling down and watching some late-night TV, something she only did occasionally, but when she did, she made it into a session.

Pascal suddenly appeared at the reception desk, still in his whites and toque. In the hushed tones and silent signals of hotel discipline, his voice, his very interruption, was a declaration of emergency.

Seeing Jojo, he looked momentarily relieved, like he was passing the baton on to someone else.

'*Madame. Madame. Vite!*'

He almost never called her *madame*. Jojo stared at him in alarm and flashed a quick look across at the guests in the dining room. No one seemed to have noticed anything, yet.

Pascal was beckoning.

'*Vite!*'

In the centre of the kitchen like a wounded bull, glaring straight ahead, was Vincent, hands by his sides, shoulders slumped, the sweat visible on his face. His very stillness in a kitchen so used to rhythmical movement was macabre in itself.

'A curse on you all,' he growled.

Everyone in the room looked at each other, unsure of who he meant or who was being cursed, or even quite why. He said again heavily:

'A curse on you.'

No one answered.

'Vincent, shut up!' Jojo shouted at him.

For a second she wasn't sure whether he was sizing her up for a punch or just trembling. He tried to stare at her but he couldn't hold his gaze.

'Urrgh,' he grunted, very quickly, as if he was trying to get something, anything out before she said anything else. Then his frame slid sideways and made for the door

66

with a final shuddering shake and lowering of the shoulder, as if to say, it's all yours.

Jojo was almost on remote control with anger.

On the floor, skewed up against the wall, lay the heavy frying pan. Droplets of hot oil ran down the tiles where it must have hit and were pooling on the angle with the floor. On the rim of the pan was a splodge of red.

Slumped like a puppet was Alastair, a white bandage oozing blood on the side of his head. One of the sous-chefs, a young Irish boy called Micky, held it in place. They looked like a tableau from the barricades of the French Revolution.

'Pascal. Take over the service. You, Micky, give him a brandy and take him to hospital. Use my car. The keys are at reception. Quickly now. Stay with him. Ring me when the doctor has seen him.'

Les misérables struggled to their feet in a muddle of arms and legs. Micky put an arm round Alastair's waist and shuffled him to the door.

Jojo moved over to Pascal's side.

'What happened?'

'He just went pop. He hit Alastair with the frying pan. Not once, but two or three times.'

'Why, for heaven's sake?'

'It happens. He has been drinking. It was not the first time.'

'What did Alastair do wrong?'

'I don't know. I wasn't listening. Probably nothing. Vincent is always picking on him, and when he has been drinking, I don't think he knows himself.'

'Christ! You men!'

Jojo went out of the kitchen door after Vincent. There was no sign of him. The night seemed to have swallowed him up.

The first chill wetness of the night was creeping into the

air. The kerb scuffed his foot. The stars and a full moon lit the field ahead. Peering through the purple blackness, Vincent could make out white shapes huddled under the shadow of the tree. He crouched and crept over the gulley behind the hedge. He could see them more clearly from here. Dead leaves rustled under his feet. Ears pricked. The flock swayed.

He could hear himself breathing noisily, and his feet creaking on the dry ground. The alcohol still burned inside him. He scratched the ground. And then he sprang. One hand leapt upwards to grab a branch and he swung through the night with a yell. He landed, backside first, on the back of one of the ewes and fell into their musty, misty midst as the animals scattered. He grabbed the ewe to his left, clenching his fist into the deep fur, his other arm round its shoulder in an iron grip.

'Got you my beauty,' he breathed in its ear.

'Baah,' the frightened creature bleated underneath him. He pulled himself on top of it, dragging it to the ground.

'You are mine. Mine. Mine,' he breathed.

He held tight and wiped his sweaty cheek along its wool and put his nose deep into the curls. He whispered into its ear:

'Don't struggle, you bitch, I have you. I can poach you. I can roast you. I can sautée your brains in black butter. I am your master.'

The sheep lurched under him. He held tight, his hand right under the belly. The heartbeat slapped hard and rhythmically in the palm of his hand.

Suddenly the animal seemed to sense his dominance and lay still, complicit, unarguing. This stillness woke dark thoughts in him. The heat of its body, its acceptance of his mastery and strength, its total passivity.

The smells of its fleece and the wet night grass reached up to him. He felt his penis rising rigidly.

The sheep squealed, tried to rise, but his weight was too much for its back legs. It turned its head away from him and looked straight ahead into the night.

'Hold tight, my beautiful. I have something here for you. I am going to give you a little stuffing.'

The animal's hips moved but it only served to arouse Vincent more. His head full of brandy and the night air and the physical proximity of wrestling with the beast, he felt wild. He thrust himself into the dark nether regions blindly, the wool, the cakes of mud and turd. He hit bluntly against flesh. And then the unthinkable, blasphemous, moist, fibrous cavern swallowed him. He was in with the devil. This was the devil's bride. He roared. He trembled so much he barely felt the sheep's movement as he thrust desperately, swiftly that all this would be over soon. Finally, he fell to the side into the grass. Released, his sheep lover sprinted forward ten metres and stopped and turned. It baahed at him.

'What, no cuddle? No post-coital tenderness? No cigarette? Was it good for you too?'

'Baah. Baah.'

'My beasty darling, you are so beautiful in the night air. Shall I buy you and take you home and save you from the abattoir?' The animal ran off. His head nestled in the muddy grass roots and his eyes closed.

Jojo waited anxiously for the call from the hospital. She conjured up the image of the spell slyly slipping Vincent an extra drink to tip him over the edge. At 3 a.m. Micky phoned.

'They are keeping him in. He is OK, apparently, but they say that about everyone. Probably let him out tomorrow. The burns don't seem too bad. It's the knock on the head they are more worried about.'

'Thanks, Micky. Thanks for staying with him. How did he seem to you?'

'Well, he never has that much to say anyway. They gave him some stitches and I guess he's dozing off with the nurses by now.'

'OK, I'll see you in the morning.'

'Do I get to lie in a bit?'

'No, I'd like you in early.'

'You're a hard woman to work for.'

'You don't know how hard, boy.'

Vincent re-emerged at eleven. By then Jojo had calmed down and organised herself. She had her whites on and they were getting on with the morning prep. She was in the middle of the kitchen, wiping a herb and mustard crust on to the fat back legs of a lamb. Vincent said nothing and headed for the chef's booth.

'Where do you think you are going?' she said.

'I have some paperwork to do,' he muttered.

'And what about last night?'

'What about last night?'

'Alastair could charge you with assault.'

'Will he the fuck? He'll lose his job.'

'He is not your chattel.'

'He is a fool. He has to learn.'

'Don't you want to know how he is?'

'He'll be fine. He's got a headache and some stitches.'

'Vincent, you are sacked.'

'I am the chef. You need me. I have shares. This is my kingdom. I do what I will. They do what I say. They will obey me now.'

'You were drunk.'

'So? Service was over.'

Jojo paused.

'I will not put up with violence. I will not work with you.'

'You have no choice. I read the papers. The greatest food writers say I am the most important cook in the

70

country. I have stars and rosettes. My office is like the pony club. Look at it. You. You would not dare to get rid of me.'

'Vincent, you are a drunk and you are a bull. You are fired.'

'You have to give me three warnings, it's the law.'

'Bugger the law, Vincent. Get out. I'll post a cheque on. You give me any trouble and I'll make sure you never work again. You take me to court and I'll make sure Alastair puts you in prison.'

'After all I have done for you? You will regret it.'

'I don't. I won't. Get out. Out. Now.'

His eyes bobbed around the room, checking the floor, the stove, back to Jojo, back to the floor again. He started chewing his lip.

'I'm sorry.'

'So am I.'

They both meant different things.

'Goodbye, boys. Cook well. Remember what I taught you.'

Then he was gone.

'You did well, *madame*, very well. I'll do the service, you get on,' said Pascal.

'Good on you, Jojo,' said Micky.

'You men, you are all crazy,' said Jojo.

'You don't know how crazy,' Micky cracked.

In the drawing room, Jojo reviewed her options. She poured herself a stiff Armagnac. At this rate she would end up like Vincent herself. She needed a shower. She could smell the sweat on herself. Perhaps she was not so cool in a crisis after all. She sat on the big green leather executive chair and put her feet on the table. Dickhead. She rarely swore, not even in her head, but all this male machismo seemed to rub off on her. She disliked giving in to it. She swigged the Armagnac. She lectured herself. You have no chef. You have no customers. The projections are down. She felt like ringing Marcel to ask his advice. No, she didn't want to tell him. He was another macho man, he wouldn't understand.

Vincent would be no great loss. She could do more cooking. She would enjoy that. He had kept her out of the kitchen. Pascal could step up. He was inexperienced but his instincts were good. But she still needed help. She finished the Armagnac and picked up the phone.

The answerphone was on. As usual. A cold female voice was repeating in a loop: 'Please leave a message. We will get back to you as soon as possible.' Very transatlantic, she thought, not even Cartier's own slurpy tones, just the Paid Voice.

She had not really expected anything else, but sometimes you got Cartier's fast, streetwise rap, lilting with sarcasm and a conspiratorial change of accents. His voice gave the impression of having cruised the major arteries of the city and holed up somewhere close to the heart where it could feel the pulse. Its pockets burst with gossip.

The answerphone voice, the faxes, the stories in the papers and from Lydia – there was another person she had not seen for a few weeks – had all put together this odd, macramé image of a man. If he had come to the Vicarage, she might well not have recognised him. Probably would not have done. It was time to see what else he could do.

She left a message asking Jack Cartier to call her, in person.

She put down the phone and poured another drink.

'Help,' she breathed to herself. In the back of her mind she heard the spell chuckling quietly.

4

THE HATFUL OF TRUFFLES

JACK CARTIER WAS drinking jasmine tea at CCK when Jojo called. Mr Woo let him have one of the big round tables in the back room before the restaurant got too busy. Mr Woo was happy to humour his valued guest. Cartier was often the introducer of good, high-paying western customers. Cartier spread himself out with bits of paper, receipts that needed logging, the week's letters to answer, bills to settle. He used the time to bring some order to the anarchy of the rest of his week.

CCK was a handy refuge away from his usual haunts. No one he knew came here so he would not be interrupted or distracted. The atmosphere was sufficiently different to nudge him into finishing his business chores. In the good days when he had had six, even seven girls working for him, he had enjoyed and needed the privacy. Now he took a certain comfort from doing all this in a neutral atmosphere. A smell of cooking oil and burnt skins of green peppers hung in the air. Thin films of blue smoke rose up from the dim sum trolleys. Cantonese versions of country and western songs jangled out of the cornicing. Behind there was the regular chinking of bowls, the tapping of plastic chopsticks on china, the sizzling of peppers on hot plates, the clunk of tea pots, a patter of voices and phones and the steady machine-gun rattle of the till.

Cartier fantasised about the waitresses as they pushed their metal trolleys round and round the cavernous room beneath the plastic chandeliers and past the spitting dragons on the walls. They each wore the same uniform of red waistcoat, white shirt, bow tie, black skirt, but each girl managed to assert her individuality. One hadn't bothered to iron her shirt. Another had tied her long hair into a fat plait that swung down across one breast to her navel. A third had a bob. Two others wore ponytails; one had tied the knot on the top of her head, the other down the nape of her neck. The ends of their hair were unilaterally and impeccably straight, as if they had all been to the same hairdresser that morning. They rivalled each other in the glare of their fake gold ornate buttons and hair grips.

The desirability of the waitresses was a long-standing ragging between Cartier and Mr Woo. They had embroidered the subject into a game they played out each week. The waitresses assumed personas as the most evil and cunning temptresses or as beautiful and innocent princesses. Mr Woo protected their honour as if with his life. Cartier was cast as the imperial opium trader seeking to corrupt and seduce them.

It was their sheer unattainability that fascinated Cartier. Why were these beautiful girls always so unapproachable? Why did they reject his advances so absolutely? They didn't even bother to say no if he asked them out. They just burst out laughing like it was the most ridiculous thing anyone could propose.

'You stop looking at that waitress and get on with your work,' Mr Woo chided.

'She fancies me. She wants to run off with me.'

'She better not. Anyway, you too ugly for her. Chinese girls no like western men, Cartier.'

'You just like to think that.'

'They like money, not men, not *gweilo* men anyway.'

'See, she's smiling at me,' Cartier said, eyeing the girl with the long plait lingering by his table. He didn't know whether she understood English or not. Or, if she did, whether she might have taken him seriously.

'She's smiling at your wallet. You know nothing. Chinese girls send money home. They got aunts. They got uncles. They got cousins. They got nephews. They want money for this business. They want money for that business. They suck you dry. You got no chance.'

'I bet in the middle of the night they think about something else, apart from pound notes.'

'Sure, they think about dollars. Besides, you western boys smell like a juicy pig to them. Me, I smell like a fragrant tea leaf.'

'Pigs dig up truffles.'

'You keep your hands off my girls. They just trouble for you. These girls are serious business for me. I don't want them out on the town with the likes of you. I want them short of money so they come here and work late and cheap for me.'

'I can wait. I'll come back every day. One day she will be ready for me.'

'That's plenty char sui buns and roast duck noodle soup for me. Maybe I let you wait. That way I get filthy rich and by the time you paid me out she be old and wrinkled and dry.'

'I bet her pussy is as warm as a shark's fin dumpling and her skin is as silky as wet noodles.'

'Your prick would shrivel up like a whelk in chilli.'

Mr Woo turned to the waitress and barked something in Cantonese. Her skin looked so soft. She giggled something back, then pushed her trolley modestly away.

'She says you got rough old skin like wun tun. Scratch her bad.'

'I have money,' Cartier said, getting a £10 note out of his pocket.

'I your friend. I save you from her. For £10 that good advice. Or she twice cook your goose, Cartier. You go out with her and pretty soon you end up upside down in the shop window hanging from a hook up your naked bottom like one of those plump soya chickens. Her brother see to that.'

Mr Woo was laughing now, his implacability disturbed like a stone thrown into a pond.

'OK. Don't lose it all on mah jong tonight.'

'That is a proper vice for a man. Maybe I win another restaurant with it. You bring me plenty more customers now.'

Mr Woo drifted away, leaving Cartier to finish his papers. He wrote out the last invoice. He noticed on the credit check that someone else had been examining his file. He wondered who and why. He picked up his papers and left a second £10 note as tip. He looked over to see if any of the girls noticed his leaving. They didn't. They never did.

He walked two blocks to the serviced office that took care of his phone calls and letters and maintained the illusion that Jack Cartier Associates International was some form of glamorous expanded intercontinental brokerage. That was when he got Jojo's message.

Vincent had not even bothered to pack a bag after the débâcle at the Vicarage. He had taken the first train to London and went on a rampage around clubland for a week, popping pills, drinking vodka, snorting cocaine.

His pride, his mind, his heart, everything ached. He had slaked himself to the point that his whole body began to tremble. He felt even more wounded when Jojo deposited such a small cheque in his account for all the fame and notoriety he had brought the Vicarage. Jojo must have spent all the profits on flowers, antiques, paintings, clothes, old balsamic vinegar, and thrown them all on the balance sheet as one fat single digital debit marked Miscellaneous. He felt betrayed.

Jojo should have made better reparation. He would show her what he was worth. He would show everyone. The last grains of his sensibilities told him to book into the Savoy and save himself.

He kissed his latest *compadre*-in-arms passionately goodbye on the mouth under the station arcade of Charing Cross and zigzagged studiously along the Embankment gardens, planting one foot on the flower-beds and then crossing the path to the grass verge and peering mindlessly into the waste-paper bins, stopping for the odd break on a park bench. In the hotel he bathed, managed a rather slewed shave, drank one last half-bottle of gin, and disappeared to sleep for thirty-six hours. When he woke, he ordered a massive English breakfast of two eggs, bacon, sausages, kippers, black pudding, mushrooms, tomatoes, fried bread, toast and two pots of coffee, and rang the bank. Within forty-eight hours he had unlocked his savings. There was a site on Queensway, a defunct, much-bankrupted Greek restaurant. He dossed under the tables as the decorators moved in. He called it the Montague after his errant ex-partner. He was resolved never to risk Aids again. The restaurant would be his memorial to passion. Grievance would furnish his ambition.

Cartier had met Jojo once, fleetingly, at a launch party for a new restaurant, but she had not made the connection. He had targeted her across the room and arrived as she was rebuking one of the backers, a city type in a pinstripe suit, pink shirt and slime-green cravat.

'I am not interested in men, you should know. Even if I were, you would probably not be very high up on my list.'

'Why is that?' the Cravat had asked.

'I don't like fat bellies,' she said, poking him with her finger. And – turning to Cartier – 'Who are you? You are a bit thinner. You look like the painter. Are you the painter? Are these your walls?'

Cartier laughed without saying anything. She was leaving anyway.

'Do you think she's a dyke?' the Cravat said to Cartier as she left.

'I think she's stunning,' Cartier said.

He had also eaten once at the Vicarage. Jojo had been preoccupied and obviously had not recognised him, or, if she had, she gave no indication. There had been no reason to introduce himself. Lydia looked after the account pretty well. But then he had had to let Lydia go . . .

And now there was this message.

Cartier disliked the countryside. He disliked the way country restaurants never had any customers in the week and were never big enough to cope with everyone who wanted to eat at 8.15 on Saturday night. He did not drive because he drank all the time. He did not like trains. He listened to Jojo's voice on the answerphone again. It was an unusual proposition. At first she had not seemed especially interesting, but people noticed her. The food at the Vicarage had been exceptionally fine. Besides, he needed the money.

The papers wrote that the downturn in the economy would only last a few months, but nothing Jojo could see supported that idea. The only projections that looked comfortable were the hotel rooms – even the county people had friends to stay and she could count on the spillover. The shooting weekends were pretty much full. Those poor little pheasants, if only they knew how much depended on them.

78

While Vincent was there, she had been happy enough to sign off bills for caviare, lobster, fillet steak, wild salmon and all the other expected furniture of a top-class restaurant. The wine bill for the sauces was lavish. Now she was in control of the kitchen again, she realised she hardly ever ate those things herself.

'They make us lazy just having them about the place,' she told Pascal. 'We rely on them. Customers expect these things but it is not what we do best and not everybody can afford them. I want a kitchen that *cooks*. We should grow things we want to cook. Why should we pay for all these things to be flown over from Paris and Milan? We can grow rocket. We can grow baby pak choi. Cooking is not just about technique. It is about what you cook.'

'Will people pay for such things?'

'They will pay for our skills. There is no profit in steak anyway. It is too expensive.'

'Does that mean I can change the menu?' he asked

'Pascal, you can change the menu every day if you like.'

'Every day?'

'Every day.'

'You are crazy. Sure you don't want to ask Jack Cartier about that?'

'Certainly not. The kitchen is my department. Cut back on the *carte* and just give people a choice of what is best on the day.'

Cutting back the menu and stopping the Paris deliveries at a stroke wiped £5,000 a month off the supply bill Vincent had run up. Jojo rewrote the business plan, including two full-time gardeners and setting up a bakery so the Vicarage could sell bread to the county. It was an act of emancipation. She had pulled the plug on the old regime. She was heartened by the new projections.

If they could sell bread, they could make money. The Vicarage would not go down. She would not let it.

Paddington Station felt like an alien terminus to Jack Cartier. It was loud and dirty, even though the scaffolding was up to clean it. It seemed like some huge needle injecting thousands of people into the arteries of the Tube. All these people, with their ordinary lives and tags on them for places like Reading, Didcot, Swindon, Kemble, Stroud, Stonehouse, where they all had wives and husbands, children and pets, and houses, hurtling towards little box offices in the metropolis where they would have coffee machines and secretaries and post boys and sandwiches. Jack Cartier did not feel he was one of this tribe.

He sat self-consciously in the smoking compartment of the 5.45 and drank a beer and wondered at the sheer scale of humanity. Perhaps it was not the country he minded, just the getting there. All this dead time, down time, like dead skin flaking off their lives.

Had Cartier still had a proper office, which he didn't, then the nameplate might have said 'By Arrangement'. He existed on one bank account, six credit cards, a Mont Blanc pen, a Sony Mars Bar phone, and a Filofax of phone numbers. The only insurance he carried was for the Filofax. The agency photocopied the new numbers each week and kept a second copy in the safe. He had distilled his world into a battered leather 10×8 folder.

Cartier slid into the world of public relations and marketing as if through a side door, with a small but blue-chip list of clients. He sustained them on large amounts of Chablis and whisky. He had been working front of house in a restaurant in Charlotte Street and had begun by doing a few favours for valued customers. And then a few more. Soon people started to come to the restaurant when there was something they wanted Cartier to fix, as much as for the food. The patron would not stand for it. He sacked him. Having spent his life in kitchens and dining rooms, the world looked a lot better from the table. The more people he talked to in a day, the better the day. He didn't push too hard. If he did someone a favour, he expected it returned, in time. There didn't seem to be anybody on this train to whom he wanted to talk.

The train half emptied at Reading. He felt better for the space. Out of boredom he went to the bar and ordered another beer. He tried to make a few calls but the reception cut out as the train went through a series of deep embankments. Eventually it hauled itself into Didcot and, with relief, Cartier jumped out and got into a battered Cortina that passed as a taxi.

'The Vicarage, please.'

The driver looked pleased to have such a good long fare.

'Nice place, the Vicarage. Expensive, though,' the driver said.

'Is it?' Cartier said. He had long since given up talking to taxi drivers.

The parish for which the Vicarage had been intended to house the pastor comprised a knot of sandstone houses with angled tiled roofs in a dip in the valley. Beyond, there were five scattered farms where the villagers would previously have worked. Only the road and its cars and the spread-out fields gave any indication that these undulating pastures were now part of a different, twentieth-century culture.

The once great agricultural valley lay fallow. Its hedges were neatly trimmed, the huge oaks allowed to tower into the evening sky. There was no evidence of ploughing or sowing. No tractors. Just grass, and more grass. 'It is all set-aside round here, bit of a waste, if you ask me,' the taxi driver volunteered. Outside the little houses were the telltale dormitory signs of Cortinas, Sierras and Vauxhalls cramped alongside the steep pavements, huddled bumper to bumper, waiting for the tide of the incoming eight o'clock commute. The fact that the Vicarage now occupied a position of prestige as a restaurant while all the surrounding food crafts were being laid off was not lost on Cartier.

The church was visible from the road, a neat boot of a building with a square clock tower and a long arched nave. The gravestones to the west were partially tended. Then the estate wall began.

It must have been twelve feet high and went on and on in both directions. It shadowed the road and gave a sense of rude impersonality. Eventually they came to a break in its monotonous, paranoiac security. And there was the Vicarage . . .

The only time Cartier had been there, it had been dark. Now bathed in the yellow warmth of a spring dusk, it stared back at him with tall chimneys smoking light. Iron-battened windows lit up invitingly from within. Pouting, abundant flowerbeds burst over their edges. The gravel was beach-clean and loud.

Trees lined the drive on both sides, big ones at that. Some kind of prunus, which this week were as pink as blancmange. One spring squall and the blossoms would fall into the gravel and stain the drive pink.

Stepping out of the cab, Cartier was struck by the silence. In the city he never heard silence. The turn of the car engine grated, but beyond it he could hear nothing, except a bird shrilling. He let the taxi scrunch down the drive and whine back down the lane, luxuriating in the tangibly calm void.

A menu was posted on the porch pillar. Cartier remembered it being strong on wine sauces – sole with

Gewürtztraminer; fillet of beef with Brouilly; rack of lamb with Pinot Noir; crayfish poached in champagne. A different hand seemed to be at work. In place of the brief two-dimensional descriptions, there were longer, more precise explanations – a salad of fresh papardelle, red chicory, broad beans and dolcelatte; a soup of Sancerre served with its *friture* of mussels, breadcrumbs and salsify. There was even, boldly, Spanish onion stuffed with fresh roasted garlic.

A small, elegant figure waited inside the door with an unsure smile. He was Asian, Far Asian, Cartier guessed, dressed in a soft grey pinstripe suit that was hand-made and a purple silk shirt. If he hadn't moved, he could have been mistaken for one of the sculptures in the hall. Neat, slightly effeminate, but a rosy, benign face. He bowed gently. The palm of his hand was showing Cartier the hallway. He said nothing. Cartier went in.

Jojo was in one of her studious moments, sitting on the footstool by the drawing room window, peering at the *Financial Times* spread out on the varnished floor. Her face was hidden in a cascade of curled auburn hair. She was wearing a Chinese silk pencil dress with a high embroidered collar. A gold dragon spat pith and hatred across her back. The sides were slashed provocatively up to her hip bone; the front flap fell like an apron in front of her, guarding her chastity. It was a squat, paddy-field-style pose, the kind they liked in left-wing-style magazines. The professional peasant.

She took off the hornrim spectacles and was immediately transformed from a bookkeeper. She swirled the long red hair with her other hand. The green eyes fixed him. The high cheekbones squeezed up underneath them as she smiled slowly, like she was waking up.

'You've met Mr Lee? He is a star. His English is a bit dusty. He is so polite. I found him in the Tuk Tuk, waiting on tables. I told him he was wasted. I offered him a job and here he is. He's a brilliant cook. You should see him carve vegetables. It's a revelation.'

Before she said hello, Jojo often gave a soliloquy, to establish mutual ground. Also it gave her a good chance to weigh up people's moods. The first few times visitors often put it down to coquettishness, but after a while they learned it was a way of acknowledging their presence. She moved across to the couch and laid herself out on its ochre length.

'Sit over there. We'll have coffee. Or tea? Or there's Chablis? In fact, I think we have everything.'

'A large espresso would be fine, thank you.'

'Mr Lee makes lovely coffee, you'll see. He's tinkered with the machine, brought the temperature down a few degrees, and the difference is quite remarkable.'

She clapped her hands. The room was quiet for a few seconds, then Mr Lee appeared at the door. She lowered her head in acknowledgement of his presence. He responded. She made a drinking movement with her wrist, and then gestured as if unlocking an espresso machine.

Beaming, he clapped his hands back at Jojo and vanished again.

'He can't make tea. Not English tea anyway. I don't think Thais understand things with cow's milk in them. It comes out as weird water. He's banned from breakfast tea.'

Cartier found her radiant. Jojo's dress matched the storm of saffron drapes falling out from the ceiling. The room was full of shades of warm, desert yellows and polished woods.

This was her room. The rest of the Vicarage had not been touched by quite the same personality. At night it transformed into a formal dining room around a long table, the lights selectively spotting the few indulgences, the Klimt painting, the seventeenth-century engraved

84

French mirror, the small marble bust of indiscernible sex. The big drapes, on occasions like that, were pulled tight, creating a massive cleavage. A spiral staircase led up to a raised office, beneath which were shelves of books. Endless rows of books, on food and cooking.

'I imagined you rather differently,' she said. 'You look wretched. You are not sleeping enough. You haven't shaved. I'm not kissing you. That stubble would lacerate me.'

If a man was to have a reputation then he should look as though he had at least earned it. In that regard Cartier looked the part. The cheeks were sallow and sunken like bread rolls, but the brown eyes were steady. He was deliberate in his actions. His hands were well manicured. His clothes were sharp, new, and showed a sense of fashion.

Jojo liked the idea of Cartier being louche. He didn't say much. He just watched her, carefully, trying to marry what he had heard with the woman who was now talking to him and treating him so quickly as a confidant. She seemed to be in a hurry to strip away the social conventions. After the scene-setting came the personal remark, or a disguised compliment, to show she had singled him out and thought about him. Very French. She did not seem to really expect a reply. It was not conversation, but statement.

'You should dress more classically. You would look good in suits. Or even a uniform perhaps. You would look good in uniform.' Jojo laughed.

She was immediately curious to find out about the Montague. Was it open? What was Vincent cooking? Would it be any good?

'It is a bit old guard for my taste. Very expensive. Lots of stocks and sauces, plenty of truffle this and truffle that. It impresses people. He has a good young pastry chef in Marylese.'

'Do you think it will be a success?'

'Probably.'

'Bah,' she spat. 'So the old bull has not slunk off to his lair to hide.'

Mr Lee reappeared with a tray of coffee. He put it down between them, then retired to the far corner where he could both listen in on their conversation and keep an eye through the half-open door on the first diners arriving.

'We have five acres. I'm hoping to buy another seven nearby. We won't be self-sufficient, of course, but we will have fruit and vegetable varieties that nowhere else has. I have been having a gay time of it rummaging through seed catalogues. We are planting yellow beetroot, mizuna, pak choi, ruffle basil, marfone potatoes. It is all picked at five o'clock, washed and served before nine. The sheer freshness is dazzling. We hardly bother to cook half the stuff. Show it the range and it wilts. We just dress it and send it out. The flavours are wonderful. You will have to eat with us. It has all changed and it is very exciting.'

'I have been here once before,' he ventured.

'How remiss of me not to see you. Why didn't you say?'

'I had an important client. We were talking.'

'I hope I am an important client. Or do we country folk not qualify?'

'Of course, but he was having a crisis.'

'Well, perhaps we are having one too. I may need to call rather more on your services. But first, I'd like to ask: what exactly is it that you do?'

'Anything.'

'Anything is a rather broad brief.' She flicked her hair behind one ear.

'Different people have different desires.'

'And you fix them for them?'

'Yes.'

'Good. I have something I want to talk through with you.'

He sipped his coffee. The sofa felt very soft for a business meeting. She stood up and walked the length of the couch. Cartier was struck, not for the first time, by how elegant she was. She smiled at him. Her smile was compelling, like the afternoon sun.

'We,' she began ceremonially.

He took that to mean her and someone else, but he later realised she meant the two of them.

'We shall make a spectacle. Something no one has ever seen before. A circus, a gastronomic circus. Music. Lights. Fireworks. And acts. Ice carvers. Sugar work. And there will be exploding cakes, of course.'

'Of course,' he said, without thinking.

'This is not a party, Cartier. I am not Zsa Zsa Gabor. We are not sending out engraved invitations to my coming-out party like I am some middle-aged débutante, or announcing my new sexuality. I have not bought a new dress I want to share with my friends. I want what is mine. I want my reputation. This is going to give it to me. That heifer Vincent will know he cannot steal my vision, my skills, my name. He is not to get away with it.'

She was quiet for a moment. Old enemies. Unfulfilled hopes.

'You don't really care about Vincent, do you?' Cartier asked. 'He is nothing. So what if a few people think the Montague is a cute place for dinner. It is not in your class.'

'No. Vincent is just a symbol, I suppose. But I want my place in their male hierarchy.'

'They know how good you are.'

'No, they don't, I don't even think I know myself. I want to cook this brilliant meal and I want to serve it on

87

a stage, like it is the ballet or the opera. It should be like going to the theatre. People will buy tickets. I have prepared a few things to show you what I mean . . .'

Cartier sat back, wondering what was going to happen.

'Would you mind moving over there? It will be better,' she said, indicating the chair to the side of the desk. He obeyed. She talked as she walked. Her hands were miming the shape of a top hat.

'We will have a box – a big hat box – and we will fill it with truffles. It will be walked around the room for everyone to smell. Truffles always smell better than they taste.'

She pulled the curtains with a flick of her forearm and the great drapes swept down, clothing the room in soft shadow apart from the one side lamp.

'Mr Lee, are you ready?' Cartier had forgotten him sitting in the corner – inscrutable in baggy pinstripes, sharp Armani waistcoat, bracelets on his left wrist and a single earring. Mr Lee moved swiftly around the room, checking the light fittings, half smiling as he moved.

'I am ready, Mistress Jojo.'

He turned to face Cartier and bowed:

'For your delectation and delight . . .' he said, and flicked off the last switch so the room was completely dark. All Cartier could see was the memory of his smiling face.

He heard hands clapping. And a bang. A series of small explosions sparkled like electricity round the room. The lamp beside him seemed to be exploding. Shards of coloured paper flashed past his shoulder towards the ceiling. From the other side of the room a vase erupted in a panoply of confetti. Then another. And another.

They were all covered in flying tickertape, the room filled with clouds, a light, acrid smell of explosives, and the conspiratorial laughing of Jojo and Mr Lee. Something bulky burst across the room on its way towards Jojo. And it was raining small parachutes. Cartier felt two, three, four, five small objects patter down on him. He looked down to his lap. They were tiny biscuits.

The lights flashed on again.

'Did we shock you?'

'I wasn't expecting fireworks.'

'Isn't it brilliant? This is how we will end the Circus. The whole room will explode in happiness. Mind you, Mr Lee, you will still have to do something about that cordite. The smell is too strong.'

'I fix that OK, no trouble.'

Jojo was on her knees on the floor, picking something up.

'Did you see these?'

She held out a palmful of little chocolates.

'Taste one,' she said to Mr Lee. 'I made them up specially. The Circus will go out with a bang. Mr Lee, you are a genius.'

She didn't offer Cartier the chocolate. He had to pick one off the floor for himself.

'Good, aren't they?' she said.

As the last plastic plane fell from the ceiling, Mr Lee bowed, grinning again at Cartier. In his hand he had a short kitchen knife and a phallus of a carrot. He carved it quickly as if he could do this in his sleep. Then he walked over and presented Cartier with a perfectly formed sculpture of a lion.

'For you.'

'Remarkable. I have seen it done before but not as neatly and quickly.'

'We have not finished yet. Mr Lee, would you tell the kitchen we are ready . . .'

Mr Lee bowed and went out of the door. A waitress slipped in and started tidying up the mess around them.

Cartier waited. Jojo was watching him and chatting. She seemed to presume they were old friends.

'It is showing off, really. Here, at the Vicarage, I just want the kitchen to cook. Whatever is the best thing to do on the day. The ingredients here are what matters. But the Circus should really be about technique, skill, all those tricks of the trade that make a good show. It is a magic show.'

A young chef appeared at the door, pushing a wooden trolley. He parked in the middle of the room and waited for Jojo to give him the go-ahead.

'Show him your trick, Micky.'

He nodded silently and started to work in the half-dark with a bunsen burner and a blow torch. He was hunched like he was telling a good story and was enjoying it as much this time as every other time he had told it. He was melting sugar. Cartier watched the blue light catch Jojo watching intently, one arm out-stretched, finger pointing, commanding silence, her foot up on the chaise-longue like the great dictator. The only sound was the quiet hiss of the torch.

The sugar became a molten caramel lump. Micky plied it in his hands and then laid it over a bowl of ice. On the trolley top were a series of bowls. He worked his way around each one. He made little sides out of chocolate. He took his sugar and spun it into threads around a carving steel so it coiled. He dipped strawber-ries in more sugar and pulled the ends into sharp arrows. In a few minutes he had assembled a dozen items. Jojo didn't say anything. What he was doing was fascinating because he made it look so fascinating. His fingers worked swiftly. There was a sense of magic about what he was making.

He spread out a napkin in front of him on the table, just as if he was a conjuror, and started to put things together. A flower, a petal, a stem, a coil of sugar. There was a little box in the centre. Inside was chocolate mousse. The walls were made of a different chocolate. He hinged them by dipping them in the warmed sugar. He took little hazelnuts and rolled them in white sugar and put them gently side by side on top of the mousse. And then he set up the flowers and the coils. He had made a perfectly lacquered little jewellery box, surrounded by spun sugar carvings, studded and filled with fresh berries. It was all completely edible.

Finally, Micky's soft Irish brogue broke the silence.

'You may taste it now.' Micky turned his head away as he offered it to Jojo, as if he could not bear to see his creation be consumed.

She plucked out the strawberry, nibbled and dismissed it. She then took a long thin knife off the trolley and slashed right through the little confection. She scooped it off the blade with her tongue.

'It is very clever,' she declared. 'The chocolate is not good enough. The balance of cocoa solids is all wrong. The casing must be made with much purer cocoa – probably as much as seventy per cent – this is too weak. The mousse must be gentler. And we must make the strawberries work harder. If they are to be eaten then they must taste of something. I don't just want toffee strawberries. I want them to blend in with the rest of the dish. It is not just cosmetic. I think you should macerate them in Grand Marnier.'

She turned to Cartier, wielding the chocolate-smeared knife from the disembowelled box.

'I was thinking that we would have five or six people working with Micky in the dining room actually making these desserts as the meal was going on. So each table would have its desserts constructed in front of it. It is so wonderful to watch it. So mysterious. And because they are out in the dining room they can quietly be slipping little presents of chocolates and fondants and tuiles on to tables as they go. It will be culinary cabaret.'

Jojo beamed. She clapped. She stalked up the room like some general planning a battle, clasping her hands together and twisting the rings right round her fingers.

'So will you help? Please say yes.'

'What do you want me to do?'

'I thought you might like to be the impresario. No going out on any of your notorious jaunts, mind you. You see, I have done my homework on you. I've had quite enough of that from Vincent. You said you do anything, so . . .'

'It'll be expensive.'

'Yes, but it is a big idea. I want people to talk. I want it reviewed. I want it on TV. I can't leave here, so I need someone who understands cooking and also who can orchestrate.'

'Where will we do this?' he asked.

'In London, of course. Right on Vincent's doorstep, probably.' She laughed and, stooping over the laquered table, picked up a fat fountain pen and passed him a cheque.

'Don't let me down.'

5

DANGEROUS LIAISONS

HE DECIDED TO walk through the balmy city evening, past the little cards for the Praed Street hookers in the phone booths, over the park and through the big squares of Grosvenor and Berkeley. It was not the quickest way to Soho but it was more interesting and would give him time to think. Cartier wouldn't have minded staying for dinner at the Vicarage, but Jojo had to cook and he didn't want to eat alone. He flicked his mobile on to answerphone. The sun was a fading violet and glinted against the sculpted grey concretes. The blank, empty offices and showrooms with their agents' numbers winked opportunity at him as he passed.

He had expected Jojo to be a force, but even so she had surprised him. It was difficult to disentangle all the different images he had of her. She used her manners like screens across the conversation and hid behind them. There was the beautiful woman he had just met: enthusiastic and inspired. There was the considerate businesswoman offering a much-needed contract. And then there was this other woman he had imagined, based on what Lydia and Vincent had told him. They cast her more as a wilful, machiavellian creature, brusque and tough. And then she was the cook. And a good one too. None of the impressions really seemed to sit easily with the other. Perhaps she was deliberately

93

unapproachable, like a nun, her private life and feelings hidden away in the convent, out of sight.

She had obviously done her homework. The Circus would be a good stunt. He could see the cast of culinary acrobats somersaulting around the dining room. It was crazy enough to succeed. He'd make sure it did.

By the time he had signed into the Groucho, Cartier was feeling quite up about the whole venture. He ordered a Jack Daniel's and sank into one of the battered blue divans to make some calls. The first was to Harriet Huss. Harriet was a harridan, but if anybody could get the Circus on TV, then she could. She looked like her name – a willowy frame, narrow mane of hair, oversized jaw, disjointed teeth, lips that never seemed to quite meet, nostrils agape ranged at an angle of forty-five degrees. Her eyes were sunk in small round sockets. In more vitriolic moments, her victims had been known to remark that at least with the fish the head was taken off before it was sent to market. Her physical ugliness was also pointed up by a rapacious, very obvious meanness.

No one could swim with her for long before she cannibalised their relationship. That's television, she'd explain. Nothing kept her from her holy grail of the broadcast image. Cartier thought she made awful programmes, but usually by the time they came out she had camped herself so deeply in the brains of the channel that she made everyone else believe they were top class. If the ratings were low, she declared it was part of her, and British TV's, commitment to quality broadcasting. Or it was the fault of the presenter and the director and she sacked them both and pocketed their fees.

Possibly he was being reckless trying to involve this piranha with Jojo. In his mind he grasped the tiller a bit tighter as he shoved the boat over the rapids.

'Yes, I have heard of her . . . but this is a bit off the wall.'

Huss was being difficult. She knew of Jojo by reputation from the Vicarage and the gossip columns which Cartier through Lydia had encouraged. She liked the colour of her reputation. She appeared to be a modern woman in all the senses she admired.

'Where do you fit in, Cartier? I just don't see you two as an item. You are not trying to get off with her, are you?'

'This is business.'

'She's attractive and rich. You can't afford to pass up a chance like that.'

'She's a client, that's all. Besides, she doesn't have time for all that. She cooks.'

'I never knew a girl who couldn't make time . . .'

'Get off my case, will you . . .'

'Tetchy . . . It would need some very big names to make it work. It is not worth my time unless it is network.'

'It'll be big, I'll make sure of that. Everyone will want to be there.'

'I can't waste my time chasing ambulances. It's OK for you to run after rich women but I'll need some hello money.'

Harriet always wanted hello money.

'You'll get paid by the TV station.'

'I don't know that I get all of this . . .'

'Put it down as a favour you owe me. If you're not interested I'll get someone else, but I thought it was your sort of deal. Go and have a chat to her.'

'OK, OK, don't hustle me, Cartier. I'm the hustler, not you.'

Harriet was interested in a crabby sort of way. She was always a bit slow to grab an idea, but at the same time she hated the thought that she might be missing out on anything remotely televisable. Jojo would do the rest. He had a feeling the two of them would get on just fine.

The city held its breath as the jets of Desert Storm flew over the Iraqi oil wells. No one seemed to dare to eat out. Except at the Montague. While other restaurants in London were empty, the Montague was full. A procession of reviewers came and reported back that the food was good. Success pumped into Vincent like antibiotics. Fame, he decided, suited him. He felt vindicated. He put Jojo out of his mind. She was a bad talisman.

Jojo took to spending more time in the garden. The walk down the kitchen path to the polytunnels had become one of her favourite times of the day. Since Vincent had gone, her routine was better. She stayed at the Vicarage most of the week. There was less money coming in, but she had trimmed back the overheads.

'All that matters now,' she told Mr Lee, 'is a good name. Everything else can follow.' That, she mused as she cut into the rhubarb with her knife, was Cartier's problem.

Her time split now into manageable chunks. When she woke she would get straight on the phone to her stockbroker. Even though the financial markets were down, it was still exciting. The spell helped her find one or two shares that kept the portfolio intact. At nine o'clock she went for a run, then showered and had breakfast after the guests. From ten till twelve she did the hotel books, the ordering, and paid the bills. She took it in turns with Pascal to cook lunch. In the afternoon she slept for an hour, then she would go out into the garden.

She thinned out the garlic and cut off the first green stems. She liked the slimy wet mud on her fingers. The garden felt like something she had put away for herself, her bottom drawer. Her incessant ambition nagged at her shoulder like an old cousin, but these simple, monastic rituals appealed too. There was something very personal in waiting for the first spears of mint; in piling fresh earth over the shoots, knowing that underneath the potatoes were fattening; in cutting the purple flower bells off the chives to colour her vinegar. The spell had no power over these rituals.

She went back to the kitchen with an armful of rhubarb, the thick pink stems sticking into her breast and the larger-than-life triffid leaves wobbling in front of her. She put them down on the table beside the afternoon's other pickings and sorted over the large, wet downs of newly washed sorrel, basil, mizuna, celery, endive, Italian flat-leafed parsley, club-headed rocket, the first tiny carrots still with their tops on. Their scents hovered in the dry, clean atmosphere, soon to be devoured by the danker, hot spume from the range when the sauces began.

Pascal ran a knife through the belly of a wild salmon which a poacher had brought him from the Usk. He flicked a finger inside, beneath the backbone, and pulled out the entrails under the running tap.

'How are you going to cook that tonight?' Jojo asked.

'I like it with the rhubarb and cucumber,' he answered without looking up.

'How many people have we got in?'

'Twenty-eight so far, nearly all with phone numbers from around here. No London people. And no VIPS. Not bad for a Tuesday,' said Mr Lee.

'Perhaps things are looking up . . .'

Jojo separated the bitter leaves she wanted for the ravioli and passed them to Mr Lee. He raised his cleaver and macheted the greens into neat little shards. This was a cornerstone of the new menu, and everyone in the kitchen played their part. The bitter herbs were diced and wrapped in the ravioli that Pascal had prepared in the afternoon. Jojo tasted the stock made from the carcasses of the langoustines.

'Micky, this is too reduced. Don't do it so long tomorrow.'

'Yes, Chef. Sorry, Chef.'

These early evening sessions took the place of any board meetings. The time was used to talk through the running of the Vicarage while they worked. Mr Lee chopped and carved the decorations for the plates.

'It's funny,' Jojo said, 'but you always think the end of May is really the summer. It should be a time when everything is blooming, but there is still precious little here. It is like a false dawn. Where are all the smells of summer? I am impatient for them.'

'There is lamb. Wonderful spring lamb,' Pascal protested.

'It's expensive,' Jojo said.

'Not if we buy all the animal. We can casserole the feet; make a stew with peas of the tails; the liver and the kidneys are nearly as good as veal at this time of year; we can make little sausages with mint from the trimmings. There is plenty there.'

'Pascal, you always like talking in terms of whole animals. If you can find some good young ones, let's do it.'

'The boy who caught the salmon said he could bring us some from Wales – thirty pounds each.'

'All right. Try him out,' said Jojo.

Mr Lee washed off the last carrot. He had transformed it into six carvings of chrysanthemums. He placed them in a bowl of water and squeezed half a lemon over them to stop any discoloration. He washed his hands and slipped back into the public areas to check on the guests for the evening.

'You look a bit down in the mouth,' Jojo asked. 'Are you all right, Pascal?'

'That bastard Vincent. He has started doing late suppers and is keeping Marylese on lates. I think he does it deliberately so she is too exhausted to see me.'

'Does he know about you two?'

'I'm not even sure Marylese knows about us yet. I hardly get the chance to see her. It is like being in love with an apparition.'

'You being in love with anyone is quite something, Pascal. I hope this doesn't mean that you won't be bringing me any more waitresses?'

Pascal had been the main source of new staff for the Vicarage, introducing students and local girls he had met at the disco. He didn't seem to need sleep. On Fridays and Saturdays he was often out all night. Jojo had come to rely on his love life as a recruiting agency.

'You know, Marylese must be making him a fortune. He has got her doing outside catering, after-theatre, lunches. He treats her like a skivvy. She just cooks and cooks and cooks. He pays her nothing.'

'She could leave.'

'She says it is good experience. She says where else could she be doing all these stages in one go? She is a dedicated woman. And she is so beautiful I could die.'

Jojo recalled that Cartier had mentioned how good a pastry chef Marylese was.

'When I ring her, I have to pretend to be selling vegetables. If he finds out he will think I am trying to steal her. Me. A vegetable seller, can you believe it?'

'Perhaps it's time we came up with a scheme to get you two together.'

Pascal's silence lent him the poise of experience. Jojo had seen him do this before on other people, usually suppliers, and didn't enjoy it being done to her. If you were going to ask a favour you had to know that, whatever happened for those few moments, Pascal would extract his price so you would not ask again lightly.

'I thought, perhaps, she could help do the Circus with me?' he said.

'Vincent isn't going to like that.'

'So?'

'We'll see. He will go berserk if he finds out. He will never forgive me. Bad enough that I steal his throne, but to do so with his favourite little girl who is going to run off with his arch-rival. How delicious. Will you fix it?'

'I'll get Cartier to set up a private booking. Vincent's too lazy to do those himself. He'll send Marylese instead. He'll never guess.' She laughed. 'I'm very happy for you both.'

Jojo's good humour over Pascal's display of emotion was momentarily interrupted in the drawing room when she read a review of Vincent's new restaurant. He seemed to be cooking some very dull, old-fashioned dishes and taking all the credit for the Vicarage. 'Victor Vincent has brought the freshness of the countryside to Bayswater.' Jojo did not begrudge him his restaurant. He could terrorise people as much as he liked in his own place. It was depressing that he seemed to be doing all the kinds of things she disliked – very rich, very elaborate. Had the two of them really been so far apart in what they wanted?

Cartier had been keeping out of Vincent's way. Sooner or later the call had to come. Vincent would hear about the Circus and he would ring Cartier to find out more. Sure enough a message was waiting for him on the answerphone. But Cartier was also keen to quiz Vincent more about Jojo. The last time they had spoken about her a vein on the chef's forehead had visibly started to throb.

'She nearly ruined me,' he had said. 'She is a talent. No one would dispute that. But she is a woman. So it does not matter. Not unless the world turns on its head. But she is not to be trusted. You be careful, Cartier. She can turn on you just like that.'

Vincent had regaled him with stories: how she was so ruthless; how she had always overridden him; how she had claimed the credit for his cooking; how she had thrown him out on the street; how she had always wined and dined the critics, so they thought she was the Svengali, while all the time he was doing the cooking.

Cartier dialled the Montague. Vincent had heard the rumour. You couldn't keep anything quiet for long. He was intrigued but conciliatory. Cartier asked:

'What happened between you two anyway?'

'A misunderstanding, that's all.'

'Pascal says you hit the kitchen porter.'

'So? You have to have discipline in the kitchen. It was nothing serious, he only had a few stitches and a little headache. It was just a trifle . . . There was no reason for her to get so upset.'

'That's not what you said last time we spoke.'

'Now I have the Montague, so perhaps I do not care so much. She is a cruel woman, true enough. She is out to ruin my reputation. But I am still the best chef in London and she knows it. But why . . . ?'

'You know Jojo, she has these big ideas,' Cartier said casually.

'But why? Why?' Vincent was agitated. He was repeating himself. 'Why? Why didn't she ask me?'

'I thought you two didn't speak.'

'I would, would have done it for her. If she had asked properly. It could have been a reconciliation. There is no reason for us always, always to be enemies.'

'No?' Cartier was surprised.

'Tell her that I would have done it.'

'Why don't you tell her yourself?'

'Cartier, I am a proud man. And I am hurt that she

wants somebody else to do things. I can't do everything, of course. We must let the young ones have their chance. But she is a clever woman and I am here if she needs me. She must not forget me. I would be unhappy if she did. Tell her that. But you must come to lunch. I have something else I want to talk to you about.'

An invitation to dinner at the Montague was not top of Cartier's list of things to do, but he was curious to see the place again, and if the invitation was from Vincent, it was not refusable, not without being ostracised. He acquiesced.

He looked at his watch. Jojo had put only one stipulation on their arrangement.

'You will call at six o'clock each night, so I know what you are up to.'

He ordered another Daniel's. Perhaps that was what was happening to him now, he mused. Jojo was using him. The Circus was her show. He was just the hired gun.

Jojo and Mr Lee gossiped about Cartier while they were cooking. They had built up this persona around him from his six o'clock phone calls. It gave a human face to all the details of the Circus. If things were going well, they chatted about him as if he was a favoured son who had done well at school.

'He did well to get that TV woman here so quickly,' said Mr Lee.

'We'll see about that. She looked a bit plastic to me,' Jojo retorted.

Or, if things were slowing down, it was Cartier's fault.

'We haven't found a venue yet, either,' Jojo moaned.

'We could always get a tent,' joked Mr Lee.

'We are not Girl Guides, Mr Lee,' she snapped.

Jojo liked Cartier's bravo charisma, the way he

seemed to have achieved his not inconsiderable reputation without having done very much.

'Do you think he is good-looking?' asked Mr Lee.

'In a rakish way. He's a bit puffy from the drink.'

'Women?'

'None that seem to stick.' Jojo cast him as a man who would console an unhappy wife every other Thursday afternoon in a hotel room. She imagined a string of brief unhappy relationships, always the bit-part player, never the central character.

Mr Lee was a supporter. He spoke up for Cartier when Jojo was sticking pins in his reputation.

'You cannot cast him like that, Mistress Jojo,' he declared. 'He is a man who has got where he has got. Perhaps he has built all he can so far.'

'And where does a man like that find happiness, then?'

'Perhaps happiness is not his option.'

'Pfah. He is probably just a waster.'

'I think not.'

'He drinks too much.'

'He drinks. But he is never drunk. Sometimes he sounds tired, but never drunk.'

'Well, that's only at six o'clock . . . Heaven knows what he is like by midnight. And what about our launch party? He was so pissed he couldn't make it.'

'It can be a long way from the street to the house, mistress.'

'Oh, very prophetic, I'm sure, Mr Lee. Usually in this country men like him drive an Audi and have a stash and kids in the country.'

'An Audi is not what I see in him. I think he prefers to drive an old Chevrolet.'

'Old for certain. He has probably got someone else looking after his kids. I bet he just puts them on Amex.'

It was six o'clock. The phone rang.

'He's on time for once,' Jojo said as she picked up the receiver.

'Cartier, what sort of car do you drive?'

'A taxi, usually.'

'Have you never had a car?'

'No. I sleep in cars. I work in cars. I don't drive them.'

'Have you never driven one?'

'Only when I didn't have anywhere else to take a girl.'

'I wish I hadn't asked. Was it a Cortina?'

'It was a Jaguar with leather upholstery, as you ask.'

'Very sticky.'

'It broke down a lot.'

'I bet. What's new?'

'I've booked three jugglers. And I'm checking out the glasses tomorrow and maybe the plates and cutlery. Oh, and Vincent sent his regards.'

'He can ring me, if he still has the balls.'

'I don't think he'll do that, but at least he doesn't seem to want to trample all over you any more.'

'*Olé*. By the way, Harriet Huss was in at lunch.'

'How did it go?'

'You can certainly pick them. She ran up a bill of a hundred and twenty-six pounds. She said she was driving so she could only have a couple of glasses, so orders half of '61 Cissac. That came to ninety-three pounds. She's not exactly short of neck. Then she wanted to be paid up front.'

'So what did you say?'

'I gave her something on condition. I don't trust her. You'd better be right about her.'

'I am.'

'We'll see. By the way, for the main course, I thought we might re-create the Dorking capon. We will use white truffles not black. These will not be the Bresse chickens half in mourning that they used to do in Lyons. My chickens will be bridesmaids dressed in white, their flesh will be white because they will only have eaten milk powder, and we will slide the truffles under the skin. They will be cooked in milk and cream, sealed in the pot so when they are open the whole room will burst with the smell of white truffles. What do you think?'

'Sounds wonderful.'

'You are slurring. Are you drunk?'

'I'm just warming up. Talk to you tomorrow.'

'One thing, Cartier, before you go.'

'Yes.'

'Mr Lee was wondering . . . Why did you never cook?'

'I can't.'

'Come on. You know about restaurants. You must.'

'Not like you.'

'Flattery now. What's the real reason?'

'All those hours locked away in a hot box with a lot of spotty adolescents to talk to. No, thank you.'

'Pascal hasn't got spots. Pascal, have you got spots?'

'No, *madame*. I hope not.'

'See, you are misinformed.'

'I'm a front-of-house man. I prefer people. Besides, you know what they say about too many cooks.'

Cartier put down the phone then decided to do something he had not done for a few weeks. He grabbed the Tube at Leicester Square, and cut up on the Northern Line to Golders Green. He bought some lilies at the florist by the bridge and walked round to the crematorium. He laid them by the stubby, well-pruned rose that marked the place where his wife's ashes had been scattered. Usually he was religious about getting up there once a week, but the Circus had knocked his routine sideways. He stood with bowed head by the rose bush as it grew dark. An attendant wanted to close the gates and brushed him away down the path like another fallen leaf.

The Montague was a brooding room full of drapes and candles, a modern incarnation of a Middle Ages banqueting hall. The waiters wore black and moved like shadows. The table lamps offered the boudoir privacy of snooker tables. Customers had their own cocoon into which pretty, frivolous plates of food were thrust. The mood was discreet, even conspiratorial, but, Cartier reflected, hardly convivial. Since the Aids miasma, Vincent had kept his homosexuality concealed. This sense of repression seemed to permeate the restaurant. The waiters stalked like pallbearers with their trolleys of plates and bottles.

Vincent escorted Cartier to the kitchen. It was still early and the stoves were active. Some tables had not finished. A few late bookings were just coming in.

It was Cartier's first sight of Marylese for some while. He had forgotten how beautiful she was, even in the bed linen couture of a chef's uniform. She hid her long black hair in a bandanna. The white cotton framed her features and made her look angelic, with large brown eyes, blushed cheeks, full-fleshed lips, her breasts bursting out of the constraints of her jacket.

Her hands betrayed her. The fingers were rough and callused from hours of manual work, the nails cut right down, and along the sides were recent unhealed cuts. She smiled shyly at him and went on with her work.

There were three other girls in the kitchen, which was unusual in itself, but Marylese stood out as she would have done anywhere. Vincent had warned him off poaching her. She must be very good.

Vincent caught him admiring her.

'I try to teach them the joy of doing simple things well. Girls are better than boys. They don't have the inspiration, but they are more diligent and faithful. They re-create what I want. That one' – he pointed to Marylese – 'she reminds me of one of those French girls who were brought up to make cheese so they could marry a farmer. She works quietly all day, never a tremor or a tantrum. I call them my little sisters of cuisine. I am their Father Superior.'

He giggled.

'Here they are safe. These boys won't touch them. We are a family. I look after them well. I pay their rent. I put some of their wages away for them. They want for nothing. Anywhere else they would be lazy slobs on the street, but with me they will touch greatness. Maybe one day I will open other restaurants and the best of them will be able to cook there without my supervision.'

Cartier wondered how many of these boys and girls actually wanted to end up cooking like Vincent or to have a restaurant like the Montague. There was something that struck him as implicitly old-fashioned about the restaurant and it seemed unlikely that these young chefs would aspire to repeat it. The Montague catered only for the very rich and the very elderly. It inhabited a stratosphere of its own, featuring in foreign listings magazines; in backhanders to hotel porters and concierges; and survived on a small number of high rollers who dispensed £800 a time on a bottle of mature Petrus or Latour without a care to the mark-up. The Montague had ceased to be a restaurant and had become a reaffirmation of status. Dishes never changed. Half the customers were too old to taste what they were eating and were happy to go through their memories of how things were or how they thought they remembered they were. Vincent was like some seaside matinée idol playing his jukebox of old sensibilities.

It was all by the book, and in French, *le canard au sang, les cailles à la dauphinoise, le saumon en croûte avec gingenmbre, le rôti d'agneau, sauce Madère, la bombe formosa,* but it did not translate into *cooking* that had anything to teach or to inspire. The kitchen was a production line replicating the same twenty-seven dishes. Not like the Vicarage, where the kitchen was thinking and moving with the garden and the markets and changing from day to day.

Cartier preferred Jojo's approach. It was the cooking that was worth paying for – everything fresh every morning, everything prepared that day. One thing going into the next. It was all about freshness – of produce and preparation. The rest of it was just catering and greed. If you want to use a truffle, then fine, use a fresh truffle and be done with it. Vincent, of course, would just open a tin, impervious to the difference.

At bottom, Vincent's philosophy wasn't really much different from the old trick of washing out the pan juices from a roast with a carton of double cream and calling it a sauce. Vincent wasn't even really a classicist. Just a pragmatist. He compromised a lot, too much for someone of his reputation. Cartier worried about what he was really teaching his team. Technically, it was probably a good apprenticeship. Spiritually, the Montague was moribund.

But there were two vintage Daimlers in the underground car park next door. Somehow the heretic was making the money.

A waiter sidled across to Vincent.

'Table six. Mrs Van Hohen. She has brought her Chihuahua. She wants him to have something.'

'Something?'

'She suggests something nice. She says he likes beef.'

'Then give it to him.'

'I have never served a dog, Chef. Shall I go next door and buy a tin of puppy food?'

'No, no. It smells horrible. I can't have that in the dining room. It would give us all BSE. The dog is a customer. If Mrs Van Hohen wants her dog fed, then her dog will be fed. It will be the best meal a dog has ever had. Every customer is equal and Mrs Van Hohen is more equal than some others. Give him the *boeuf bourguignon*. And use the silver service. Give the dog some water too. Make a fuss of it. Put a napkin on it.'

The waiter did not blink. The instruction flew round the kitchen. The waiter took the salver and the bowl.

Vincent and Cartier were back in the dining room when the waiter arrived at the table. He put the tray on the trolley. He took a napkin and Mrs Van Hohen lifted up her little dog. It already had a pink ribbon on its head. The waiter gravely tied the napkin round the Chihuahua neck. He put the bowl of water on the floor and went to fetch the plate.

'Poppums will have some proper food today. Just like Mamma.'

The Chihuahua salivated.

'You like some beef, don't you, poppums?'

Mrs Van Hohen cuddled the dog. The waiter put the *boeuf bourguignon* in front of her. She dipped the little dog into the bowl and it ate, happily suspended in mid air. The plate was clean in less than a minute. Mrs Van Hohen lowered the dog to the floor for it to drink. Then she looked up, smiling.

'I'm ready for my grilled sole now. I do hope it is from Dover. The best soles are from Dover, you know. I can tell the difference if it is not.'

Vincent seemed unfazed, concerned only that the waiters had behaved correctly. The Chihuahua had hopped happily back on to his mistress's lap as she toyed with the fish.

As she finished, Mrs Van Hohen remarked:

'I don't think that was from Dover, you know.

Brighton, perhaps. It tasted a little south coast. Channel waters are a little warmer. Not quite the same thing. Was *your* water all right, poppums? Not too many chemicals in it, I hope?'

She patted the Chihuahua's little head and adjusted the bow. Vincent turned to Cartier, who was trying to suppress his laughter.

'This thing with Jojo . . . Will it be big?'

Cartier shrugged, trying to look innocent and recover his composure. 'It is for her. We'll see.'

'I wanted to talk to you about something else, but you tell Jojo if she wants anything then she only has to come here for lunch and ask me. She never comes. It's a pity.'

Cartier, toying with a very solid gelatine-laden green mousse, could imagine why she didn't.

'The Montague serves the best food in town. And yet I still have to pay the suppliers. Why should I? It is their privilege to have their foods served here. I don't think I should pay them. It is only a small bill for a butcher. He could be credited on the menu. My customers would become his customers. My customers are wealthy. They can afford such things.'

Vincent's little goatee beard quivered with avarice.

'What do you think?'

'I think they will laugh at you.'

'They wouldn't dare.'

'Restaurants, even well-known ones, are just small beer.'

'Think of the publicity. You could fix that.'

'I don't think so.'

'You know lots of people. Find somebody.'

'I'll think about it, but frankly, Vincent, the idea sucks.'

Outside, the dusk was shunting in over the roofscapes,

casting an unlikely mellow glow over the dust and brick of Queensway so that even the turmoil of taxis and coaches was caught in warming pastels. Cartier was walking south towards the Chinese restaurants. As he passed the Olympiad Café he glimpsed a scene in the window. It was touching and unsettling at the same time, as if the real world was suddenly tugging at the sleeve of his less than real existence.

Marylese was sitting talking to someone. She was out of her chef's whites and just wearing a blouse; her long black hair fell freely to her shoulders. He saw the hand of her companion move across the table. She leant forward and kissed the fingers. Then she slipped the hand under the blouse on to her bare flesh, pressing her breast to the palm of Pascal's hand. They didn't think anyone could see them. They looked so happy. Cartier moved on quickly, feeling untidy for intruding on them. He was embarrassed. It had been a long time since he had been embarrassed, he reflected. Too long.

Soho was Cartier's Alamo, the last stand for the coffee roasters like the Algerian and Angelucca, the wet fish trader Richards, the delis like Randall and Aubin, Camisa and Lena, and the fruit and vegetable stall holders. The young-gun restaurateurs, Lander, Henderson, Little, Preston, Worrall Thompson, Cavalier, Holihead, were shuffling into the empty spaces on the barricades. And they were full. Fuller than the Janus sex shop, fuller than the Maximum Perversion video shop, fuller than the £1 peepshows.

Cartier's day was spent cruising the streets, speedballing on espressos, catching a beer at D'ell Ugo, a duck noodle soup down at Lee Ho Fook, a bottle of wine at the Soho Brasserie, or a bowl of pasta at Pollo. Even if he had only strayed as far as the Ivy in Covent Garden for lunch, Soho always felt like coming home.

He saw the geography physically in his mind as the shape of a hand – Old Compton Street was the knuckles, and the five streets going north to south – Greek, Frith, Dean, Wardour and Berwick – were the fingers just touching Oxford Street at the tips. The hand led into the arm at Chinatown and the shoulder of the West End.

He had composed comfortable images for each street. Greek was respectable, post-war middle class: the perennial Escargot, Victor Sassie's love affair with the left wing at the Gay Hussar, and the Resistance-style patisserie of Maison Bertaux. Frith was where the new boys were moving in, Alastair Little, Soho Soho, upstairs at the French House, Anthony Worrall Thompson on the old Braganza site, Morgens at Est Est Est. All the media crowd seemed to just cross over from drinking in the Dog and Duck for a bowl of noodles in the Rasa. Dean was asleep still, save for Amin Ali's cavernous Red Fort; Wardour was a mess as they busted down the Marquee. Berwick was the thumb, with its street markets, gauntlet of sex shops and cinemas, and the last visible signs of prostitution.

Sitting outside the Bar Italia or Café Nero he watched the sex business in a great stand-off with the restaurant universe. Recession in Soho wore a different face from the rest of London. A few years ago all had seemed lost to the raincoat tourists looking for a red-light zone, but the sleaze had been pushed back. Now there was a visible transfer of power over to media companies and the food shops again. There were still small red neon signs declaring MODEL, but you were never quite sure if they led to a dimly lit boudoir or a design studio which had kept the logo as a memento.

He headed for the Groucho and found a quiet corner, which meant the sofa with the broken springs, ordered a bottle of white wine and got to work. The

Circus had a menu but no venue. The big hotels insisted that their kitchens did the cooking. Jojo was adamant:

'We have to do it. It is our show. Get one of those brigades to work on the meal and suddenly you'll get schmaltz, you'll get tomato rose garnishes, you'll get yesterday's pastry, you'll get tinned asparagus, you'll get halves of lemon. And they will all look aghast that you think something is wrong. Imagine Vincent doing it. He would do it all the day before and let it go stale in the fridge overnight. Urgh.'

Pascal and Micky would run the brigade, with Marylese looking after the pastries and bread. Cartier had already booked a team to support them. He tried the clubs and private rooms – the Wellington, the Garrick, the Travellers', the ICA. Each had its own contracts sewn up and unbreachable. His mobile was sticky from the endless phone calls. He rang her as usual at six to report his further failures.

'You'll find something. You'll see. Keep at it.'

She was in a hurry.

'Tell me, Cartier, all these stories one hears about you. Are they true?'

'I like to let them fester. They are good for business.'

'Is it true you pimp girls for chefs?'

'It's a bit of an exaggeration.'

The story was that Cartier had stolen a head chef from one group by holing him up in a hotel for two weeks and supplying girls to entertain him.

'He had a weight problem and needed to get away. It started out as a cure, but one of my girls, Marie Louise, became rather over-enthusiastic about him. It's nothing to do with me what the girls do in their own time . . .'

'I see,' Jojo said noncommittally.

Cartier finished the wine and wandered over to the bar to order a Jack Daniel's.

Gazing out of the window at the scaffolding on the opposite side of the street, he remembered a cavernous loft conversion. It was perfect. Acres of untarnished, unsold virgin conversion work. Perfect floors. He had not thought of it before because there was no kitchen. But there was space. There was room to put one in.

Within five minutes he had trawled through his address book, found the agent on his mobile at Quaglino's, run through the details in a painstakingly drunken fashion, eked enough yes's out of him; and given the man twenty-five tickets for his pains to invite would-be tenants. He rang Jojo with the news.

She was busy. Probably in the dining room. He looked at his watch. It was 8.50. He felt piqued. He wanted her to be there for him with his news. He drained another large double. She kept her distance. Very neatly and tidily. She was such a sensual woman and yet there never seemed to be any attachments. The phone rang in his pocket. It was Jojo.

'I was cooking. It's Pascal's night off. What's up?'

He told her.

'That's brilliant. Well done. I knew you'd find somewhere.'

'Are you busy?'

'Yes. We've fifty-six in — not bad, eh?'

'Can I ask you something?'

'Sure.'

'Do you have a boyfriend?'

'You can't ask me questions like that.'

'You must have admirers.'

'I have arrangements.'

'What sort of arrangements?'

'Are you propositioning me or gossiping?'

'I want to know.'

'Why? It's not really any of your business, is it?'

'Perhaps I'd like it to be.'

'Since you ask, Cartier, I don't really do that sort of thing. Or didn't you know? I have still got twelve covers to do. I have to go. Well done. Ring me tomorrow, usual time.'

She had already left a message on his answerphone when he woke next morning.

'Come to dinner on Sunday. Let me know if you can't.'

Encouraged by the invitation, he resolved to implement another strategy he had been toying with. Harriet Huss, TV producer extraordinaire, might enjoy Vincent's proposition rather more than he had. It was her sort of deal. Vincent would see the glimmer of a chance to be on the box. She would get a free meal – probably quite a few. She could do the rounds of the suppliers. They would be flattered. It was the sort of barter they were both into. He'd have to persuade her to talk down the Circus a bit. He did not think she knew about his treachery over Marylese. She was used to double-dealing anyway. A mistress at it. He rang her as he walked down the street and got her out of bed.

By chance he passed Dillons on Oxford Street and saw the new editions of the guides in the window. The big guides like Michelin, the Good Food Guide, Maschler and Egg on Toast didn't appear until the autumn, but these slimmer private editions from Hardens and the French Gault Millau usually gave an important steer on what people were thinking. Hardens was made up from customer reports, Gault Millau by professional inspectors. He grabbed them quickly, retraced his footsteps to Soho and devoured them over coffee outside Café Nero. This was business. The winners he could take credit for. The losers he could tout for work.

Vincent had done well. The Montague had picked

up toques and capital letters in both guides. The previous year's enthusiasm for the Vicarage had been tempered by reflection and by the defection of Vincent. The ratings were on a par, but the tones were different. Vincent won out in the optimism of a new beginning. 'Victor Vincent has re-created the 17th arrondissement in WC2 . . . Very powerful intricate dishes of classical hauteur.' Customers writing to Harden reported 'lots of enthusiasm for a decent new restaurant in Queensway . . .' There seemed to be only hints of the fundamental changes in the cooking philosophies of either restaurant. Cartier had the Montague down as recidivist and the Vicarage with its new-found energy out of the garden as radical. The differences were skated over. The Gault Millau noted the fact by marking the Montague in black type to indicate traditional food and the Vicarage in red to mark modern. That was OK, but Jojo would not take Hardens' reserved praise very well: 'There have been changes and few reports on the new regime, but nothing bad . . . Service is a bit slow.' The French inspectors judged the Vicarage cooking 'light and dazzling, on the edge of fashion, less classical since the departure of head chef Victor Vincent (q.v. Montague), ably succeeded by the young Pascal Pommier under the strict eye of the charming Jojo Coltrane. Note the preference for vegetable juices in place of stocks.'

She took an age to come to the phone. He was watching the urban drift kick itself into gear for one last push before the twelve o'clock rush to the bars.

'I was in the garden,' she apologised.

He read out the listings.

'Don't these people *know* anything?'

'It's not a bad result. You keep your rating – and you need it more out there than he does in town. Remember these are London guides, so you are only in there on sufferance.'

'Pfufff.' He could hear the exasperation in her voice. She was standing in her wellington boots and a dirt-smeared T-shirt, holding the phone with her only two partially clean fingers through the kitchen window. She had been weeding the salad beds after a deluge. Her sleeves were rolled to the elbow and her forearms smudged with mud. As she held the phone the back of her hand accidentally rubbed more mud down her cheek.

'I'm standing here in the garden trying to grow waxy potatoes, little baby leaves of pak choi, shoots of fresh garlic . . . Can they not taste the difference?'

'You don't have to do that yourself . . .'

'I like doing it. When you see these little baby shoots coming through, when you can taste the flowers on the thyme, the difference between the lemon thyme and the rough Portuguese, these are the little details on which the cooking hangs . . . not those great horrible cauldrons of stocks that Vincent likes so much. He probably buys his vegetables from Sainsbury's. Some-times, Cartier, I despair.'

'You kept your seventeen out of twenty. It's not too bad.'

'We are worth more.'

'You confused them. They probably didn't have a chance to fully assess what you are doing. It reads to me like a holding entry. I'll talk to the editor.'

'Make a point to invite them to the Circus.'

'Sure. Thanks for asking me to dinner.'

'Don't get your hopes up. It won't be a romantic tête-à-tête.'

'Pity. Perhaps we can have a nightcap afterwards.'

'I'll find someone nice for you to sit next to.'

Lunch ticked away like a Swiss watch. Vincent was solicitous in the extreme. He had put on weight since leaving the Vicarage and, although he had stopped drinking, his complexion was taking on the hue of a pork chop. Harriet was full of deadly flattery.

'I think you would be marvellous on television. You could present. Perhaps your own show.'

'At last, someone who understands my cooking,' Vincent gurgled.

'It is wonderful food. Don't you agree, Cartier?'

Cartier nodded. Part of him felt like Judas and part of him was pleased to have organised the two dangerous mavericks into one pigeonhole.

'We could do a programme around each of your suppliers. They tell us about their foods, then you cook it.'

'And they supply me for free.'

Harriet ate greedily. Vincent offered her a succession of different dishes to try.

'Sweets are really my thing, Vincent.'

'Then you shall try them all.'

'You are outrageous.'

She had him on her line and was not going to pass up a chance to fill her boots, her stockings, her knickers, her girdle, her bra. Cartier fiddled politely with the food without eating. He consoled himself with another bottle of Muscat.

Vincent beamed. He would happily have spent the whole afternoon coercing more food down this wonderfully appreciative woman's gullet.

'You can eat here any time you want. Any, any, any time you want to bring any important clients, just ring me and you are my guest.'

'How nice of you. I will.'

Cartier raised an inner eyebrow, conscious that invitations to Harriet would not be disdained. She slurped her spoon through the maquise of chocolate.

'Cartier, you are a genius for introducing us. I

wonder if I could rearrange my five o'clock into dinner on Thursday? I don't know which I like better – the strawberry tart or the chocolate maquise. Let me try them both again. Vincent, you are a master.'

Vincent purred. He watched each spoonful disappearing into her mouth, then combed her face for a response. Cartier left them to it. Three had suddenly become too many.

Behind the drape, as he made a phone call, a hand touched his sleeve.

'Mr Cartier. Could I ask you a favour? Will you be seeing Pascal?'

It was Marylese. She looked anxious.

'Would you give him something from me? I won't be able to get away this weekend. We have a big festival at Brighton. If you could, I would be very grateful.'

She passed him a little square patisserie box.

'Don't put it near the heat. Leave it in the fridge if you can't get there tonight.'

'I'll look after it.'

'Thank you' – she hesitated – 'so much.'

Kissing the tip of her finger, she drew it across his cheek and disappeared in the darkness.

If there was one time to be out of London it was Sunday afternoon. The pieces for the Circus were falling into place. On the train Cartier held the patisserie box rather self-consciously on his knees.

When he arrived at the Vicarage he took it straight round to the kitchen door. Pascal was poaching some pears in red wine for dinner.

'That was a nice gesture for you, Cartier, to bring it all the way. I appreciate it.

'The bad news is she can't see you tonight. Vincent's sent her to Brighton.'

'He treats her like a skivvy. Bastard.'

Pascal flipped open the box. Inside was a small loaf of bread baked in the shape of a heart. He smiled and broke it open. Inside were nuts and raisins. He ate a corner.

'She soaked the raisins in eau-de-vie. You must have got this today?'

'At lunchtime.'

Cartier wasn't being offered any. This was a very personal gift. Pascal lifted the cake to his lips and sniffed it. He kept his spare hand underneath to catch any crumbs, munching slowly.

'Gregory crashed his van outside Dover yesterday. He's our courier. He delivers here and he delivers to the Montague. He takes messages from me to her and from her to me. But he's in hospital with a broken leg.' He ate another piece of cake. 'She is a wonderful baker, Marylese.'

'She said she was doing a festival and wouldn't be around.'

'You see why I am so unhappy? No father could ever be as strict as him. It is like being in love with a cloud. One moment she's here and then she's gone. I hardly know her. She sends me these presents like she is thirteen. It is so sweet. Do you know, we have not even slept together? I haven't slept with anybody since I met her. Me! We have these illicit moments. We hold hands. We kiss. We touch. Then she is snatched away from me again.'

'You will see her for the Circus.'

'Heavens, I can't wait that long. I have red blood in my veins – not your English sang-froid. But, as you say, Jojo's big event will also be ours.'

Cartier left him with his crumbs in his hand and his frustrations, and went off to the drawing room. He had hoped to find Jojo alone. Far from it. There were thirty people or so, some of whom looked as if they had been there all afternoon. They were not hotel guests. Jojo was presiding at the epicentre of the throng. His expectations of a small private dinner in the country were dashed. He moved through the crowd towards her.

'Ah, and this is Jack Cartier, our ringmaster, so to speak. Jack, please come and meet . . .'

The names spun past him in a sea of nodding faces.

'. . . Be nice to them, Jack,' she whispered. 'They are going to help us with the Circus.'

Jojo moved to the left to talk to another circle. They were mostly financial people. Jojo's business contacts, as far as Cartier could guess, smart, elegant, safe. He felt like he was selling tickets. He probably was.

Jojo stayed at the far end of the room until dinner. Cartier held back and caught up with her as they went through.

'I was rather hoping we might have a night off from the Circus.'

'These people are serious. We need them. Work them.'

'Circus. Circus.'

'Humour me.'

'I always do.'

'Then get on with it. Don't give me all this man-woman nonsense. Besides, I've put somebody next to you you might like.'

She had placed him down the table, about as far away from her as possible. Next to him was a voluptuous, lipsticked Brazilian. She introduced herself as Maria.

'Jojo has told me a lot about you,' she said.

She was divorced, loud and liked slapping his thigh or grabbing his elbow to jostle the conversation along. She smelled of oranges and mangoes.

Pascal cooked a fashionable bake of tuna fillet on a bed of those waxy French potatoes Jojo had been so proud of growing, seasoned with quail eggs, fresh anchovies and olives and covered with a heap of chopped flat leaf parsley. Cartier recognised the olive oil as Jojo's private supply.

Jojo was philosophising at the top of the table:

'The English are engineers. They like doing things that are mechanical on a big scale. You can't have good food like that. It is great for conquering the world and going to war but it is no good for anything else. Half the people in the food industry in this country couldn't even cook their own dinner.'

'So how would you improve our food?' asked the man on her left, politely.

'Diversity. You must have small craft businesses. With a lot of small trades you get quality and you get protection from the dangers of mass production like salmonella, listeria, and BSE. Food has to be about people and the quality of jobs and life and looking after the land we live on.'

Cartier distracted himself by flirting mildly with his Brazilian neighbour. She regaled him with stories of her ex-lovers.

'With Miguel we were always making love on the train. We would rendezvous for the overnight sleeper to Penzance. So romantic, so old-fashioned, don't you think? So much more exciting than a hotel.'

A tall, suave man in a dark blue Armani suit got to his feet to propose a toast.

'Bravo to our hostess, bravo to the Circus, may it be a huge success.' He drank its health in Puligny-Montra-chet and the whole table followed loudly.

The party was breaking up. Jojo had disappeared, ushering her guests into their coats and saying her goodbyes. Cartier slipped out quietly to the kitchen to talk to Pascal.

'Did you enjoy the meal?'

'Excellent.'

'I used to do it just as a salad without the tuna, but it looked a bit sparse for the restaurant and everyone seems to like tuna these days.'

'Are you going out tonight?'

'I have no one to go with,' Pascal replied morosely.

'Cartier, I thought you might like to take me . . . home.'

Maria had followed him. She was standing almost on his toes. He could smell the coffee on her breath, and a splash of fresh cologne.

'That's nice of you, but I don't drive.'

'I do.'

'I have an early start.'

'Then it would be better to be in London, not here.'

As he closed the car door he knew it was a mistake. Huddled in the front of the Peugeot 306, he wrapped his forebodings around him.

He should have stayed. If he had waited, Jojo might have reappeared. Why was he so impatient? Another voice told him not to be so crass. She owed him nothing. She was away with one of her – what was the word she had used? – arrangements.

The smell of Maria's perfume was thick. The voluminous padded sleeves of her mohair jacket scraped against his shoulder as she changed gear, a vicarious, arbitrary, uncontrolled, unfeeling touching of clothes. He dozed.

At Maria's flat, he fought with himself not to be embarrassed. He had accidentally opened a whole cupboard of guilt. Suitcases of angst tumbled on top of him. The infidelity hurt. Or perhaps he just wanted it to feel like infidelity?

Somewhere, he had missed a turn. All his sixth senses nagged and tried to drag him back, but it was too late now. He was geographically misplaced. And besides, what would he be going back to? A hotel where everyone was asleep.

Maria made instant coffee. She gave him a whisky. She chattered endlessly about people he didn't know. She didn't seem bothered that he just nodded and smiled. She was not pushing him. She stroked him occasionally. Brushed past him. There was a generalness about her approach that did not seem to be overly confrontational.

She hadn't even bothered to offer to drop him off at his place. He didn't want all that performance. Not the tubes of cream, and the Durex. He wanted to relax. Maria seemed to sense that.

She led him to the bedroom. It was all pink and chintz with cushions and drapes and a hundred and one little bottles and boxes on the table and a phone. A single framed picture of a man on the beach beamed out of a blue wooden square, neatly allotted his two inches on the second shelf, otherwise the room was completely feminine.

Maria sat on the far side of the bed and patted the space beside her.

'You look tired. Perhaps your heart is not really with us. No, do not answer that. Just relax. Don't talk. There is no need. Do you want to look at me?'

She unbuttoned her dress as she talked.

'You like what you see?'

Her body was Botticellian, folds of softness.

'Give me your hand. Feel. There.'

She stroked his head.

'Here.'

Her other hand slipped his under the band of her knickers. The tips of his fingers ran into the dank wiriness of her pubic hair. Instinctively the tip of his forefinger slipped between her lips and found her erect clitoris. Agilely her other hand slipped the knickers off and the movement of her hips filled his hand. He flicked idly, gently, hardly touching at all, just brushing a few millimetres, catching the nib of her sex with his nail. Her mouth was on his ear.

'I like that.'

They were not touching at all now, apart from the light brushing of his fingertip over the bud of her sex. He could hear her arousal from her breathing. He could feel her wetness oiling his finger.

'That's nice.'

For Cartier the sex was abstract, but Maria continued to whisper encouragement. He could feel how warm she was.

'That's good. More . . .'

Her body arched lightly. She shifted. Her hand reached down and two firm fingers grasped his and shoved him deeper into her. He ran his finger back and forth through the wetness of her sex no more than an inch.

'Yes.'

Her excitement was infectious. But she was ahead of him. Well ahead of him. Her back arched and thrust her hips up on to his finger. She came. He could feel the frisson down his arm. She fell back.

'Thank you. I needed you to do that. You have such a tender touch.'

He must have fallen asleep. Maria was snoring by his side, her dress still on. The mix of feelings inside him wound like a piece of cloth into a tourniquet. He awoke without passion. Slipping off the bed he went to run a bath. He wanted to wash himself clean. The running bath must have awoken her.

'You don't like me?' Maria was at the door.

'I probably need more foreplay.'

She crossed the room and sat on the loo.

'You can stay if you want. You have such magic fingers. I wouldn't want you to leave unsatisfied.'

'Another time, maybe. It has been a long week and I am not really up for a grand romance.'

'Is that what they call English reserve? Or perhaps you need to play some games? Perhaps you want me to pee on you.'

'No, it's OK. But thanks for the offer.'

'Good, I'm bursting. I don't think I could have waited.'

He could hear the stream of liquid rushing out of her.

'Would you like me to dress up for you next time? And perhaps we should go somewhere more interesting than a bedroom.'

There was this strangely comfortable, unmeaning understanding between them. His lack of passion did not seem to offend her. There was just friendship. She was almost maternal. She seemed to recognise the deep unease and tiredness he felt, and the confusion. He was happy for that, at least. He wondered what Jojo was doing.

'I have an early start.'

'I make you some coffee and something to eat.'

He was standing at the kitchen door. She was hovering between the food processor and the cupboard. He had watched her take a tin of baked beans, one of tuna, one of anchovy, one of sweetcorn and tip the contents carefully into the mixer.

'Maria, what on earth are you doing?'

'I am afraid I am not such a great cook as your Jojo. But I get hungry in the middle of the night. Ah, that will do nicely.'

She pulled out a tin of drinking chocolate and measured two tablespoons and lobbed them in as well.

'I like to invent things. A little tomato, I think. Could you put some mayonnaise on the bread?'

'Is this actually a recipe, Maria?'

'No, it is just a lot of things I like. I put them all together and usually it works out OK.'

She pushed the switch and the machine whirred violently. She peered in.

'It looks a little wet and messy tonight.'

She took a big strainer and emptied the reddy-grey contents into it.

'There. Now we put this on some sliced bread with mayonnaise and a leaf of lettuce. I confess I am not a very good cook, so I don't try. Does that offend you? My first husband left me because he said I couldn't cook. But I say why cook when you can eat in restaurants? The trouble with London is there are no restaurants open in the middle of the night. Go on, try, it is not too bad.'

She thrust the bean-tuna-anchovy-corn-chocolate-tomato sandwich at him. It was almost falling apart in her hands it was so big. Cartier thought it tasted of everything and nothing, just a pile of slosh that he had to navigate carefully to his mouth so it didn't fall on to his clothes.

'I've tasted worse.'

'I promise I won't tell anyone. It wouldn't be good for your reputation if people found out you had been eating things like this. I will keep your secret. Would you like some ketchup with it?'

'No, thanks.'

'Brown sauce? What would Jojo say? She would be horrified. Oh, I'm sorry. You like her, don't you? Still, you can't be serious all the time. Life would be no fun. Besides, she is not free anyway.'

'Not free?'

'There was someone. He was killed. It all happened

very suddenly. She doesn't have the same ambitions as other women. It changed her.'

'I didn't know.'

'Well, I have told you her secret. Perhaps one day she may tell you herself, but don't count on it. Mustard. That is what is missing. I must have some mustard.'

She reached to the cupboard and took a knife and smeared a layer of yellow on. It was the last straw. The sandwich collapsed on the table.

'Damn. I will have to use a knife and fork. That is how I know when it is done, when the whole thing falls apart.'

She laughed.

'You can come back and see me again when you have a hard-on and I will make you something even more outrageous. There is a really disgusting concoction I do with chilli and Battenburg cake and pineapple chunks . . .'

The unholy alliance of Vincent and Harriet had flourished across the dining-room table. She had taken up his kind offer of entertaining whoever she pleased five times in less than two weeks. Far from feeling put upon, Vincent found himself relishing the occasions and this woman who could do so much for him and who so obviously enjoyed his food. She had eaten the entire summer menu. As she was leaving, he caught her ear.

'I have some new dishes that I would like you to sample. Nobody else has tasted them yet.'

'Vincent, that would be gorgeous.' Harriet's face was alight with greed and anticipation.

They arranged to dine together after the main dinner rush was over. On the day Vincent was in a state. He was shouting at Marylese.

'The stock is too bitter. It has been over-reduced. You must not let sole bones cook so long. Turbot you

128

can. But never, never, never sole. You have been doing too much outside catering. You have forgotten cuisine. All those pastries have gone to your head. You must remember. Throw it all away. No, on second thoughts, thin it down – it will have to do. But I don't want it for my new dishes with Miss Huss.'

He stuck his finger in a passing saffron sauce for red mullet.

'There's no salt in this. Send it back. What is the matter with all of you? Have you forgotten everything I have ever taught you? Do you not listen? Do you, do you, do you not listen, airheads? My soufflés. I, I, I clap my hands and you collapse on me.'

In the dining room he became a different man, restrained, neat, fiddling with his cuffs, wiping his brocaded signature in case there was any fluff, nodding politely to customers. Tonight everyone felt more like guests than paying punters.

As Harriet walked in, he saw her in his mind like one of the frontispieces from his old cookery books. She was surrounded by a halo of new dishes – the snails *en beignets*, the sweetbread torte with the tomato coulis, the terrine of langoustines (he hoped she wouldn't know that he had borrowed this), the choux pastry swans with peaches and vanilla ice cream (his private homage to her, like Escoffier's peach Melba for his diva Nellie), the mousse of chocolate (made with 73 per cent cocoa solids in the casing) surrounded by a raspberry coulis. She was a vision. She was wearing a loose floral dress. He was glad to see it. She would have no restraints.

'I have chosen some of my favourite Sauterne for you,' he cooed over her.

'I'm sure it will be lovely, Vincent. You are such a master of taste.'

The dishes arrived. Vincent sat patiently beside her, watching, waiting for her judgement, perusing her features as each mouthful made its way between her lips.

'You are not eating?'

'I am too nervous. I want to know what you think.'

'The snails were superb – so clever to put the garlic with the cream in the pastry case. Delicious. So inventive. Try one.'

There were two of thirteen left on her plate. She pronged one and moved her fork towards him. It wobbled off. She caught it in her other hand. The snail nestled in her palm in a splattering of sauce.

Without thinking, if he had thought he would never have dared, Vincent caught her hand and lifted it to his mouth.

'Go on, big man,' she said softly. 'Eat.'

He brought her hand up to his face and licked the snail and the sauce out of the cup of her hand. Her skin felt divine. His sauce was divine. He wiped her hand clean with a napkin before letting go of the wrist.

'That was a beautiful thing to do,' she said as she devoured the last snail herself, so they were both joined by the same flavours at the same moment.

As the dishes were brought before her, she became more daring. She wanted him to share her pleasure. She fed him with a fork for the sweetbreads, just a little. It was too good to waste too much.

The choux pastry swan she picked up in her fingers and pushed into his mouth. By the mousse everyone had left. They were alone. She had drunk two bottles of wine. She put her finger into the mousse and sucked it off. And then she repeated the ritual, only this time she offered him her finger covered with a swirl of dark, egg-filled softness. He leant forward and licked his creation off her finger. It was as if eating off her flesh was the final, missing, sensuality to his cooking.

'You must cook for me one night at home, I think, Vincent,' she said.

6

A DAY OUT

JOJO AND MR LEE had planned their day away from the Vicarage as though it were some momentous occasion. There were things she wanted to check. She was anxious to confront Harriet and discover what progress she was making. She also, to her surprise, wanted to see Cartier again, not just talk to him on the phone. From what Maria had said, and from his rather off-hand manner on the phone, she feared she might have offended him in some way. She wondered, idly, if he had been discriminating enough not to sleep with her. Maria had been vague on that point. Usually she was pretty candid with those kinds of details.

'He didn't like my sandwiches very much. I quite horrified him, I think.'

'Did you sleep with him?'

'Sort of, yes and no.'

'Yes or no?'

'Sort of no, but yes, you know.'

'I don't think I do.'

'Another time. You are not interested in that sort of thing anyway. I'll tell you if it gets juicy.'

And then she had run off, chattering about who she could bring to the Circus.

'You are not interested in him, are you?'

'No. No. I just wanted to know.'

Perhaps she did want to know. If he had slept with Maria then at least he was safely ensconced nearby and she would not have to worry about him. If he hadn't, then it might be encouraging, but tricky. The spectre of him eating one of Maria's famously gunky sandwiches in the middle of the night evoked a plethora of confused emotions. She set them aside. She toyed with the idea of gatecrashing the Montague to see what Vincent was up to, but rejected it.

Mr Lee spun the Mercedes 500 off the road and on to a private drive. The suspension waddled as it took the weight of the potholes. A rumble-tumble string of dilapidated barns encircled them on three sides. The two on the end were a heap of fallen mossy-green lichen-covered slabs. The main porch appeared to be the only section still intact. A woman peered out of the open door and then came to greet them with a bright, lippy smile.

'Chickens,' Jojo declared, as she got out of the car.

Mrs Hateley was built in stages, huge bustling biceps almost the size of her bosom, hips that only just fitted through the door frontways, calves that curved like pistons. Her fashion sense, or her money, had run out sometime when big flowery patterns were in vogue and had been sustained with patches from other flowered prints from the same period, so she looked like she was dressed in a spring meadow.

The two women were about the same height but that was all they had in common physically. Mrs Hateley bulged in places that Jojo did not have. An alien biologist might have mistaken them for different species.

There was evidence of children everywhere – bikes, toys, games, dolls, puzzles, a football were strewn across the yard and the floor – but none around.

Large red Warrener chickens scratched around a rusty swing, perched on the windowsills and scuffed about the flower borders. In the kitchen, a week-old baby lamb lolloped its head happily out of the bottom oven of the range, watching the strange visitors come in. Rows of neat preserves lined long shelves beneath a cobwebbed, flaking ceiling.

Jojo endeared herself by asking to taste the pickled walnuts and the home-made raspberry vinegar. Mrs Hateley made a pot of tea and served it in chipped pink floral cups. Like her clothes, the cups seemed to be relics of another era, probably her wedding day. She offered home-made bread and cake. She heaped four spoons of sugar into her own tea. Busy faecal farm smells swarmed around her after the antiseptic air-conditioning of the car.

Mrs Hateley was used to powerful country ladies. She put Jojo down as the kind of woman who would normally chair the committees she sat on.

Mr Lee nodded quietly in the corner, enjoying this exotic scene of English country folk. He looked totally out of place in his black suit and bowler hat, but then, like Mrs Hateley, there was no side to him.

Jojo produced an envelope and began to count out £300 in £5 notes and laid them on the table.

'Mr Charles, he takes all our animals for his butcher's shop,' Mrs Hateley said. 'He pays good money. And he pays on time. So if he says he wants you to have a favour, that will be all right with me. You don't have to show me your money.'

Jojo smiled, but left the money where she could see it all the same. The two of them started talking chickens.

'We used to keep about fifty chickens. I don't like to have more than that. That's plenty for us and a few for the farm gate. But since them mad regulations came in we have to get them all checked for salmonella. You can't do that on fifty. So we have to go up to about two hundred and fifty and use the bottom fields. I don't hold with it myself. Crowding them and all. It ain't natural. They don't like it. And they aren't happy. We live in the country because we don't want to live like chickens cooped up in a high rise and now this government is telling us to put our chickens in high rises. It ain't right. I been telling my man Ben that we should have to stop selling them eggs. It ain't moral.'

'I want fifty chickens,' Jojo explained. 'They must be not less than a hundred days old and not more than a hundred and thirty. I'd prefer cockerels that have been castrated. They will be fed on milk powder. They will drink milk not water – nothing else apart from what they can scratch up, and some corn. I want them happy and unstressed. And I will want them the first week of November.'

'I'm not sure if the Minister allows us to chop their balls off, these days.'

'Mrs Hateley, I don't care what the Minister says. If he wants to send somebody round to have a look at their testicles, then we will worry about it then. I want them off. Besides, you don't want them pecking at each other. It will calm them down. I'll pay for the fencing. I'll pay for the diet. And then I'll give you ten pounds a bird. And I want the livers and the necks and the giblets, even the combs.'

'The Minister won't like that. There's definitely a law on that.'

Mrs Hateley was impressed by the money sitting on the table but was not going to let it show. Jojo laid out another £50 in notes. But Mrs Hateley did not intend to demean herself by picking up the cash.

'After that the Vicarage will take five birds a week from you; that way you can keep the flock down to a manageable size. I want happy chickens.'

'Have another cup of tea. My granny used to talk about raising chickens like that. She was in Guildford.

They used to send them to the banquets in the City. They got huge, you know.'

'For the last week I want you to bring them inside and pamper them on nothing but milk powder. Let them live their last days like kings.'

'That's what Granny used to do. It must be some banquet you have got planned.'

'It is,' said Jojo. 'We have to go, I'm afraid. We have some other calls to make. Come and have lunch with us at the Vicarage, Mrs Hateley. I like our suppliers to know what we are doing.'

'I haven't been out to dinner for years. I don't know that I have got a dress.'

'Come all the same. Lunch isn't formal.'

Cartier planned to meet Jojo for lunch with Harriet Huss. Having missed the first meeting, he was intrigued to see how they got along.

Jojo phoned as he was making his way to CCK for his Thursday ritual. She was in a fashion shop in Notting Hill, picking out the drapes for the walls. The warehouse conversion for the Circus was bleak. Jojo wanted to cover the walls in exuberant silks.

'I want your opinion, Cartier. Could you meet me here? We can go on to lunch together afterwards.'

Cartier took a cab. The shop was down a back lane and the driver had to slow down to avoid people walking off the kerb. It was busy in an aimless way. A few boys were hanging out on the street, getting in the way of older people going to the shops.

Inside, the shop seemed deserted. There were just walls and walls of long rolls of different-coloured cloths. An assistant in black appeared from the back room.

'I was looking for Jojo Coltrane . . .'

'She's expecting you.'

Cartier followed the assistant through a dark corridor into a neat, well-lit showroom.

Jojo was waiting for him, leaning against the wall. She was naked except for a length of vermilion cloth still attached to its roller on the floor. It was draped across her diagonally. She let it drop so her left breast was exposed.

She was laughing. She was laughing at him.

'What do you think?'

'You look great.'

'Is this bright enough? Do you like this? And the walls will be draped in this.'

She picked up a run of crimson flecked with ochre arrows and crests. The first roll fell from her. For a moment she was completely naked in front of him. She waved the second cloth in front of her like a veil.

'And the tables in this?'

She pointed to the vermilion.

'And I will be in this.'

Jojo dropped the roll and in a single swivel pulled the end of the crimson roll round her hips and tied it tightly round her stomach. She pulled the cloth up and bound her breasts in it, but even as she did so the other end pulled taut and revealed the inside of her thigh. She was a little girl in an Aladdin's cave. Cartier could smell her nakedness. She was treating him like a lover. She was enjoying it. The shop girl indulged her without comment.

'Do you think I will look OK?'

'Stunning.'

'Good.'

'Why are you teasing me like this?'

'I like teasing you, Cartier. It gives me pleasure. Don't you know that? I like you watching me.'

'It bothers me.'

'It wouldn't be much fun if it didn't bother you, would it?'

She turned and disappeared into a changing cubicle as

if she had been discussing the weather. He waited for her while she dressed. She emerged in a man's grey pinstripe working suit that didn't fully fit. The wall was up again. He had been auditioned. But he had no idea if he had got the part. They picked up Mr Lee who had been waiting in a side room and headed back into the daylight.

The gleaming Mercedes had attracted a crowd. A bison of a man with a split-open shirt was leaning on the bonnet.

'Pretty woman,' he said as he saw Jojo approach. She stared at him in surprise that anyone would talk to her like that. Some of the crowd sidled away. He stayed.

'That's my car, if you don't mind,' she said.

The man looked through her at Cartier just behind.

'How much you want for the woman?'

'You couldn't afford her,' said Cartier.

'I got money. I give you a monkey for French. I be quick. You guys have another beer, take it easy. Listen to the music.'

Cartier noticed Jojo's shoulder tremble, but he couldn't see her face to know whether it was from fear or anger. Mr Lee slid sideways round the back of the car. Cartier stepped in front of Jojo, and eyeballed the man, who just leaned back further on the bonnet and ran his finger down the chrome.

'I don't want a beer.'

'Nice motor too.'

'But I could use a smoke. What you got?'

'Prime Jamaican.'

'How much?'

The man slid his hand in his pocket and took out a cellophane slab the size of a cigarette packet. 'Half an hour with the babe, and it's yours.'

Cartier flashed a £50 note into his hand and reached for the packet. The man smiled.

'You cool, dude. That's cool.'

'You too, man.'

Cartier bundled Jojo into the back of the Mercedes. Mr Lee was at the wheel, his hand twisting the ignition like he was going to break it off. Cartier sweated.

'You bring her back here see me, you hear. Such a pretty woman. I get me some more money.' The man swaggered back on to the pavement.

Mr Lee revved and the Mercedes sped away into the street.

'Christ, don't they have police around here?' Jojo yelled. 'What you want to buy that crap for anyway, Cartier?'

'Better than getting mugged.'

'He was a very big man,' said Mr Lee.

'He was a stupid man,' said Jojo. 'If he wanted sex he just had to ask properly. I quite like black men. We had room in the car. We could have taken him back with us.'

Her sudden laughter broke the tension. Mr Lee laughed loudest. He was driving fast, weaving through the traffic.

'He look good on the door of the Vicarage.'

'I thought you didn't like real men, Mr Lee,' Jojo asked, curious.

'He should have asked me. I would have done it for fifty pounds,' joked Mr Lee.

'Really?'

'Sure.'

'Really?'

Cartier felt her hand on the back of his head, stroking his hair. It was the first time she had touched him.

'Thank you for saving me, Cartier.'

'Another tenner I might have thought about it.'

Harriet was waiting for them and beginning to feel

irritable. She had drunk half a bottle of wine. The ashtray was full of olive pips.

The Square was fashionable enough to attract people other than the auction house bidders from across the road. It had been a good choice, Cartier reflected. They fitted easily into the pseudo-Parisian 'ladies who lunch' ambience. It helped dissipate the hysterical atmosphere in the car.

'What do you recommend?' Harriet asked.

'I've never been here before,' said Jojo.

'I'll have a salad then,' said Harriet dismissively.

'The chef here, he can cook,' Cartier interjected.

'All right, I'll have the brill then,' said Jojo.

'Me too,' said Harriet.

Jojo wagged her finger. 'We have to have something different. Try the quail with miso, it's almost a salad, I guess.'

Cartier watched, entertained, as Harriet and Jojo sparred around each other. Harriet was smiling, unctuous, even solicitous. Jojo was withdrawn, polite and businesslike.

'Nobody is quite sure what this Circus is going to be,' Harriet was saying. 'If there had been one before then they might understand it.'

'Isn't that the whole point?' Jojo answered. 'If there had been one before, then there wouldn't be any point doing it.'

'Well, sometimes something has to happen twice for television. It is the only way to make it happen in people's minds.'

'We may never be able to repeat it. Besides, don't the suits know who's coming?'

'Frankly, if it's not Sharon Stone they don't care.'

'Who on earth is Sharon Stone?' asked Jojo.

'Blonde. Open legs. Hollywood.'

Cartier wasn't sure if Jojo was joking. He chivvied her along.

'You know. *Basic Instinct.*'

'I never go to the cinema. I hate plastic art. I want to see real people or I'm not interested.'

'At least a few TV celebs?' Harriet pleaded.

'Should we pay for it? Would that get it on?'

'That's not allowed, darling. We could try for a sponsor, I suppose. A supermarket might be interested.'

'A supermarket! Harriet, this is something special. The idea of a load of grocers flogging frozen chapattis and Black Forest gâteaux . . .'

'I'll think of something, I promise. But it's not easy. It takes time and money.'

'You have had quite a lot of money already. The deal is simple, Harriet. No TV, no bonus. We all want you to succeed. We are all rooting for you. Go and do your devious best.'

Harriet preened herself, wriggling inside her cash-mere polka dots, crossing her black ski trousers, pursing her large lips. She had been visibly warmed by the compliment and the reminder of the reward for all her travails. She left the restaurant with her mind focused cleanly on the Valhalla of air time.

When they were alone Jojo said to Cartier:

'She really is a nasty piece of work, that one. I would not like to be her grandmother.'

And then:

'You are distracted. Are you upset with me?'

'Not upset. Unsure, perhaps.'

'You have no reason to be unsure of me, Cartier. Do you? No reason at all. There are two things you need to know about me. That I was an only child and that I went to an all-girl boarding school.'

'What's that supposed to mean?'

'That I'm difficult, self-centred and have an unbal-anced attitude towards men.'

'I wouldn't say you were that unbalanced.'

'You just haven't tipped the scales.'

'Is that an invitation?'

'No. Just some good advice.'

She leaned towards him across the table, looking him straight in the eye. Her breath smelled of parsley. Her lips finished the sentence on his. She left them there for a second, lingering on the kiss, taking a moment to smell what he was like, like a deer sniffing the wind, he sensed, in case of danger.

She withdrew.

'That is cruel.'

'Perhaps I like being cruel to you . . . You are a man. Anyway, you're far too dangerous to mess with.'

She banned him from his own feelings. There was still a table between them.

'Did you sleep with Maria?'

She was smiling. Those eyes held him. He didn't see the hand take the cup, nor the arm pull back. The first he noticed was the black coffee splattering across his shirt and face.

'What did you do that for?'

'It'll help cool you down. Serves you right if you did sleep with her. Either way I don't want her hurt. Mop yourself up, it's time to go.'

Jojo left him standing on the pavement. In the car Mr Lee cross-examined her.

'Are you frightened of Cartier?'

'He's just a handsome rake.'

'No, but maybe you frightened what he could do for you. You are like the girls I used to work with in Bangkok. You do not connect with other people.'

'I do. Not like that, perhaps. Not the way you mean it.'

'You mean woman to him.'

'It'll keep him sharp. Anyway, I'm not some geisha girl trying to get him back to my tub.'

'Maybe you judge him wrong.'

'He's not that much of a pussy cat, either.'

The mortality of a restaurant was not unlike that of a love affair, Cartier reflected. People got into restaurants the same way they fell in love, which is to say for no good reason. They were both high-risk enterprises.

Jojo's animated behaviour – the striptease, the grilling of Harriet, throwing the coffee – had revealed at least the other woman behind the demure and rigorous taste mistress. Doubtless, if she had stayed long enough, she would have said in one of her cryptic asides that she was just drawing a line. Blush. Smile. And give him the hard stare. As it was, she had hurried away and left things unsaid.

Cartier bought a new shirt, changed in the street and dropped the soiled one at the dry cleaner. Then he went up to CCK to do his books and post (which he had meant to do in the morning). Afterwards he picked up a reception at the Meridien for a new book – there was hardly anyone there he knew – caught dinner alone upstairs at the French House then set off east for some serious spirit drinking. Cheap wine at receptions always made him thirsty for something harder.

Recession at first had been good for business. No sooner did one restaurant close than another opened. Everyone wanted Cartier's advice. It was when they closed again that the banks got involved and kept them shut. The Vicarage, Cartier calculated, was just about saleable. And probably Jojo would sell it eventually. She was too creative to be constrained by bricks and mortar.

Meanwhile, Cartier gathered up unconsidered trifles. He traded in the twilight area between other people's passions and misfortunes, a dealer in hopes, and yet a hostage to other people's fortunes. (JCA had come unstuck, he reminded himself painfully, when two clients stopped paying their bills. In the space of a few weeks he had skidded from an office and staff of twelve back to his own resources.)

Jojo's sudden flirtatiousness was both disarming and destructive. She was young, beautiful, seemingly unattached, and he was without commitment. It would have been impolite not to proposition. Her response was instinctual but the door had neither been open nor shut, it just batted back and forth like it had been kicked very hard.

Sitting at the bar at the Hothouse he flicked through the detail of his Circus notes and frightened himself – 2,600 knives, 2,600 forks, 1,300 desert spoons, 650 teaspoons, 650 napkins, 3,250 wine glasses, 3,900 plates, 6,500 candles, 95 floral table displays, 85 serving salvers, 65 trolleys with lamps and burners and blow torches, 115 butter dishes, all to be sourced, transported to the warehouse, washed and returned unbroken within forty-eight hours. Plus six ovens, four stock pots, five griddles, seven deep-fat-fryers-cum-steamers to be added to the rudimentary arrangements in the basement. Beyond that the room itself was bare, and, even with the fabrics that Jojo had chosen, there was a need for tables, chairs, ornaments, chandeliers, lighting, air-conditioning, sound system and plans of waiters' walk-throughs, how the guests would find their seats, how the dishes would get upstairs. Cartier had set up new restaurants before. Each time reminded him how much work was involved. Doing it all for just the one night was a daunting prospect. There was the staff on the night to be considered. The key players he had in place, but he was still in need of 65 waiters, 17 sous-chefs (Pascal's estimate), 20 washer-uppers-cum-bus-boys, eight hat-check girls, four greeters, seven carvers. The £200 ticket did not seem so much set against this long and expensive list.

Cartier was feeling pensive. He always did on cognac. If Harriet inspired Vincent to some awful act, Jojo would detect Cartier's hand in it and blame him in some way. His scheming would look like treason. And then there were the young lovers, Pascal and Marylese. They seemed as destined for each other as he and Jojo were not. It rankled that Jojo had set him up with Maria, then punished him for it.

It was 11.30. He had come to ask Peter, who was running the front of the house, to be one of the carvers at the Circus.

The last customers were still clinging to their glasses and gazing at each other through the flickering candle-light. The late shift shuffled around in the shadows tidying tables and trying to make just enough noise to make it clear it was time to go home.

Some designer had had the rather obvious notion of doing the room out in hessian to associate it with its former life for storing tea. The idea had been that it would be buzzy and trendy, but the new tenants of the neighbouring flat conversions worked late and ate late, which made the waiters bad-tempered.

On impulse he decided to ring Jojo. It rang ten, twelve bleeps. Cartier persisted. Reception eventually put him through.

'Can't it wait till the morning?' Jojo sounded bored and sleepy.

'I wanted to see you. Nothing to do with the Circus. I just fancied seeing you.'

'Where are you? In some bar, I guess. Have you got yourself a clean shirt yet?' She laughed. 'Are you drunk?'

'I could come over.'

'You've missed the last train.'

'There's one at twelve-oh-six. I checked. I could just make it.'

'No, no, not here,' she said, too quickly. 'What about the Sultan Club? They keep your kind of hours, I suppose. Time for me to have a shower and do the M4. I'll see you there.'

He put the phone down and panicked. He was wearing jeans. The Sultan Club would not let him in. For a second he had this vision of standing outside on the street, waiting for her to emerge with her winnings.

'Peter,' he called out across the bar.

'Yeah, what?'

'I want your trousers.'

'I thought you'd never ask. This must be my lucky night. First you offer me a job for no money and now you want my trousers. You want my shirt as well? My underpants any good? I've got a nice signet ring you might like too. Only one owner. What's the deal here?'

'Just lend me your trousers and jacket. You can have mine. I have to go to the Sultan Club.'

'I've had some strange propositions in my time . . .'

'Where else am I going to get a suit at this time of night?'

'Haven't you got a home, with a wardrobe? You know, where ordinary people keep their clothes?'

'I know it sounds daft, but everything is at the cleaner's.'

'Well, if you are going up West, I guess you can give me a lift.'

'Deal.'

They changed in the shadows of the dimmest corner of the bar while the last couple looked amorously at each other, unaware of the striptease ten feet away.

The suit was hardly the greatest fit. Cartier fixed the waist with string and buttoned the jacket across. Peter could hardly fit into the jeans. He had to pull the shirt down to cover the bulging flies.

'It'll be OK where I'm going – don't fret! But where the hell did you get these jeans? They're antique.'

'Swinging London, sixty-six. That's why they look so good. They're faded with real life.'

The cab was an old Cortina with burst seats, rusted wheel rims, a radio that spouted wires and crackled incomprehensible messages. The driver was a huge African who barely fitted in the seat himself. He leaned a quarter of his torso out of the window as if he was keeping the door on with his elbow. He had not washed for a few days. The front seat was scattered with empty Opal Fruit packets.

'He's cheap, he's open late and he's here, so don't go complaining,' said Peter as they got in. Cartier told him to take them to Park Lane.

'How you expect me to know where that is? There's a hundred Park Lanes. You want Brentford, you want Bow, you want Hackney?'

'Park Lane, Park Lane . . . Park Lane. Just go west, I'll show you.'

'You know the way, that's fine. You don't know the way then I ask my radio. He don't know, we ask someone in the street.'

'We know the way.'

The rusted jalopy swung out of the tall warehouse terraces of the docks and sped through the empty city streets. A journey that would have taken an hour in the morning was a ten-minute spin.

As they lurched to a halt outside the Sultan Club, Cartier shoved a wodge of fivers into Peter's hand and leapt out, holding on to his waistband under his jacket.

'Enjoy yourself.'

'And you. Don't do anything I wouldn't do!'

'In these trousers?'

Cartier slunk past the doorman, trying to look as suave as Noël Coward and telling himself people would think he had his hand in a sling. He signed in jerkily and made for the bar, where he could sit on a stool without his trousers falling down.

Jojo arrived at two o'clock. She looked as though she had just stepped off the catwalk. The dress was a simple scarf of crimson silk that was strung from her left shoulder to her right knee. Her body swelled and broke like waves beneath it, revealing slices of tanned flesh. A sofa full of Arabs ogled her every movement.

Cartier was aware, in a sort of resigned way, that she had trumped him again. He had just wanted the warmth of some intimacy to end the day. Somebody to chat to. She had taken him for his word and was ready to kill. She was going to outpace him.

'Would you like a drink?'

'Not yet,' she said. 'You got me out of bed. Let's gamble.'

She offered him her arm. He took it with his one free hand and they went upstairs.

'I don't often play the tables – but tonight I thought it might be fun. I could do with a big win. Shall we play blackjack or roulette? I prefer blackjack. It always seems a more intelligent way to lose your money.'

'I guess that makes me pretty intelligent.'

'You seem to be in danger of losing something else.' Jojo eyed his baggy trousers.

'I'm hanging in there.'

'I shouldn't have bothered to make an effort. But then these places are always so glum. I didn't want to look like your tart. If any of those Arabs come cruising around, you will have to pretend to be my minder.'

The gaming room was half full, and there was a funereal hush. The women on display dressed like they were twenty, though most were pushing forty, even fifty. Dull-eyed beneath their make-up, they casually lost their stake money on mindless pitches at the dice. Their glasses were rimmed with lipstick. Cartier wondered, were they losing for the sake of it or hoping that some millionaire might take them away from the crowd

147

and show them how to lose even more money? Or were they management stooges?

Jojo gestured towards a particularly frumpy redhead, whose dress had slipped to reveal her cleavage, as she shot a double three at the crap table.

'Now she looks just right for you,' she said.

The heavy rollers were stuck into the tables, surrounded by admirers and hangers-on. There was a gaggle of tourists, by the look of them lost souls from the marketing department. The croupiers were pretty and blind.

'I'll get us some chips,' he said.

'I'll get my own, thanks.'

'Suit yourself . . . Shall we have some champagne?'

'We'll celebrate later. I want to play. I want to beat that little black girl over there on the blackjack. I want to make her worry about her job.'

Jojo sidled on to the middle stool. To her right was a pinstripe from the motor trade. On the other side was a blue-rinse old enough to be his mother, who looked like she had been *in situ* for a couple of hours and was about to ask for credit. Jojo piled her blue and red chips on the green baize and eyed the girl with the cards. There was no seat for Cartier. He waited at Jojo's shoulder, while she played herself in, safely without risk.

Then he drifted away to the roulette table for a few minutes and lost a stack of green chips very quickly. He edged across the room to the Chesterfield. It was deep and comfortable. Cartier hadn't realised quite how tired he was.

'Can't stand the pace?'

Jojo kicked him awake. She stood in front of him, smiling, with a stack of chips in her hand.

'I find the numbers come up better when you are asleep.'

'For you maybe . . . what happened to the champagne?'

148

'What time is it?'

'Three thirty.'

Cartier raised his hand at a passing waitress.

'The vintage – not the ordinary.' She joined him on the sofa.

'You didn't play?'

'I guess the day just ran out on me.'

'What did you want to talk about?'

'Not about anything in particular. I just wanted some company. I wanted to see you. Why did you come?'

The champagne arrived before Jojo could reply. The waitress poured two glasses. Jojo downed hers in a single gulp. Cartier sipped. The bubbles knocked the sleep out of him.

'I don't think I like being your hired gun. I'm jealous of all the time everyone else gets. I'm even jealous of Mr Lee.'

'My, Cartier, I didn't know you could be so candid. You got into it because you needed the money.'

'Did I?'

'How many women do you have, Cartier? Do you really need another one? You're charming and you're clever. But you drink like a fish. You keep the hours of a pimp. And you don't even have a proper place to live.'

'So?'

'Do you think I want to cook and darn someone's socks? Do you think I want to argue over which TV programme to watch? Do you think I don't have my own emotional baggage – of which, incidentally, I am quite fond? Why would I want to share my feelings with you, or anyone else?'

'I want you,' he said.

'I am not for wanting.'

She stroked his cheek lightly with the back of her hand.

'Cartier,' she said, 'you do not know what love is.'

Outside, the pale yellow of the dawn was running a clean line across the horizon above the grey Edwardian brickwork. Mr Lee stretched out across the front seats of the Mercedes, fast asleep. He woke the instant Jojo touched the door.

'Good evening, Mistress Jojo.'

'Good night, Cartier,' she said finally. 'Thanks for the game.'

As Cartier walked down Piccadilly he tried to remember her scent, but the smell of the morning was already washing it away.

7

SECRETS

THE BARRIERS JOJO had so carefully erected might have been mistaken for pride or even conceit. To anyone not privy to her inner humility, to the virtuous karma that her celibacy inspired, the surrounding protection, as Cartier had found, was a dense bush, barbed with her wit and her sense of self-preservation.

Jojo's looks attracted overtures. She patted them away, often callously.

Mr Lee was not a threat but a confidant. It was a contractual relationship. Cartier did not fit so easily into the same constraints. She enjoyed the ambition of his approaches, but she was a spectator. Their conversations ebbed back and forth, like the tide. The beach was never covered for any length of time.

Jojo liked the ordered day of the kitchen, she liked to be in private, she liked the country, she liked to have space in her head where she could invent a new dish, or redesign a corner of the garden, or create an extraordinary vision like the Circus. The present was of little consequence. She lived in the past and had set a course for the future.

Cartier lived almost exclusively in the continuous present. His beloved Soho, his never minding whom he met with, or where, or what they thought of him, his unscheduled and unsolicited moments of brilliance, his rampant drinking. He lived through other people. There was no house, no furniture, none of the usual trappings. (Had she known, he actually had less than she imagined, only a rented garret on Frith Street where he kept two wardrobes of clothes.) None of the normal, tiny pleasures of life which most people set so much store by. The spurious Jack Cartier Associates International was not much more than a business card. And Jack himself was like the wind. Sometimes he gusted strongly, sometimes he was just a breeze.

She appreciated his meticulous scrutiny of the tiniest detail, his huge network of contacts, his knowing exactly where to go for something, his second-guessing where the problems would be, his staying up till God knew when to catch someone, his incessant, ruthless telephoning.

People expected her to be at the Vicarage, to cook at the Vicarage, to be the Vicarage. She expected herself to be there. How else could she guarantee the performance? She could not, she now conceded, have done it without him.

Her ambition did not need feelings. It didn't need sex in the middle of the night. It just needed her. If she took Cartier as a lover, would that secure anything? Or would it risk everything? For all his fancy, handsome, chancing appeal, would he really support her? That was one chance she could not take. A snatched night. A messy crumpling of emotions. Egos. Tears. Baggage. All the usual complications. Better that he took all that out on someone else . . . She had no enthusiasm to rekindle the spell with its devious ways. Or even to expose him to it.

She remembered the trauma of losing the baby. She had been stunned. She had found love, womanhood, companionship, sex, adulthood, motherhood in the space of a few short weeks. Suddenly she had been knocked back into childhood, as if some supernatural force, which she now accepted it was, had said: You travel too quickly.

They were travelling too quickly now. It would not take much for it all to miscue. The danger, though, she had to admit to herself, was erotic.

Jojo had a sudden need to talk to him. He was a good barometer of what was happening, and he had been more accurate than anyone else in his forecasts. The papers were all chattering about an upswing in the economy. The Vicarage figures were neat and tidy but modest. She had plundered her savings to keep it afloat and fund the Circus. There was not much margin left for error.

She found Cartier at Christopher's, the fashionable place of the moment off Covent Garden. It was four o'clock. He was still on lunch.

'Stay there. Have another drink. Mr Lee has got some things to do in London. He'll drop me off.'

The traffic was bad. By the time she reached Christopher's the early evening drinkers were clustered in the bar of the old bank vaults. Cartier was in the corner, talking to the owner over another bottle of Chablis and half watching the American baseball repeats on the TV monitor. She judged he must have drunk three or four bottles. She didn't notice the empty whisky glass on the table that had not been cleared between shifts.

All the figurework and coffee had made her hyperactive. She was glad of the change of atmosphere. Questions that had seemed so important an hour earlier as she mooned over the books were blurring in her head. Perhaps she just felt out of touch, marooned in the country, out of the swim . . .

Cartier looked at her admiringly. She was wearing a flying jacket, jeans, neat white bobby sox and luminescent green trainers.

'I don't see why you should be the only person allowed to get drunk all afternoon.'

'Would you prefer to go to an office? I find restaurants are cheaper than offices and a lot more fun.'

'Do you want to eat? It's less crowded upstairs.'

'OK.'

Jojo took the bottle and slipped through the drinking mêlée. He was swaying like an old bear, she noted. There were only a few other people upstairs, mostly going on to theatres, though the big mirror on the wall made it seem busier.

'I've got some catching up to do,' Jojo said as she sank the first glass. The waitress hovered by them with her pad.

'Order me something messy. I want to eat with my fingers. And another bottle of wine. This one isn't going to last.'

'A plate of soft-shelled crabs,' said Cartier.

'And some chips . . . with mayonnaise.'

'I didn't think you ate things like that.'

'When I'm in the mood. Why not? I've been going over the figures all afternoon and I've had enough. I can hardly get ratarsed in the Vicarage, can I? The guests might get quite peeved.'

She refilled her glass without waiting for him.

'The recession doesn't seem to be having much effect here.'

'Restaurants always do well in recession. People save on the big things. They don't buy cars. They don't go on holiday. They need to cheer themselves up. So they go out to eat.'

'Well, they don't in Oxfordshire. They all seem to stay in and watch TV.'

'You'll be OK. Good restaurants survive.'

'Is the Vicarage good enough?'

'Probably.'

'Probably? What's that supposed to mean?'

'Yes.'

'You don't have to be polite with me.'

Cartier raised an eyebrow.

Jojo had drunk more than half the bottle already. Cartier wasn't sure what mood she was in. She was bickering. She ran off a list of jobs she wanted done for the Circus, in a bored, bad-tempered, nagging way. The other tables were filling up now. He reached for a Marlboro. There were only two left in the packet.

'Urgh. I wish you wouldn't.'

'Why? Are you going to kiss me?'

'I might have done, but not now.' She paused for a second, then:

'Is that what you were thinking? That I was going to get drunk and drag you into the ladies' loo for a quick grope?'

'It's not such a bad idea.'

Jojo finished her glass, and poured another.

'Shall we?'

'Now?'

'There's a hotel over the road.'

'I own a hotel, Cartier.'

'Let's go there, then,' he said. The alcohol had loosened his tongue.

'I've only just got here.'

'Don't you like me?'

'Liking hasn't got anything to do with it, has it? The princess and the pauper; the politician and the whore; the croupier and her boss, you know the kind of thing. The sort of thing you shouldn't do.'

'Those are love stories.'

'They are foolish stories.'

The waitress arrived with a heap of crabs and a basket of chips. Jojo was hungry. She tore into a crab and wiped it in the mayonnaise.

'I was in love once. That was quite enough, but thank you for offering.'

'What happened?'

'He died. In a car crash.'

'I'm sorry.'

'There's no reason to be. It was nothing to do with you. At least we have something in common.'

She ate more slowly now, her fingers dancing over the food, picking one chip at a time, dipping it in salt or mayonnaise or leaving it bare alternately. Cartier just watched her without speaking.

'I suppose, because I cook for everyone, I must be partially in love with all of them. I make things I love for strangers. Get me another bottle of wine. And a cafetière of coffee. And an Armagnac,' she said, beckoning to the waitress. 'You can leave those. I haven't finished.'

She laughed suddenly:

'Do I embarrass you, Cartier?'

Her hand slipped under the table and felt his groin. It was not done with affection, but more a surgeon's matter-of-fact examination of an organ he was going to operate on.

'Can't you even get horny for me, Cartier? Are you too pissed? Don't you think, Cartier, I'm worth a hard-on? See. I *can* shock you.'

She took her hand back. She was smiling all the time.

'Do you always treat people like this?'

'You are not people.'

'No. I'm just the hired gun.'

'God, I'm sorry. Do I really treat you like that? I'm sorry. I didn't mean . . .'

She sucked pensively on a crab claw.

'I thought you liked hurting people.'

'Only you.'

She threw the empty shell back on to the basket and shoved the whole thing away from her.

'You can smoke if you want.'

He lit up the last cigarette.

'You know,' she began for no obvious reason, 'that Thai sauce, the one with the fermented fish? The one Mr Lee likes. I think it is horrible. It just smells like decomposition. Mr Lee loves it. I can hardly stay in the room with it. If the Thais really like that, then no wonder they like going to bed with anyone. Maybe I have a highly developed sense of smell because I cook. I mean, if men and women smell differently then they won't care for the same kind of foods, will they – like they won't leap into bed with just anybody . . . Do redheads smell differently from blondes?'

'Yes.'

'Really? Tell me. Don't be shy. I want to know. What do they smell like?'

'Blondes smell like yeasty vanilla, or the crust on sour cream when it has been left open for a couple of days.'

'Yuk. And brunettes?'

'Tomato soup.'

'What about those Chinese girls?'

'That might be different.'

'Why redheads? Could you do it with a red-haired man?'

'Do what? No, I don't think so.'

'See, my point, men must smell differently.'

Then she asked quickly:

'Would you like to have sex with me?'

'Jo, I hardly know you.'

'That's what girls are supposed to say.'

Cartier shrugged.

'You called me. Jo. I like that.'

'I call you all sorts of things in my head. Josie when I think you're fucked up. Jojo when you are being sassy like now. Josephine when you are being businesslike. Jo when I'm feeling fond of you.'

'I don't mind you calling me Jo, when it's not business.'

And then she said:

'Don't you want to do it? Just have me now and be done with it? No, don't answer that, I don't want you. I was only asking.'

'You make it sound like some sort of jousting tournament. I am the knight fighting for your favours.'

'Just because I let you wear my colours does not mean you have proved yourself yet.'

'I didn't realise love was about proving anything.'

'Even dough has to rise, Cartier.'

'Is that why you knock me back down all the time? To improve the fermentation?'

'You will be better for it. It takes time to turn wheat into bread. There's no point rushing it.'

'It is the baking part that is worrying me.'

'I was looking forward to slashing the crust. That's the artistic bit.'

She paused. 'I am not like you. Easy come, easy go. I need to know. I need to know the flour is strong enough.'

'And if it isn't?'

'I'll throw it away.'

'Jo, you're drunk.'

'I would need some form of commitment from you.'

'Commitment?'

'It would have to be unconditional.'

'Is this another challenge?'

'Something very personal, that only the two of us could share or even know about, that no one else could guess at . . .'

Cartier stubbed out the cigarette and leant back in his chair. He felt calm – probably the wine – and beguiled. There was a steely sense of purpose behind her coyness.

'Do you agree?'

'To what, exactly?'

'It might be anything, but you are not allowed to know or it would be unfair. Do you agree?'

'Probably.' Cartier wanted another drink but he didn't dare take his eyes off hers to check for a waitress.

'Is that a yes or a no? You can wait if you want. I'm not pressurising you.'

'No. It's a yes.'

'To anything, whatever it might be? Even if it is painful, even if you don't understand what it is I want or why?'

'Sure.' Cartier wondered what trapdoor he had just unlocked.

She growled. He smiled back at her. The curse was there at her shoulder. She knew it. She could sense it. But she knew that she had to push things further. She needed him to show that he was strong enough. She grasped the bottle of wine by the neck and put her elbows on the table either side of his outstretched hand. She lifted the bottle, then, in one stabbing millisecond of wrath, brought the thick base down on to the tip of his forefinger.

'Christ!'

The bottle cracked at the base and showered the hand with deep green splinters. The finger swelled up and the blood burst through the nail.

'Be thankful at least that you didn't fuck her,' Jojo said.

The girl at the next table flinched. She bit her lip in horror and turned away. The waitress swooped and was kneeling on the floor, picking up the broken glass.

Cartier couldn't see Jojo's face. Her red hair hid it. She was bent over the damaged finger, like a nurse now, tending it. She was flicking the shards of glass away from the wound, tidying her work.

'Did I pass the audition?' His finger was starting to throb.

'It won't happen again. I'm not a sadist. African tribes cut themselves to show their loyalty. They wear their scars with pride. So can you.'

Tenderly she stroked away the damaged flesh and grasped the base of his hand. When she looked at him again, the steeliness was gone from her eyes.

'I seem to remember you not approving of employers hitting employees.' He winced.

'You are not an employee.'

The pain streaked down his arm. He hardly dared move the hand. The finger might well be broken.

'Watch,' she said. She took a broken shard and cut across the wound so the blood spurted over the cracked nail. She touched the tip of her finger to the running blood. A red pool stayed on the end and she lifted it to her mouth and licked it off.

'See.'

'You said this was going to be something we could share.'

She didn't answer. Instead she put her palm out and scratched the heel of her thumb with the glass shard so her blood ran. She held it over the wounded finger and let the blood drip into the wound and mingle.

'There.'

She bent her head and gently kissed the wound.

'You may find it painful to use your mobile phone for a few days. You have to understand, there are some things between a man and a woman that have to be exorcised.'

'Some people just make love.'

'That is too easy . . . and too pleasurable . . . too complicated.'

'This is quite painful.'

She picked up the brandy glass and poured the alcohol on the wound, and then wrapped a white napkin around the hand. Cartier winced.

'I don't really get any of this, Jojo.'

'I thought it was pretty straightforward. It's not about violence. It's about us. It's about you trusting me enough to let me do anything to you, even break your finger. It's about you knowing that I will never have to do it again because it has already happened. It's not about love but about the pain of life and how far I might go for you in return.'

'How far is that, exactly?'

'Do you want a flirtation or a love affair? Can you tell the difference?'

Cartier downed the last of the brandy.

'Does this mean we are lovers, then?'

'No. It means I have shown you what I want and what I expect.' She stood up, a little unsteadily. She smoothed the front of her T-shirt down over her stomach. There was a spat of mayonnaise on the front and her sleeve had blood on it.

'Good night, Cartier.'

Jojo skipped through the rain to the car. The wash of the rain and the cold night sobered her. What had she done? How could she have? She threw herself in the back seat.

'Home, Mr Lee. Quickly.'

'Are you OK?'

'No. Yes. I'm fine. Don't mind. Just drive.'

Guilt and venom leached out of her on to the leather seats. Suddenly she wanted reassurance. This whirlwind had just swept her up. Now that he wasn't there, normality was returning. What had compelled her to do such an outrageous thing? She was looking down a long corridor, aeons ago, and at the end a chestful of half-remembered feelings.

It was almost as though she had taken his virginity. She had made him bleed. Pleasure would come later.

The sharing of the blood was symbolic. It bound them together. Christ, she might have Aids . . .

She remembered the blood on the sheets of Didier's hospital bed. The hanging litre of blood dripping vainly into his arm. The blood of her miscarriage. His blood. Her blood. Their baby's blood.

She felt sick. Intuitively she rubbed the cut on her own hand. For a moment it seemed her only possession of worth.

She rang him.

'Are you all right? I didn't realise. I mean. I didn't mean to go so far.'

'I'd feel better if you were still here.'

'Can you forgive me?'

'Well, I won't forget you for a few days, if that's what you mean.'

'Does it hurt?'

'Only when I move it.'

'Do you think it's broken?'

'No, I can still move it, which is why it hurts. Where are you now?'

'In the car. We're just coming to the motorway . . .'

'Why not come back?'

'We've done enough for one night, don't you think?'

'Maybe you have . . .'

'Yes, I have. Good night, Cartier.'

'Good night, Josephine.'

She looked at the thick stripe across the heel of her hand. It was vivid red still. She thought of their bloods mixing. It was the sort of thing Red Indians did. Had she become so savage?

At ten o'clock the next morning, Cartier had a call from the Vicarage. An invitation to dine.

'Would you mind terribly if we ate Oriental?' Mr Lee had asked.

'No. Why?'

'To be truthful, I am finding all this French food a little too much. What you call French cooking or English cooking, it is all about meat. Meat with this. Meat with that. For me it is the rice or the pasta that is important. These are the things that make you feel good. They are bland but they respond to spices and herbs.'

'As long as I don't have to use chopsticks.'

Mr Lee walked through the doors of CCK, casual in cashmere and jeans, a gold bracelet ostentatiously on one wrist, a small cane in his hand, very *Vogue*.

'Normally on my night off I go to see some friends in Hendon. But I think they have become a little bored with me. And so I am very glad to get away, and to have a chance to talk man to man, so to speak. What have you done to your hand?'

'I caught it in a taxi door. Smashed the tip.' Cartier lied.

'Is it painful?'

'Awkward.'

'I hope it gets better soon.'

'It is better already.'

Mr Lee ordered a bottle of Courvoisier.

'We drink properly, not like *gweilos*. It is in fact the only time I drink brandy. It goes well with Chinese food. I have four interests in life – food, boats, sex and staying alive. Which would you like to talk about?'

'Boats,' Cartier said, as it was the one he knew nothing about.

'The sea links me to my home. And has always been lucky for me. Our village was a fishing village. My first money I made in Bangkok getting tourists on to taxi boats. I once lived on a houseboat with a rich man. I dream of big yachts. I have posters up in my room of boats, you know?'

'To boats,' said Cartier, raising his brandy.

'To Jojo,' said Mr Lee. 'She would be offended if you did not drink her health.'

'All right then, to Jojo.'

Cartier had drunk half the bottle by the time the two of them had consumed the crab with black bean sauce, a huge mound of fluffed rice, and a side dish of pak choi with oyster sauce. Cartier ducked out of the sweets. Mr Lee ate like someone expecting to discover something, a sailor checking out each inlet and cove. He ploughed into green and white jellies and wobbling liquorice allsorts with a ruthless determination to seek out their last essences.

'Is Mr Lee your real name?' Cartier asked.

'It is a very good name, don't you think? I use it all the time. It serves me well in all situations. It is like wearing a top hat. It stays in people's minds. Funny, that, for something so ordinary.'

He poured himself another brandy.

'I left my village to make money for my family. I worked the streets and then in the brothels. I swept the floors and tidied the rooms. The girls mothered me. I was only ten or so at first. As I got older and more sexual my presence became more of a threat. To hide me from the man who owned the brothel, the girls began to dress me in their clothes. They made me very beautiful. It was a game we played in the long hours waiting between customers.

'And then, one night, a Frenchman, Jean Pierre (I even remember his name), picked me out of the crowd. I was terrified. I could hardly tell him the truth and he was sure to find out. If he told the owner then I would be out on the street, or worse. I went with him. He was quite drunk. The girls had shown me what to do – or what they did when they not like a customer. They make him come quickly with their hands. So that is what I did. He was so drunk he didn't realise. This does not offend you, I hope.'

'I am fascinated.'

'I can't say I didn't enjoy it. You have sense of power. Some people are victims, but for people like me it is a game. The next time I wasn't so lucky. The man was furious. I thought the owner was going to kill me. He didn't. Some men, he said, would pay a lot more for a boy who was a girl. If I would take some hormones, he would give me my own room and I could stay. Pretty soon I was making more than the most beautiful girls in Bangkok.'

'Well, you are pretty good-looking, for a boy.'

'The girls taught me how to dress. I can disguise myself, like a chameleon.'

'How did you get out?'

'I was not a poor streetwalker, Cartier. My clients were generous. They took me out to restaurants. I saved for the air fare. They told me I make much more in Rome. And that is where I was going until I met Jojo. There was all this Aids scare. I thought perhaps I look after myself better and find another occupation.'

'And are you pleased with your new career?'

'Oh, yes. Jojo has been so kind. The Vicarage, the Circus. Most intriguing.'

'How should I address you? As a man or a woman?'

'That depends on my mood. At the Vicarage I do not think it would be helpful, but in London, well, I did not want to surprise you too much in one go tonight!' He laughed.

'How did Jojo take all this?'

'Sometimes I think she finds it easier to treat me as a sister.'

They fell silent while the waitress cleared the table and brought some jasmine tea. Mr Lee was the first to speak again.

'I have taken you into my confidence, because I have some things I would like to ask you, if I may?'

Cartier nodded.

'You too are not what you might seem,' he announced casually.

'Who is?'

'You have no address. Some accounts. No history. No business. No employees. No family. Just acquaintances. You are invisible man. I could turn around and you would not be there. I check the newspapers. That is more interesting. A few pictures of you with beautiful women. A piece about a client who sued you for promising something you could not deliver. You lost that one, I noticed.'

'There's always one woman you saw in half by mistake.'

'Perhaps, but, unlike me, you did not just arrive off the boat one morning. For a man with such a reputation, you seem, forgive me, very short of credentials.'

'Credentials for what? What you see is pretty much what you get.'

'You work also for other clients.'

'I also need to turn a trick or two.'

'So whose man are you?'

'My own.' Cartier eyed him carefully.

'There were a number of debts, in your wife's name.'

'It is not much of an obituary, is it, to have a line of county court judgements against your name. She was good with a credit card, though.'

'I noticed. Quite imaginative,' said Mr Lee. 'Were you very close?'

'Close enough.'

'I am prying.'

'Not really. We were not married very long. She died very suddenly. Blood poisoning. You would think it couldn't happen in this day and age. She was in India.

She cut herself. It got infected. She didn't realise. She died on the plane. We had hardly got used to each other.'

'How sad.'

'Yes, it was . . . Are these your questions, or Jojo's?'

'Mine.'

'I live for today, Mr Lee, that is all. I have a past but it is all jumbled up, and as for the future, well, who knows, and perhaps who cares?'

'But you are successful. You could plan?'

'There are two ways to make money in this city, Mr Lee. Your daddy gives it to you. Or you deal in cocaine.'

'Jojo said she thought you were involved with drugs.'

'Everyone who made it in London in the eighties – who made it without any help – did it through coke. It was the quickest way to get a client list. For some of us it was the only way.'

'Do you still?'

'Now it is just kids. The risks are too high. Besides, it does not mix with food. Most of my people got respectable and went to the country. Or their jobs got serious and they had to think all day. Once they stopped making money out of houses, they all panicked.'

'Why didn't you go to the country?'

'Too boring. Too dark at night.'

'Are you afraid of the dark?'

'Only that people go to bed early and so don't do restaurants properly.'

'Is that all you care about?'

'It's all I know about.'

'I know about brothels. It doesn't mean I wanted to stay in one.'

'I love restaurants.'

'Maybe it would be better for you if you loved somebody. You can't be a hired gun forever.'

'Gunslingers, to use your words, don't love people, they shoot them.'

Mr Lee clapped.

'Bravo! You are a strange man, but I like you. One day maybe you hang up your guns. We get you a little ranch in the hills with a good woman to cook your supper and I come and see you and she shout at us for drinking brandy on the porch together.'

'You are a romantic, Mr Lee.'

'Why do you say that?'

'Some people would say that another word for a gunslinger is a psychopath.'

'Or a hero . . .'

'Heroes are redundant, Mr Lee, or hadn't you heard?'

'There's always somebody who needs protecting. Or rescuing. Surely.'

Cartier continued to check in religiously with Jojo each evening. Their conversations became increasingly brief and pragmatic. The Circus consumed them. As the day approached, Jojo confirmed the number of bookings. They etched a picture of a side of her life that he could only guess at. Whether they were friends or just people who had heard of her growing reputation, the list was taking on awesome proportions. 'Mohammed is coming,' she announced one evening. 'That's our first bit of royalty. His Excellency will be bringing three wives.'

'How many has he got?'

'Six or seven at last count. He adores women. But only plump ones. He feeds them up like seal puppies. Only one will be allowed to accompany him. The others must be fed in their room. They would be very upset to miss out. He has sent an extra cheque to cover for them.'

'He doesn't sound very modern-thinking.'

'Mohammed's view is that being fed by him is rather

more attractive than starving in Somalia. There are worse fates than being one of his concubines. I've got some more replies here, I am just opening the envelopes . . .'

The line went quiet.

'Where do you know all these people from?'

'I met them on the bus, where do you think? Oh, look, Monsieur Gaston Piquet is honoured to accept. So we have at least one serious French chef. No, we have two, no, three . . . Monsieur Le Maître wonders if he may bring his friends from Coulommiers and from Chambery. Of course he may.

'And from Italy, yes, the Conte and Contessa Sonnino, and from Modena, yes, Michelangelo will be here and he will bring with him his amazing vinegar. By my calculation we now have three hundred and seventy-three firm guests. And we must have a few tables extra in case, for the press and other hangers-on.'

'You promised twenty to the fabric warehouse,' Cartier reminded her. 'And I've promised another twenty to the developers.'

'We're getting there. We're getting there.'

'There'll be a few stragglers at the end.'

'How is your hand? Mr Lee said you had it in a sling.'

'What do you expect?'

'I didn't mean to cripple you.'

'What did you mean, then?'

'Just to mark you, that was all.'

At the Montague, Vincent made the sausages himself. He minced the veal and the goose liver. He mixed in the cream. He added the port and the ginger. He liked ginger. It was not classical but it was something of himself. He pounded the mix until it was so smooth it was velvet. And then he piped it into the casings from the ox stomach he had ordered specially for the occasion.

This would be one of his great meals. The setting might not be perfect, but he would be prepared. He made another mousse, this time of passion fruit and lychees. And he set it in the centre of a pastry tart surrounded by fresh fruit on a crème anglaise. To start, he could not make up his mind. Certainly not soup. Nor a salad. He decided on fish, two fillets of lemon sole filled with a mousse of lobster. He had one in the fridge he had made yesterday.

At 9.30 he absented himself from the Montague and made his way to the South Bank and presented himself at the top floor with his little polythene box and two bottles of wine – a Gewürztztraminer in his jacket pocket and a vintage Mumm in his hand.

The room was blank, without any stamp of personality. Even the shelves were nude of books. It looked as if it had been hastily tidied. The waste-paper basket was brimming over with old newspapers and spent faxes.

A bare table was set in the middle of the room with a single candle. To one side was a tiny kitchen, and to the other, fenced off by a metal curtain rail, a half-made bed.

'How lovely to see you,' Harriet said. 'And your little box. Let me see.' She peeked in. 'Delicious. You will cook. I will choose how we eat.'

She gave him a glass of Mâcon Lugny and dispatched him to the kitchen area. She sat down and he laid a fresh cloth on the table in front of her. The oven had not been cleaned, but it would have to do. He took a small, battered pan and washed it carefully, then began beating the butter into his flour.

'You are such a clever chef. You should really be appearing at Jojo's Circus. It will be the worse for not having you.'

'I thought it was just a private little affair.'

'It's a bit more than that.'

'Really? Tell me later. Are you ready to eat?'

He came bearing the soles sandwiched around the pink mousse, with shiny translucent sauce around and two large prawns at the edge.

Harriet was wearing a crimson blouse and a wrap-round skirt.

'Sit next to me,' she instructed, plunging her fork into the aspic.

'It seems so long since I tasted your cooking. I will eat both of them. You are not to eat – not until I tell you.' She smiled conspiratorially and passed him a glass of wine.

Vincent watched her, the dutiful puppy. She took her time, conscious of his eyes upon her. As she wiped her lips with the back of her hand, he went to fetch the *boudin*.

'No, no, not yet. I want some pudding. Something sweet. Put that back. It must not spoil. And keep it warm.'

Vincent obeyed without a word. He returned with his tart.

'That's better. But you should eat something, to whet your appetite. Cut me a slice. Just one, and bring it here. Kneel down.'

He knelt. Harriet loosened her blouse. She was naked underneath.

'I am going to feed you. Open your mouth. You like the taste of my skin, don't you, Vincent?'

He licked the cake off her hand. She gave him another piece and stroked the back of his head as he ate. She slipped her breast out of her blouse and gave it to him. His lips took the nipple greedily. She moaned quietly as he licked and squeezed, unfamiliar with the fleshiness of a woman but captivated. With her finger she scooped some cream and pushed it into the corner of his mouth as he suckled. She stroked his hair. His beard tickled.

'That is good. You like eating me, don't you, Vincent?'

171

His head nodded in her hand, not leaving the breast. She tweaked his hair to pull him off.

'Now we want some more food. Bring me the *boudin*. Make sure it is warm, not cold.'

He was back in seconds with the plate. The two large *boudins* gleamed warmly. She inspected them carefully, running a finger along the sides.

'This one will do fine. Quite firm enough. Kneel down. Right down. There.'

Between two fingers she took the *boudin* and felt it, judging it. She shifted, and parted her skirt. She was naked underneath. She ran the sausage down her body, pretending to suck it and then deliberately using it to point out her nudity. A light glistening trail of grease dribbled across her stomach into her pubic hairs. Vincent was transfixed. His knees hurt. He could barely keep steady.

She lifted her left leg and slowly inserted the *boudin* between her thighs. She moved it in and out as she spoke.

'Do you like me, Vincent? Do you like your *boudin*, Vincent? Do you like watching me do this?'

He nodded. He felt part of some black witch's ritual, and he ached from his position on the floor.

'Are you hungry, Vincent? Do you want to, Vincent? Do you want to pleasure me, Vincent? Eat me, Vincent. Eat me. Eat your precious *boudin*. Eat us both together.'

She pulled his face between her legs. He almost toppled into her. She held his head tightly with two hands as her thighs squeezed around his black hair like a vice. Her voice became distant as her flesh filled his ears. He couldn't see. She was stripping him of his senses except his mouth. A long way away he heard her say:

'Eat. Eat me. All of it. Lick the juices. Lick.'

She howled like a wolf as he ate.

8

THE DANCE OF THE BOUILLABAISSE

THERE WAS NO one on the front desk, it was still early. Cartier walked slowly through to the drawing room, hoping to catch her alone. It was empty. He went through to the kitchen. They were all there huddled together. Instead of the perpetual motion that characterises all kitchens — hands cutting, soups being ladled, people stretching to reach something, clearing a space, lifting something to taste — everyone was still. Something was wrong.

Jojo didn't notice him come in. In her hand she held a coffee cup. She walked over and held the cup under the steel piston bar of the espresso machine. Everyone watched.

On the table was an open carton of milk and a sealed glass jar filled with the small, round, knobbly beige truffles.

Jojo held the cup under the metal frother and switched on. There was a violent hiss. Steam poured over the edges. She held it there for thirty seconds, then swung round to face Pascal and Mr Lee, looking very glum.

'You see. There's no smell. Just burnt milk.'

She bent her head down and sniffed deeply. She dipped her finger into the frothy bubbles. It came out draped with a pliant length of tuber, which she ate.

'Nothing. It doesn't work. The cooking just burns it out. It's hopeless. White truffles don't cook. Why doesn't anybody write this down? Only black truffles cook. I have to find out the day before the curtain goes up that my capons are not going to have a white wedding after all. They are going to get a damp bath and come the time we take the lids off there will be no climax, there will be no aroma, there will be nothing but hard little bits of leather which the milkman might as well have left.'

She noticed Cartier for the first time, and thrust the cup under his nose.

'Smell this. We have ten thousand pounds of white truffles and a recipe that doesn't work. Aargh!' she screamed.

Cartier sniffed the cup. It was just warmed milk.

'Aaargh!' she screamed again, and, wheeling round, leapt on the bench in frustration. She paced across the silver table, one hand on her hip, peering down at them like a bird with a broken wing.

'It could be worse,' said Cartier quietly.

'Don't be ridiculous. What could be worse? We have six hundred guests and no main course to speak of . . .'

'So?'

They looked at him in hope rather than expectation.

'So, if it doesn't work, it doesn't work. We have white truffles and we have capons. You can still do something.'

'What?' Jojo said morosely. He had never seen her so deflated. He had not expected her to be beaten down by something like this, something so ordinary that any home cook might panic over.

'You can still poach the chickens. Do it the old way. Very simple. Very classic. The chickens can still be carved at the table. And do a classical Parisienne, but use the stock from the chickens, not veal.'

'Nice, but not special or modern. And what about the wretched truffles? We can't throw them away,' said Pascal.

'Keep the eggs with the truffles; they will take on the flavour. Then use the yolks to liaise the sauce. It would be a triumph. It's the same principle – just the other way round.'

Jojo's mood was immediately transformed.

'And then we still have the truffles. They can be walked around the tables and shaved on top as garnish. The smell will be fabulous.'

'Yes, it works,' said Pascal. 'But what of the rest of the meal? How will that balance?'

In the space of five minutes, they rewrote the whole menu.

Mr Lee said: 'I like the bouillabaisse.'

'Do we dare do that for the French?' asked Pascal.

'A very small, very clear, clarified, very intense bouillabaisse,' Jojo answered. 'With tiny croûtons. We don't serve the fish with it. Instead we will have turbot, the king of fish, and it will be our little joke. As if the finest fish of all has come out of this peasant stew.'

Jojo's usual brio was returning.

'Cartier, you must get the biggest turbot you can find. We need good chunks of flesh. Pascal, the red wine sauce must be the same colour as the bouillabaisse – but we only want a dribble on the plate. You could use a little verjus or sherry vinegar to acidulate it, which will create the contrast with the soup. A few capers too. We will taste it together. We need to see the red of the sauce, the green of the seaweed – that will remind them also of the bottom of the sea, and the Italian flag, which will please the Conte. And the spices. The skin must be crisp. Pascal, you must make sure that each piece of fish has the spices rubbed hard into the flesh or the effect will be lost. What spices will you use?'

'Mace, coriander, ginger, cinnamon and pepper. I

would like to make a Chinese-style five spice, to make it a little more exotic,' said Pascal, rediscovering his enthusiasm. Jojo nodded.

'You could finish the joke by serving a little *rouille*, perhaps with saffron, to one side,' Cartier interjected.

They grinned at each other, like climbers who had fallen off the mountain and managed to pull themselves back from the crevasse.

Jojo turned to Cartier.

'That is the second time you have saved us, Cartier. You should come here more often. You are a useful man to have around.'

A large shark had swum through the waters of Vincent's inner consciousness. It had been many years since he had been intimate with a woman. He had not liked it then and had planned for it never to happen again. He had not realised that his relationship with Harriet was a seduction. He had been too focused on the power she wielded in television and her delight in his food. He had enjoyed the conspiracy. Now he had gone further than he had expected with someone whom he absolutely had no wish to offend. He worshipped her, but not like that. He thought of all those feeble excuses women always gave in soap operas for being unfaithful. I didn't mean to. It was an accident. He had not meant to. *It had been an accident.*

Also he was scared of how a woman might respond in this situation, let alone a woman like Harriet. The naked outpouring of instant emotion was one reason he avoided women. He never knew how to respond. Now, inadvisedly, he had guided himself right into the eye of a storm.

It was her fault. She had made it all happen. He had been an unwitting accomplice. She had never mentioned the subject and then it was too late. He had fallen into her trap.

On the floor of her flat, he had tried to broach the subject. If anything, this had made matters even worse. She had hardly altered her position throughout their intimacy. She was still in that chair, open to him, only now she was smoking a cheap cigar. The sour smell filled the room. He sat miserably at her feet. Occasionally her hand wandered out to pat his head, as if he were a pet dog.

'Harriet, you know that I am gay.'

'Of course.'

'I haven't been with a naked woman for years.'

'Is it horrible?'

'No. No, it's not.'

What could he have said? That someone else would have enjoyed it more? That someone else might have been more up to the occasion?

'You seemed to enjoy yourself, as I recall. Are you frightened that I might ask you to do something you might not like?'

'Yes, perhaps I am.'

'Have I done that so far?'

'No.'

'Trust me. I understand you. I would not betray you. Where would any of us be if we did not do what our friends wanted? Do you understand me, Vincent?'

He nodded, meekly, not totally reassured. Her nakedness was threatening.

'Perhaps you would like to go now? It is late. We both have things to do tomorrow. I will not be offended if you go.'

It was more a direction than a question. He got up, shuffled into his clothes and tidied his pots and pans in the semi-dark. She seemed to be meditating, moving only occasionally to suck on the cigar and let the yellow smoke rise up in the moonlight. He kissed her clumsily on her hair in the dark, unsure of where she was. He realised they had never actually kissed, except when she had taken the last piece of sausage from his lips. Prostitutes were never supposed to kiss. The chasm of the sexes yawned in front of him.

He wanted his privacy back. He didn't know what she wanted and she did not seem inclined to tell him. She seemed to be indifferent and already sinking into sleep. The act was over. Most of all Vincent didn't want her to make any more demands on his body. He didn't want to penetrate her. He wanted to go passively into the night. He had wanted their relationship to peak with the food. She was as still and relaxed as a cast bust. The storm in him bellowed and threatened to burst out of him and spew all over her.

'Ring me tomorrow.'

Thank heavens. He closed the door, unsure whether he was leaving behind him a wrathful, frustrated siren or a friend with whom he had just shared a bizarre but momentous closeness. The stairwell looked invitingly safe and empty.

Had Vincent known Harriet better, he might have realised she only had a few more days of use left for him. Had he asked her, she would have told him that she did not care much either way. She had her commitment. The condemned man had had his last supper.

The other disorienting factor was the welling sense of foreboding about the Circus. Vincent seemed to have been completely ostracised. That in itself did not matter. He was the best chef in London and that was no easy status for anyone else to take from him. But people were talking. Harriet had mentioned it again. One of his valued customers had asked if he was going to be there because they had taken a table for four – now at £500 each! What was Jojo up to?

To compound the sense of rising misery, one of the

diary columns pointed out that among the guests for this event was to be Conte Antonio Antinori. Vincent had seen him once fleetingly at the Vicarage. If he was coming, then Jojo was taking this Circus very seriously indeed.

He paced his kitchen, a mantle of loneliness cast around his shoulders. The world was on the move. And it was not taking him with it. In the corner Marylese was working methodically kneading the pasta. At least she was with him.

He tried to ring Harriet. She was out. The answerphone was not specific. He left a message. He tried again an hour later and left another message. Then he didn't dare ring again in case she took it the wrong way.

He tried to ring Cartier. Another answerphone.

He tried to get a ticket.

'I'm sorry, sir, all the tickets were taken weeks ago.'

'Are there no returns?'

'We are not expecting any.'

He rang Pascal.

'What's the menu?'

'I'm sworn to secrecy.'

'Come on.'

'No chance. Jojo would kill me. Mind you, she has changed it once already. She might change it again. Who knows?'

'You can't cook for five hundred people like that.'

'Six hundred and fifty covers now, in fact.'

'Perhaps I'll come round to the kitchen later, after we close, and see how you are getting on.'

'You'll have to get a pass. The security is pretty tight. There's some heavy-duty dignitaries coming.'

'They know me, they'll let me in.'

Pascal made a mental note to be sure that he had spirited Marylese away before ten. The others could have the glory. He had a more important assignation.

Vincent's fish supplier could not find any turbot.

'What do you mean, you cannot find any turbot? There is an ocean out there, full of them. Where have they gone?'

'Someone has bought the lot.'

'You can't buy all the turbot in London.'

'There's not that much of it about.'

'I only want one fish.'

'I promise you, Vincent, I have tried. It is all booked and gone. Forget it. Put a sauce on it and give them brill. The brill is lovely.'

'Brill is not a proper fish for a proper restaurant.'

'It is very popular these days.'

'Not with me. Not at the Montague. Sole and turbot are the only white fish allowed in here. Everything else is banned.'

Vincent slammed down the phone

Harriet finally answered one of his messages. Mercifully she spoke in conciliatory tones.

'Are you feeling all right? We didn't do anything too outrageous, did we? I hope not. You are such a talent. I have just been so busy.'

'Harriet, Harriet, Harriet, please tell me, what is happening at this monstrous Circus?'

'Well, it is all quite mysterious, which is making my job to sell it to TV almost impossible. No one knows the menu. No one knows the wines. We know there are a few dignitaries. But Jojo is being so cagey, it's impossible. Frankly, unless I make something happen it is hardly going to be worthwhile hiring the camera crew.'

'Why don't you come over and have something to eat at the Montague and tell me about it?'

'I can't, Vincent. Honestly, I'd love to but I'm just up to my ears at the moment. I'll ring you later and perhaps I'll have some more news. It's such a tragedy you are not cooking there.'

★

Unless something dramatic happened Harriet was going to be lucky to make the local news network. She wanted her bounty money. More than that she wanted her screen credit. And for that she needed something on film, not just a gastronomic Circus, but something that would make a really big splash. Something that would make the channels run it.

She didn't want to have to use Vincent. He was too volatile. But she might not have any choice . . .

The first eddies of dawn willowed up in the sky. A horizontal red beam of sunlight streaked across the fences and fields and caught the edge of the Vicarage sandstone. On the horizon a crescent of pale lemon opened up the darkness.

Mr Lee woke Jojo at 5.45 bearing a breakfast tray, averting his eyes from the satin sheets and busying himself opening the curtains to the shaking light outside.

Sleep came and went as easily as a train to Jojo. She was instantly awake with her feet on the floor and one hand tying herself into her kimono.

'Do you know, Mr Lee,' she said (the thought had been with her all night like a mantra), 'that it is only a hundred and thirty-eight days since I first rang Jack Cartier. And now here we are, from nothing, on the eve of, well, we shall see . . .'

'It is going to be success, I sure.'

They had closed for two days so the brigade could prepare. Even at this time of the morning, when little usually happened, the Vicarage felt eerily deserted. There was no sensation of sharing the hotel with other people, even if they were sleeping. There were no reassuring small noises coming out of the kitchen as the taps were turned on by the cleaners. It was just her and Mr Lee. It reminded Jojo uncomfortably of how it had been when she had first seen it. It felt like a lonely building again.

Every detail of the Circus was itemised in her mind like a great till reel. She went through the list with the precision of a Shakespearian director. She would not relax until the evening, when every actor had been finally rehearsed, every line run through again for nuance, every crease in every costume checked, every fuse in the kitchen and the dining room renewed, every sauce and every seasoning tasted, every chocolate wrapped in its paper, every guest name properly spelled out at each seat.

She showered briefly and wrapped herself in a neat, businesslike cerise tunic. Mr Lee straightened the room from the night before and sat down to share some of the fruit he had brought. He was eating a melon off a knife. A second melon was left out for her, sculpted into a ceremonial fire-breathing demigod.

'Will you do the dragons tonight?'

'Of course. And polar bears, and leopards, and kingfishers, and monkeys . . . and roses.'

'No, not roses. I hate roses. They are so hackneyed. Stick to the animals. What time are you due at the market?'

'Plenty of time yet. The plane from Bangkok not get in until ten. I asked Mr Wong to reserve me some good things. He's an OK man, for a Chinese. Any time before ten will be OK.'

'I thought you were going to Nine Elms.'

'Mr Wong better — closer to Soho, anyway. Less racial. Those old boys down at Nine Elms think because you got dark skin that you have no brain. Besides, I don't think they know much about food. Mr Wong, he know plenty, for a Chinaman. He don't do fuckee-fuckee with the clients.'

'Fuckee-fuckee?' Jojo asked.

'You know, mistress. You do business with him – he fix you up with girls.'

'I didn't know they were so imaginative down there.'

'Oh sure, they know how to fuck you OK. They fuck you this way. They fuck you that way. They fuck you every way. I stay with Mr Wong all right. Then if he try and sell one limp old lettuce and start asking for backhanders, there's no problem when I say no deal.'

'Everything must be edible – no potatoes or raw parsnips, you understand me,' Jojo said, getting back to the point.

'Sure thing. I just use melons and pineapples, mangoes if they are ripe. Mr Wong he knows. They will be good and refreshing. Lift you up plenty. Lift *you* up at the start of the day. Maybe he will have some durian.'

'Too smelly.'

'It's beautiful.'

'But it stinks. Definitely not, Mr Lee. No.'

Huge cleavages of sun were starting to carve up the monstrous clouds.

'We had better get our skates on. Drop me in Soho first. I'll ring Cartier and Pascal to make sure they are up.'

'I already did. They are waiting.'

'Let's go then,' she said, swigging back the coffee.

The Mercedes slipped easily down the empty motorway. They were on Oxford Street in twenty minutes. The only people about were street cleaners and two policemen on horseback keeping an eye on the dossers tucked up in their cardboard boxes in the shop doorways. Mr Lee swung the car right, into Dean Street. The testimony of the previous evening lay, untidied, on the pavement, broken bottles spilling dark shadows on the concrete, a hat and gloves spiked on to railings, a couple cuddling in a doorway, a broken-down car parked on the kerb, a mess of chop suey where someone had dropped a takeaway, a packet of Durex in a phone box. Steely grates covered the sex shop windows, incarcerating the posters of naked girls. The market traders had already begun to muster around the coffee bar. Boxes of fruit were piled high on the pavement. The odd bent figure hurried down an alley to work. A bus stopped on Shaftesbury Avenue and dropped off a posse of young men, the first shift for the restaurant kitchens.

And out of her Mercedes stepped an elegant red-haired woman, who had pinned all her hopes and ambitions on one single, outrageous stunt.

Pascal was already in the kitchen. He was making sure that Micky would take over the service after the second course, so he could escape with Marylese. Most of her work would be done in the afternoon anyway. The two men were laughing in a conspiratorial way, but came to attention when Jojo arrived, as if they had been caught out.

'Would you like coffee?' Pascal asked Jojo.

'I'm not sure. Have you any cognac?'

'I can find some.'

'I will have a coffee and a cognac. I may need some courage this morning. Have you done the sauce bases?'

'They are waiting for you.'

She went straight across to the range and dipped her index finger into the first pan. She tasted.

'That's fine – let's try a little with the truffle and see how we get on.'

She moved across to the red wine in the fish stock.

'Damn. I should have tasted the stock first, before we added the wine. We'll need to check this later for contrast when we have got the bouillabaisse.'

Pascal had taken the egg from the jar where it nested

with the truffle. The sweet, dry smell wafted around the kitchen.

'Phew, you can't really taste anything with these things around. They're dynamite.'

'Glorious.'

Pascal closed the jar quickly and the intoxicating aroma was contained. He cracked open the eggs and separated the yolks from the whites.

'These are good eggs from that funny farm lady. Very fresh. Look, you can see the way these yolks hold up. Beautiful.'

He took the whisk and rattled the deep orange-yellow around the white bowl, then slid the contents into the beige liquid in the pan, whipping all the time. Jojo stayed close by him, under his arm, smelling, perusing, checking.

'OK, let's taste.'

They huddled their faces across the copper pan. Their fingers dipped at the same time. Jojo nodded. Pascal raised an eyebrow as if to say, I should think so . . . The first pillar was in place.

Upstairs, Cartier was slumped at a table with a coffee. When he had arrived the day before, the dining room had just been a long corridor of bare floorboards, rough-edged, naked red brick, with a curved and much-trellised window, beneath fat timbers and a murky unseen apex. As he walked, his shoes left prints in the dust. A sparrow had lurked in the eaves and there were bird droppings on the floor. Cartier made sure the whole place was vacuum-cleaned with industrial c49s disinfectant twice over. Then the floor was washed again with warm water and vanilla essence.

The room that now confronted Jojo had been miraculously transformed. The brickwork was swathed in thick drapes of vermilion and ochre cotton. The walls were dotted with antiques, a woven elephant, a roaring tiger, figurines of naked black boys, marble busts of nymphs with pouting hips and unchipped breasts, huge vases, some filled with plumes of dried flowers and others empty, waiting for the fresh blooms to be delivered that afternoon. Chandeliers hung down like medieval flagbearers. A space had been cleared to the left side for the serving trolleys. The tables were still bare except for the saffron cloth neatly ironed across each one, waiting for their decoration. At each of the four corners of the room were cannons from a galleon pointing into the centre. Jojo headed straight for them.

'Do they work?'

'Mr Lee assures me they have a range of twenty metres.'

She tapped one appreciatively and turned to look at him.

'Cartier, you look dreadful. You smell of garlic and whisky. And you have to get a haircut. If you look like that tonight I won't let you in.'

'I haven't been to bed yet.'

'Evidently.'

Jojo looked around the extraordinary room. It had been large to start with but now it was larger than life, an impossible Felliniesque set. She patrolled round.

'What flowers here?'

'Irises.'

'And here?'

'Orchids.'

'And here?'

'Lilies.'

'I like lilies. Where will the carvings and the sugar works go?'

'I have made little plinths for them. There are sixteen in sugar. The fat ones will go at either end.'

'What are they?'

'There is a four-foot crane in sparkling greens and blues made out of sugar; a whole musical set in black and white again in sugar. The fat work is two nudes – a man and a woman . . .'

'Good. I wouldn't want us to be sexist about this.'

'Five feet long and reclining.'

'You did say I wanted him erect? I can't stand all those marbles with broken-off willies . . .'

'I don't think you'll have to complain about this one. It is being delivered at three. The chocolate statues will be kept in the fridge, ready to be brought out after the cheese. They will be elephants, lions, monkeys, bears and horses – two for each table.'

'We must make sure people eat them. If everyone sits around full of English reserve then they will melt. The waiters must be told to offer them quickly. And you will have to gee them along too.'

'The flower displays in sugar and the miniature work will go on the tables. The guys must have been working all week.'

'They will be rewarded after tonight – when they see what we have done. Now get yourself off. Take some pills and set your alarm. I want you back here at three, all pressed and shining, to check over everything with me before I disappear.'

Cartier lifted himself out of his chair, slurped back the dregs of his coffee and made for the door. He was shattered. He ambled carefully through the tables, bleary-eyed, but buoyed by the sheer sense of having worked a kind of miracle.

Marylese arrived at eleven, her knives rolled up in a blanket under one arm, and a small briefcase in her hand. She was wearing whites with a miniature rose in her lapel.

'I'm here. I'm yours,' she said to Pascal.

'At last.'

He kissed her on the cheek.

'I brought you a little gift.'

She gave him the red rose.

'I will work until it wilts. And then I will not work any more.'

'I'll get a glass of water. We will disappear when the first petal drops. I have had your work area cleaned and ready. I can see you from here. So if you have any problems you have only to shout.'

Marylese smiled at him and crossed to the cooler room. The tables were covered with marble. In a pile were eggs, flour, milk, stacks of Isigny butter in their blue packs, Valronha chocolate in their black.

She opened the briefcase and took out a phial filled with long black stringy pods of Madagascar vanilla, and a full bottle of eau-de-vie de cerise. She busied herself around the table, covering the surface with flour, working with her hands, occasionally glancing into the next room where Pascal was directing operations, smiling at him when he caught her looking. After half an hour he came through bearing two trays of chocolate-dipped cherries.

'I hope these are OK. I made him follow your instructions precisely. They are Morello as you asked. The chocolate is according to your specifications as delivered to us.'

'Have you tried one?'

'Of course.'

She picked one out for herself and took a small bite.

'That is fine. Thank you.'

She smelled of the shower and shampoo. He moved towards her to kiss her. Her finger stopped him.

'Later. We have work to do.'

'I'm impatient.'

'You can wait. We have both waited so long.'

Since it was a French dish, Pascal felt it was appropriate for him to give Micky a lecture on how to make bouillabaisse.

'Bouillabaisse is something people should wait for. It ought to be brought to the table brimming hot. In Toulon we used to have it with potatoes too. But they make it a bit murky. We used to eat it hot on our summer holidays. It was wonderful to get rid of the first day's sunburn. It must be a big soup. The biggest. It needs strong seasonings. It is a man's soup. It must have balls.'

By his side, Micky chopped rhythmically as he had done for the last half an hour, slowly building up piles of neatly trimmed vegetables – one hundred onions had been transformed from golden globes into white dice; fifty leeks had been pared into lime-green circles; eighty bulbs of violet garlic had been broken upon and each one neatly topped, tailed and skinned. The bin by his side was piled with the golden skins of the onions, the deep green of the leek heads and the parchment skins of the garlic.

'We will take that back and use it in the restaurant next week. It will make wonderful soup and stock – but not for tonight.'

On another surface lay four hundred tomatoes, each one blanched, skinned and deseeded, and chopped so there were two piles, quietly drying now, one of crimson-fleshed cubes, the other a squidgy, smooth mess of skins and stalks flecked with yellow pips. Lined up behind them were heaps of fennel, of bay, strips of orange rind, a clump of thyme from which each tiny leaf had been plucked and the stalks thrown away, a cellophane envelope of saffron and five bottles of extra virgin olive oil from Nyons.

Pascal did not so much cook this soup as attack it. It was a violent, flamboyant ritual dance. He threw the neat handiwork of his commis into the giant copper pans in great handfuls. The vegetables were first.

Then he grabbed a huge cleaver and, wielding it over his head, carved his way through the firm fish that were laid in front of him. First the eel was sliced into large wheels as deftly as if it were cucumber, the lobster was halved in one strike, and the claws torn off. Then he addressed himself to the box of crabs, ripping them apart like a showman opening telephone directories and passing them to his left for Micky to strip out the dead men's fingers. Then Pascal picked up his cleaver again and smashed their backs and slung the debris into the pot. The little shards nicked his fingers and he bled from the small cuts. The blood went in the soup too.

Pascal had five cauldrons in front of him. He moved to each one in turn and buried his long spoon into the middle, hurling the tiny fragments of vegetables and fish across the diameter above the spitting heat. He shook the cauldrons and struck with the spoon as if it was a spear. He might have been battling with some unseen, animate foe. He took a pace back and then ceremonially doused each one of the cauldrons with a whole bottle of olive oil. Flicking up the fire, he gestured to Micky to add the water.

'Heat, we must have heat. If you do not create a tempest then the fish and the vegetables will never marry each other. This is a shotgun wedding. They must be forced into each other. It is the only soup in the world that must boil. It must almost burn with intensity.'

Plumes of steam rolled out from under the lids, filling the kitchen with pungent flags of fishy vegetable smells. Pascal was working with a knife on the white fish, trimming them quietly now, as if the anger of making soup had passed and he was contrite.

'OK, Micky. It's yours now. Give it four minutes more, then strain it off through the muslin. The kitchen will eat the fish in twenty minutes for lunch. Clarify the rest. We will season it later. Keep some thyme and saffron ready.'

Harriet rang the Montague. Vincent was in a terrible state. What had begun as an irritating itch had developed into a festering wound. The idea of this Circus was driving him mad.

'Don't be such a lamb,' Harriet said. 'Have a drink and get over there. You cannot let the insult pass. You must be part of it – any part will do – otherwise everyone will think you missed the boat. Say something. Anything. Make sure you are part of the proceedings. Do you understand me? Your career will be ruined if you are not there. You will be forever that other chef.'

Her words echoed around the cavern of his fears. Tears welled up in his eyes. She was calling to him like a siren. Of course he had to do something, but he was catatonic. He wanted to do nothing. He wanted this damned Circus to just vanish.

He poured himself a drink. A little martini. It was the closest thing to hand. He let the lip of the glass hang on his teeth and smelled it morosely. He wanted the alcohol to consume the world. He wanted to feel calm again. He did not want to get embroiled with these two powerful women who seemed to be dragging his life this way and that like opposite poles of a magnet. Was it the Circus that bothered him? Or Harriet? Or Jojo? He didn't know. Probably all three. He poured another martini. He just wished he could go back into the kitchen and content himself with cooking a turbot. But there had been no turbot in the market that morning. They had all gone.

Jojo arranged and rearranged the statues and ornaments in the dining room. She phoned each invitee who had taken a table. Downstairs, Pascal and Marylese had been joined by a brigade of twenty-three. Marylese would look up from time to time to catch his eye as she worked, but there was always someone else talking to him. She saw Jojo coming down the stairs and taking him off to one side to discuss the menu again.

'Are we sure?' Jojo was saying to Pascal. 'Can we print the menu now? We can still change it. Is there anything else? Anything you want to change?'

'There's nothing else, Jojo. It's fine. Just as we discussed. We can't start changing now. It will be magnificent. Have confidence. It is done. Print the menus.'

'The *rouille* will not be too strong for the turbot?' Jojo asked one last time.

'No. No. It is a good joke. I've made it very gentle with the seeds of the tomato only. There's only a very little edge to it from the chilli, nothing to distract from the saffron. You can taste it again if you like.'

'No, it was nice. Shall I go ahead and print?'

'OK. I suppose, I suppose so . . .'

Jojo Coltrane welcomes you to

The Gastronomic
CIRCUS

<u>MENU</u>

CONSOMME
of bouillabaisse

Champagne *Cordon Mumm Vintage '87*

ROAST TURBOT
with its bones deep fried,
sauce rouille with saffron,
garniture of steamed seaweed

Tokay *Faller '86*

BRAISED CAPON
with white truffles

Montrachet *Calvet '88*

INNES GOAT CHEESES
(affinés)

Ch. Comtesse de Lalande *'86*

DIVERSE FRIVOLITIES

Ch. Y'quem *La Tour Blanche '89*

COFFEE AND COMBUSTIBLES

9

CIRCUS

GREEK STREET WAS closed. Wardour spat one or two cars out into Oxford while at the other end more and more cars poured in. Taxis whirled round and round on each other, jamming the side streets, drivers glaring at each other over their elbows. The early evening pavement throng spilled out on to the roads and blocked the traffic. All the world had come to Soho. The patrons of the Circus were discernible by the cut of the men's coats and the shine of the women's heels. They massed by the red door.

The queue was as ordered as an airport security check-in. Politely, the guests handed their coats into booths on either side of the stairs as they went up.

Pascal walked quietly around the kitchen, checking every last detail. He felt like a station master. This was not the sort of cooking he was used to. It was a feat of organisation. Everything had to be on time. The tannoy was hooked to the dining room so he could synchronise – first course 8.23; second course 8.45; main course 9.08. And then he was free. Micky would do the rest. He glanced towards Marylese. Her head was bent over her hands as she tied another ribbon to a chocolate eclair. He waited for Cartier to summon him for his bow. He could hear the strains of the 'Marseillaise' brushing over the clatter of conversation from the stairs.

Harriet occupied a position in the far corner of the dining room where the shadows of guests filed past her into the enrobed plum darkness. Girl greeters in long black dresses with cleavages down to their navels led each party into the glimmering candlelight. This settling of guests always took such an age, Harriet thought impatiently. She was looking for faces she might recognise. The men looked anonymous in their dinner jackets. The women's dresses loomed colourfully but their faces were only half visible. Harriet checked her angles. Her cameraman beside her was silent in the dark, mute. No flash, Jojo had ruled.

Mr Lee's fingers gently twisted the dimmer switch to let another notch of half-light into the room, to hurry the guests along.

Cartier waited at the podium, like some high priest watching his flock gather. He was wearing an enormously tall top hat and in his hand was a long leather riding whip.

Jojo greeted at the top of the stairs, curtseying, clasping hands, kissing a cheek, smiling, welcoming, waving down the stairs, pointing groups to their tables. The final stragglers were through and she swung the curtain on the door shut and nodded to Cartier.

The controls for the spotlights and the music were in front of him. He let the music rise. The voices ebbed away as the overture from *Carmen* filled the room. Cartier held the moment, waiting for them to be still. He lowered the volume again and with his right hand swept the whip behind his head and let it flick out over the heads of the nearest tables with a huge CRACK. His tones were measured, viscous, like treacle running down the side of a wall.

'My lords, Emirs, ambassadors, bishops, ladies and gentlemen . . . welcome to the world première . . . of the world's finest . . . the world's most fabulous . . . the world's first . . . the world's least frugal . . . the world's most felicitous . . . most fragrantly flamboyant . . . the world's most fantastic . . . most fanfarous . . . most fandangorous phenomenon . . . that is . . . Jojo Coltrane's Gastronomic Circus . . .'

He paused for breath. The silence was fat. Mr Lee gave a huge whoop. 'Bravo! Bravo!' he shouted. A clatter of clapping slunk round the room. Cartier picked up the pace:

'Put your hands together, please, tonight for your mistress of ceremonies, the radiant, the ravishing, the righteous, the remarkable, the rampatious, the redolent, the resplendent, the redoubtable, the rumbustious, the rascalious, the rememorable, the regina of this culinary regatta herself . . . Miss Jojo Coltrane . . .'

He flashed the spotlight on her. Applause lit up like a match. Mr Lee shouted: 'Bravo! Bravo!' at the front. Jojo stood to the applause and waved. She looked stunning. The emerald drapes of silk made it appear as if she had just stepped out of the huge swathes of material along the walls. The dress was cut like a long toga. Every movement shifted the angles it clung to on her body. Down her naked arm she wore a series of gold armlets. Her red hair tumbled in glorious waves.

Cartier killed the lights, cracked his whip again, and returned to the microphone:

'Assisted tonight by the the punctilious professionalism and prodigious potential, the post-prandial perfectionism of that culinary prestigitateur himself, that peerless practitioner of the puissance of the peripatetic palpitation, the prolific . . . Monsieur Pascal Marmotte . . .'

Lights. Whip. Applause. Pascal appeared at the door, took one bound into the room, bowed deeply to huge roars.

'And on desserts and pastry . . . the marvellous, the

magical, the moving, the mind-enchanting, malevolent, mysterious maestroess Marylese Black . . .'

'Bravo! Bravo! Hurrah! Hurrah! Bravo! Hurrah!'

'. . . and for pyrotechnics and manual dexterity of the deftist kind, the august, the inscrutable conflagrator, the wizard himself, Mr Lee.'

Cheers thundered back to him. Mr Lee had been adopted immediately by the tables around him. He took a huge bow to even more raucous applause. Cartier raised his hand for quiet. No one noticed. He cracked the whip again, this time harder and louder, and they came to heel.

'Bear with us, good guests, for the evening will be suavely salacious, secretly salubrious, scintillatingly sensual, and filled with sententious supplications, serenades, symphonies, even, to the serendipity of the senses.'

By now the audience had warmed to the show and picked up each outrageously long description with cries of 'ooh' and 'aaah'. Cartier toyed with them.

'Be amazed . . . Be comforted . . . Be comfortable . . . Be amorous . . . Be kind . . . Be friends . . . Be yourselves. But most of all . . . enjoy.'

As his words died, the lights went up to reveal the dining room in all its finery. The room as one caught its breath. Each table place was set with cut glass, with arrangements of flowers, some real, some in pastry, little hidden parcels, tiny decorations . . .

To a collective moan, Mr Lee plunged the room back into flickering darkness. The side doors flew open. The candles bent and their light beamed madly across the walls. To the sound of the 'Marseillaise' now, a column of waiters materialised. Plates were slipped in front of guests. Wine glasses were filled. Napkins were laid across laps. On the last trumpet note the lights flared on again. Cartier put his lips back to the microphone.

'Your first course is the brilliant, the beautiful,

bounty of the barbarian seas, the most corruscating consommé of the most banquetable bouille-a-baisse.'

Before each guest was a large teacup of steaming soup, and the waiters were laying out separate tiny croûtons of Gruyère and pesto.

'Ladies and gentlemen . . . the Circus has begun.'

Prompted by Cartier's lead the room had begun to perform like a well-rehearsed act. Waves of convivial conversation flowed from one wall to the other with sprays of 'oohs' and 'aahs' as guests noticed the sculptures of asparagus and carrots among the trumpets of nasturtiums.

Cartier stepped back from the microphone and sipped the soup that had been left for him at his raised podium. Even though his was only in a chipped tea mug, the clarity of the taste and scent was intoxicating. It brought tears to his eyes.

He surveyed the assembly from his lofted perch. Few of the diners knew each other or had any connection except tenuously through Jojo, and even that link was flimsily extended to friends and acquaintances. Some of the faces were familiar from newspaper cuttings and flashes on TV, or their status was picked out by a drape of ermine or a jewelled turban. Collectively the 648 people represented some form of mass endorsement, but as a group they were as arbitrary as a crowd at the races.

Next to table 48, where the women were dressed in the primary colours of some exotic African bazaar, Cartier noticed three monks and two nuns. They had not changed out of their habits and retained their sense of decorum, heads slightly bowed. They said prayers as the first courses arrived and nodded respectfully at each other before falling hungrily to their feast.

Table 35 had a man dressed in a Lanvin dinner suit. Cartier knew that bulky style. Beside him was a girl with a choker and jewelled lead, and a catsuit that was cut to reveal her bony hips and back. There was less cloth than flesh or straggly blonde hair. The man held her lead. She positioned herself like an obedient dog resting her cheek on his shoulder. The man occasionally broke off his conversation with the androgynous cleric opposite to spoonfeed her. She seemed in a dream.

Table 20 was a collection of crumpled suits and loud, ill-fitting dresses. That was the press table, and Harriet's gaggle of producers.

Hannibal Tetris had been elevated to a table of his own – number 5 – and was holding court to a conspiratorial gang of authors and agents. They were consuming huge quantities of wine and had already broken into the chocolate sculptures.

The cut of the suits gave some tables more distinction – number 6 looked Italian, number 17 Middle Eastern, number 40 strangely corporate.

The Palisters at table 19 had been begging to meet both the chef and Jojo. Cartier thought he recognised one of the party from Mr Lee's garage. Mr Palister had stuffed a £20 note into Cartier's pocket to bribe an introduction. It would be handy for a taxi later.

After the first fanfares, there had been an expectant hush. It was the sort of lull that might have consumed the whole evening, but the prattle of conversation had picked up and bubbled round the room. It made Cartier think of groups of excited children on a treasure hunt. He flicked the control and let the opening moments of Shostakovitch's Leningrad Symphony build quietly until he was ready.

Jojo was the only figure not sitting. She moved around the tables, draping her arms around some guests, whispering to others, stroking heads with the back of her hand, laughing. In the far corner she lingered with a dark, red-lipped woman in black. It took a moment for Cartier to recognise Maria.

Not for the first time, he wondered if Jojo might be gay. There was something in the snakiness of her body movements that suggested normal lines of decorum did not apply with Maria, whose hand lingered on the curve of Jojo's buttocks.

Cartier was deeply bored with his own jealousy. He distracted himself by peering across the heads of the room to where Mr Lee was entertaining a party of fourteen with his carving of a watermelon into a fishing boat.

Jojo was in a whirl. Her emotions had as many sides as a cut diamond. She loved the spectacle. She loved the food. She half wondered: did the sight of so many people eating together cross the line between erotica and pornography? She wanted to sit down and enjoy the meal herself, but she had tasted each component so many times that afternoon, and so many more times in her mind, that she couldn't. She was sated. Besides, she had to be hostess. She felt exiled from their enjoyment.

Her great idea was being devoured before her eyes. In no time, it was passing from its glorious conception into something else, over which she had little control. It was becoming, she could see clearly, a business. Her great statement was being corporatised. The artist in her wanted to rebel.

She beckoned Cartier over.

'Maria, tonight could not have happened without Cartier. I have been so cruel to him. He needs warmth and love and I have refused him. Look after him for me, will you?'

The Brazilian woman's brown eyes surveyed Cartier as though she was measuring him for a suit. She proffered a bejewelled hand. As he bent to kiss it, she said:

'I like tall men. Tell me, do you like my breasts?'

Cartier grinned.

'You are a reserved Englishman. It is very becoming. I'm sure Jojo should not discard you too easily. Sit with me for a minute and tell me how you pulled off this magnificent evening . . . and tell me why you have been so busy that you have not even phoned.'

Jojo slipped away and stood contemplative in the centre of the throng. There was a sense of maternal pride at being able to feed such a large crowd of people. But what were they taking from the evening? Was simple pleasure enough, or would there be a spontaneous combustion of desire, satisfaction and some other magic ingredient? Her misgivings, she knew, were just nerves. Was the food really that good? She couldn't tell any more. Could food ever be that good?

To her side at one of the work stations, a chef in whites slipped the knife through the grey-black skin of the huge turbot and flicked open the gleaming white flesh off the bone, laying the fillet on the grey plate (it had to be grey to achieve the colour contrast, Jojo had insisted), and another pair of hands arranged the green leitmotif of seasoned seaweed around it.

She overheard an Italian relating the famous story of his first night with his wife at her parents'. She had heard the tale more than once before.

'So we went to Carla's parents' house, in the hills above Florence. We were not married at that time and the house was small. So Carla slept with her mother and I with her father. I had just managed to lose consciousness when I feel this nudging. Luigi, he says to me, quick, I must show this to my wife, look. Be quiet, I say, it is the middle of the night, she is asleep. No no no, he says, feel this, I have not had an erection like this for years. I must share it with her. That's not your erection, I tell him, you have got your hand on my prick . . . now get it off.'

Jojo glided through the room to find Marcel. Brigitte

sat by his side in a leather skirt so short that the rim wiped the cheeks of her bottom. Above it she just had on a scarlet bandanna. Her lipstick was a matching red. The two women kissed hello.

'Brigitte, you look sensational. Will you not be a shade cold dressed like that?' Jojo enquired.

'The turbot is brilliant, my dear,' Brigitte replied.

'Did you approve?' Jojo asked Marcel.

'I did not come all this way to expect my star pupil to be serving hamburgers. It is superb. The first two courses are exact. And the room and the occasion is sensational. You could do this in Paris, you know.'

Marcel looked flushed. He had been drinking freely. Brigitte stared at him icily.

'It would be difficult for an English girl though, would it not? In Paris. Who would believe she would be serious?'

'We could help her, I am sure.'

'And what about your reputation?'

'Shopping has not agreed with Brigitte. Everything seems to have been too heavy, too warm, too thick, too something.'

'It is not their fault the English cannot design for the sun, I know. They have no sun here. Your colour, Jojo, is not what it was when you were with us. This grey climate does your complexion no good. You wilt in it.'

'Brigitte!' Marcel was embarrassed at his wife's bad manners.

'It was not meant to hurt. You know that, Jojo. Everything is charming. Ravishing. But there is something I'm dying to know. Your Brazilian friend, we met her on the way in, does she like women or men?'

'Why not ask her yourself?'

Jojo caught Marcel's eye and for a moment she saw the deep sadness of his marriage.

'I may do that.' Brigitte smiled brightly.

★

Harriet had dispatched her cameraman to cruise the edges of the throng. She had done a few interviews in the anteroom where the light was marginally better. There was nothing for her here so far. A few famous people but no story. At this rate all she would get would be a home video.

Cartier returned to the microphone.

'Ladies and gentlemen, your centrepiece tonight is the capon raised in the style of Dorking, which had previously gone out of fashion in nineteen ninety-two but here tonight is revived – each bird fed on milk. It will be served not in the French style, in mourning, with black truffles from Périgord, but dressed in the white truffles of Alba, for its wedding feast. The birds have been poached *en vessie* with their vegetables in white burgundy and are served with their soup to the side and a white truffle *velouté* . . .'

The carvers had practised, following the descriptions in the *Arte of Carverie* dated 1598. They had chosen especially long Sabatier knives. Each chef worked with two knives at a time. He showed the bird to the table and then flicked it out of its pig's bladder. He skewered it on the point and held it aloft with one hand while the other sliced through the air, once for ceremony and once to whip through the joints and drop them on to the salver below. The tables were enthralled.

Downstairs Pascal and Marylese wiped down the work surfaces after finishing the *velouté*.

'Come on,' she said, taking his elbow. 'It is done here. It's time to go.'

'You don't want to wait to hear the verdict of the guests?'

'There is no need. We both know it is a brilliant meal. Come on. Take your knives and let's get out of here. Besides, look, the petals on our rose have all fallen off.'

They slipped out via the fire exit.

Jojo carved for Marcel and Brigitte. Deftly she laid the chicken on the plate, and arranged the tiny turnips and carrots to the side.

'And just for you two. The Conte brought it especially from Modena. His oldest. Fifty-six years.'

She flicked some spots of black balsamic vinegar on to the white truffle *velouté* and whisked it in.

'For you both. My most special guests . . .'

Pascal and Marylese ran up the stairs to the second floor and almost fell into the bedroom. They tried to kiss but were both too breathless.

'It is not quite the Ritz, is it?' said Pascal.

'Who cares? It is ours.'

Marylese strode into the bathroom and turned the shower on full force. She stripped like an athlete ready for the starting block. Pascal watched her, awed by her nakedness.

'Come on. Don't just stand there. Take your clothes off and come in here.'

'I was admiring you.'

'There will be plenty of time for that later. I want you here.'

He picked her clothes off the floor and hung them on the back of a chair, then pulled off his own. As he stepped into the warm water she grabbed him by the hips and pulled him to her. The water poured on their faces as their tongues touched. She filled her hand with shampoo and stroked it into his head and down his body.

'Wait for me on the bed. I must dry my hair first.'

'We haven't time for you to dry your hair.'

'You can't expect me to make love with wet hair and to taste of shampoo?'

★

Hannibal Tetris was holding forth to his table. Blind to the decorations, his mind was aflame with the cooking.

'That woman is the most brilliant cook, to understand turbot like this, the balance of the flavours in the colours of the Italian flag. Brilliant.'

'You think all your discoveries are brilliant, Hannibal.'

'Jojo is in a league of her own.'

'I thought this was all down to Pascal.'

'For really great cooking you need an orchestra with soloists, but she is the composer and the conductor.'

'If only you could see what she has done to the room,' said his companion.

'I do not need to. I can smell it. I can feel it all around me. I can feel nothing but joy. Where is my wine? I must drink to this.'

His companion guided his hand to the glass and he drank deeply.

'Ahh, Montrachet too. How divine. How subtle. She has perfect pitch, this woman. You are in the presence of genius, gentlemen.'

'To Jojo.'

'To Jojo.'

Pascal watched from the bed as she dried herself. She stood in front of him with the towel strapped across her hips, handling the hair dryer like it was a gun, half concentrating and half smiling at him in the mirror.

He opened a bottle of Montrachet that he had secreted away with his knives and poured two glasses. It was slightly warm now. He offered her one. She gestured to the table. There could be no words above the hair dryer. He sat again, and drank. She was watching his every move in the mirror, each muscular ripple. She was admiring his neck, his chest, his hip bones, his half-erect penis. She watched the wine flow down his throat and disappear into his flat stomach.

How could he cook so well and yet have a body without a trace of fat on it? He was ivory bones and dappled skin.

She flicked the hair dryer off. The silence slapped into the room.

'Now I'm going to have what I want. You don't think me immodest?'

Slipping off her towel, she knelt in front of him on the bed.

'Marylese, you do nothing wrong in my eyes.'

She held him firmly. The long hours in the kitchen had given her unusual strength in her arms. Her hand moved faster. He grew in her hand and then all at once she could feel the warm sperm coming in spasms and the softness returning. She kissed him hard on the mouth and looked in his eyes, which he had screwed up. As they opened again she fell into them.

'This is what I wanted,' she said.

She took her hand away and let the sperm run into the palm. It pooled like an oyster. She lifted her hand to her mouth and licked it.

'I wanted to taste you. You taste like Brie.'

The unscheduled and uninvited figure who squeezed through the door at 10.35 glared at the assembled tables. His chef's whites had got him through security. No one ever thought of a chef as a person, let alone as a security risk. He snarled at their merriment. Not being recognised amounted to another lonely rebuke. He held himself steady for a moment against the wall. The beard twitched. Beneath, the skin was flushing from red to purple. Through his belt was a cleaver that hung menacingly down the side of his thigh. In his hand was an open bottle of Hennessey XO. His gaze rested on the huge Daliesque vision of a wedding cake in the centre of the room, four tiers decorated with tiny birds.

★

Cartier moved from table to table, filling glasses, shaking hands, pointing out small things in the sculptures people might have overlooked. In the far corner, Mr Lee took out his chain saw and began to hack into an eight-foot block of ice. Soon the square block was bearing wings of an eagle. Some guests from the far end had moved up to watch him.

Suddenly, the figure at the door let out a Samurai scream. The right arm spun and sent the bottle of cognac flying up towards the ceiling and into a swathe of silk which broke its fall. Drawing the cleaver from his belt, Vincent raised it over his head, and charged.

A few unconcerned heads turned. The night had been extraordinary. This was just another extraordinary event. There was no sense of danger. What was this new entertainment?

Cartier spotted him from his pulpit.

The distance between the intruder and the centre-piece cake was thirty metres. Vincent was listing like a car spinning off a motorway after a puncture.

'Aarghhh!' he yelled.

Cartier leapt from the pulpit in a vain attempt to stop him.

The cleaver slammed into the top half of the cake, and Vincent somersaulted head over heels after it. His face slewed into a sea of cream and pastry. Fruits and profiteroles and sculptures of birds decorated his head.

Split asunder, the giant cake let out its great secrets. One. Two. Three. Four. Six. Fifteen. Twenty-two tiny aeroplanes whirled out of their inner hangars and flew up to the ceiling. Conversation ceased as the rafters filled with the humming of these tiny craft. And then the fireworks exploded, shooting out streamers of pink and blue rice paper. The little jets let go their parachutes of chocolates and almond cakes while the cannons at either side exploded with a confetti of sugared baubles.

Mr Lee, ever alert, flicked the music back on, and the whole room erupted like a New York tickertape parade. Everyone cheered. They got up to dance. New York had met the carnival at Rio.

Vincent slumped to the floor, listening incredulously to the applause. He had committed an act of gross vandalism and yet here the blood of his revenge was being sucked out. No cries of horror. No tears. Only laughing and dancing. Had he gone mad? Gentle arms cradled him. It was Jojo. He steeled himself for his sentence.

'I wanted to spoil your party.'

'You couldn't, Vincent, even if you tried.'

'Will you ever forgive me?'

'There is nothing to forgive. It is a party.'

Tears filled Vincent's eyes. The nose of Harriet's camera appeared over the table and brought him into frame, immortalising his shameful act forever.

'What have I done?' he sobbed.

Cartier watched Jojo. So, she could forgive. She had compassion in her after all.

'I'm sorry, I'm sorry, I'm sorry. It was such a beautiful cake,' Vincent said. He had cream all over his face and was sobbing uncontrollably.

Little planes continued to drop their bombs of chocolates. Above Vincent's head the table shuddered as nuns leapt to dance with monks.

And all the while Harriet's camera kept rolling. In her mind the credits were rolling too. Mad Chef Runs Amok at Banquet. Vengeful Vincent Slays Rival's Masterpiece in Kitchen Vendetta. She had her pictures. She had her TV. She would get her air time. She would make them all famous.

Cartier wondered how Harriet had managed to drive him to this. He couldn't help feeling some sympathy for Vincent's desperate act of self-humiliation.

'Vincent, get up, get up,' Harriet implored. 'Give the cake one last shot with your cleaver for the camera. Please, Vincent. For me.'

'Leave him alone, Harriet.'

'He's got to do it, Cartier, or he will look even worse. He's gotta do the whole thing. Do it once again, Vincent. Do it for me, Harriet. Now.'

Vincent looked at her and started to get up. Then he stopped himself, and fell back into the carcass of cream.

'Harriet,' he said, 'I am not a buffoon.'

With these final words the cognac hit him in the brain, and he rolled over on the floor and fell sound asleep.

Across the road, at exactly that moment, Marylese closed her eyes and stroked Pascal's head as he thrust into her with long, loving, even-paced rhythms and gasped:

'I love . . .

'You.'

She could sense Pascal quickening. She moved with him and squeezed. The harder she pressed the faster he moved. She wanted to extract the seed of their lovemaking from him. And then, as he poured himself into her, she imagined she could hear applause, hundreds of people shouting, cheering and dancing in joy, and all in happiness at the love the two of them were sharing at last.

The last guests left about four. Jojo, Cartier and Maria sat in the debris, waiting for the clean-up team. They were drinking champagne from the bottle. If Cartier had been less exhausted and had not drunk most of the four empty bottles in front of them, he might have noticed that Jojo had let her guard down and was slumped on the chair like a trucker, with her feet up and a vintage bottle of Mumm between her legs. Her dress was spattered where she had rolled the cold bottle against her chest to cool off. Vincent was snoring loudly at their feet.

'So, was it a success, Cartier?'

'It was a great success,' said Maria.

'Cartier, speak to me.'

'He is too tired. He is too old a dog for these games.'

'He's not. Wake up, Cartier.'

'I'm not asleep, I'm smoking.'

'I hate it when you smoke.'

'Give me one, Cartier,' said Maria.

'Don't you dare, Cartier. I won't have both of you ganging up on me,' said Jojo. 'Where is Mr Lee?'

'He left with that tall American.'

'Good for him,' said Maria.

'I thought Brigitte was going to kill you.'

'She asked me to lunch.'

'They left very early.'

'Marcel told me it was a wonderful evening,' said Maria.

'Did he? Did he tell you so?' asked Jojo.

'What about those nuns dancing on the table?' Cartier said, to no one in particular.

'But do you really think Marcel liked it?' Jojo asked again.

'Even someone with no taste buds like me thought it was a dream,' said Maria, running her foot over Cartier's ribs.

'Why did Pascal not come out for his bow?'

'He had something more important to do,' said Jojo.

'What do we do with this one?' asked Maria.

Vincent snored on.

'I'll sort this out,' Cartier said, and dropped off the table. He yanked Vincent to his feet and shuffled off towards the door. Laying the body in the porch, he went outside to get a cab off a tout.

'You're not leaving him in here like that,' the driver said as Cartier stuffed the semi-comatose chef into the back. 'Either you come with us or I'm not taking him. Not in that state.'

Cartier wondered about going back but thought better of it.

'You said you didn't want him,' Maria protested.

'I said I had been cruel to him.'

'So let the man have some pleasure.'

'He's mine.'

'He's more me than you.'

'Why, for heaven's sake?'

'He's just a bit of rough.'

'Well-hewn rough, mind.'

'It's never bothered you before.'

'I can't be celibate forever. I hope not, anyway.'

'You do fancy him!' Maria exclaimed, partly disbelieving. She swallowed the last dregs of champagne and kicked a paper plane across the floor.

'You are not well matched. You're a nun and he's a rake.'

'I'm not a fucking nun.'

'Oh, all right. A princess in her tower, then.'

'You don't really think that, do you?'

'I just want to see you happy. Besides, if you go off with him, you won't be able to introduce me to any more of your admirers. I like your cast-offs. You are quite useful in that way.'

'You make them sound like old clothes.'

'That's all men are really, dear,' Maria said, trying to sound sage but swaying as she stood up. 'Emotional clothes.'

10

FAME

THE ANSWERPHONE WHIRRED. The message tape wound itself back again. Click. It reset itself. Cartier could hear it vaguely in the back of his dreams. For state-of-the-art technology it was pretty noisy. Whirr. Clunk. There it went again. That and the prattling of vans braking at the junction four floors down. He tried to ignore them and go back to sleep, but the noise was relentless.

He gave in and swung his feet on to the floor of the garret. He looked at his watch. It was nearly three. He had not slept in that late for as long as he could remember. After he had somehow managed to heave the comatose Vincent back into his flat, he had returned to the Circus to check the cleaners and get-out boys had cleaned everything out. Jojo and Maria had already gone.

Cartier had had time for a last coffee at Café Nero with the breakfast shift before he had realised they were all up and ready for the day while he was shaking with a cold tiredness. Getting a hotel room at seven in the morning was one of life's impossibilities.

His Circus suit was flung on the floor. He stuffed it back into the shiny Adney and Jones carrier – very nice carriers they gave with their clothes – ready to go back to the hire shop. He showered and shaved. The razor was blunt. The toothbrush was worn down. The paste was dried out.

This place would have to go, Every time he stayed here, he promised himself he would get rid of it. The bed was wiry and uncomfortable. The curtains said it all. Two dirty miniskirts dangling from a bit of plastic. The only thing you could say in the place's favour was it had hot water and a clean bathroom. The bedroom was crowded out by an overly large wardrobe that bumped into the bed. There was no space to move. Cartier went through to the other room, which was equally sparse and dark, lit only by a dirty skylight. The neon green of the answerphone display blinked at him. 2.48 p.m. Twenty-six messages. It must have gone on the blink.

He pulled on a new pair of dark blue Levi 501s, a black Café Nero T-shirt, a Paul Smith button-down-collared beige shirt and an old soft black leather jacket. He snapped the battery on to his mobile and flew down the stairs. At Café Valérie he ordered two glasses of orange juice, a large pot of coffee and two croissants and cruised the columns of the *Daily Telegraph*. The mobile rang.

'Message waiting . . . Please dial one-six-six,' said the monotonous voice. The screen flashed up thirteen calls. Thirteen calls? They could wait. He would get over to the message bureau and get them to fix the answer-phone in the flat and find someone to give the whole place a once-over with Dulux.

As yet he had not really considered if the Circus had been a success. It was a job done. And he had taught himself, through painful experience, not to be senti-mental about work. Tomorrow he would rustle up something new. He wondered about ringing Josephine to see how she felt things had gone, but decided that could wait.

There was nothing about restaurants in the paper. He paid up, left a £10 tip so the girls would look after him next time, picked up a packet of Gauloises at the kiosk and headed to the serviced offices.

Emma on the front desk looked at him as though he had returned from the dead.

'Mr Cartier. Are we glad to see you.'

She was a large black girl, and when she spoke, her teeth flashed behind the straight lines of vermilion lipstick, which gave the impression she was always smiling when she talked. This time, he thought, she really was smiling.

'I don't know what you guys got up to last night. But you kicked up one hell of a storm. Paula hasn't done nothing but field your calls all morning. She's been trying to raise you for hours. She be real glad to see you, I can tell you. She's crawling the walls. You better get in there and deal with her. Tell me, what was this Circus thing, anyway?'

'We just had a few people over for something to eat.'

'Must have been some dinner.'

Cartier walked into the back room where four girls worked a switchboard next to a row of green-screened Amstrads and some clunking, rattling printers. Paula was the dark-haired one on the end of the row.

'Mr Cartier! Where have you been? You always answer my calls.'

'I was catching up on some sleep.'

'More like a beautiful girl, I'd say.'

'If only.'

'Well, you've got some catching up to do now. You'd better grab a chair and some coffee. You're going to be here for a while.'

The phone rang. She stopped in mid sentence to answer it.

'Jack Cartier International. No, I'm afraid Mr Cartier is in a meeting. I hope to see him in the next half an hour if you would like to leave a message. Yes. Yes. Yes. Yes. Spell that, please. Yes. We'll get back to you.'

She scribbled in shorthand on the pad. Cartier

couldn't make out what it said. He could read T-line –
he had taught himself when he was a waiter. She was
doing Pitman.

'Well, well, well,' she said, smiling. 'Do you want me
to summarise or do you want to take it a call at a time?'

'Just tell me what's up.'

'Well, six newspapers want to interview you or
Josephine before their deadlines, Thames want you in
the studio by six. There are four offers of rights for the
Circus, one in Birmingham, two in London and one
from Paris.'

'What does Jojo say?'

'She's been dead to the world too. The Vicarage say
she hasn't come in yet, and they don't know where she
is. I tried her mobile but the message service is on. I
tried your flat. And your mobile.'

'What else?'

'Vincent Victor has rung twice. He sounds pretty
het-up. Four other people rang to say thank you for last
night and there's a really weird message from Harriet
Huss.' Paula flicked a switch and Harriet's bothered and
high-pitched tones called out: 'I'm doing your job for
you. Where the hell are you? Call me, you tosser.'

Paula gave him the fierce stenographer's stare that
said, 'I'd like to go home some time and I'm not going
to be able to unless we get started pretty quickly.'

'Where do you want to begin?'

The phone rang again.

Harriet supplied the last pieces in the jigsaw. Her
footage of Vincent hurling himself, machete in hand,
into the cake, somersaulting over the top and setting off
all the fireworks, before crumpling in a bespattered
creamy heap was destined to turn the Circus from a
private evening into a worldwide spectacular.

Harriet had worked hard for her fix of air time. After

Vincent had collapsed she had gone straight to the editing suite. She bribed her way into the on-line suite for half an hour, where they were cutting something else, sliced and edited, did a quick voice-over and was back at her office before midnight. Then she got on the phone. She was still on the phone by the time Cartier had woken up.

She had travelled the time zone round the globe. First New York, then Boston, Miami, Chicago, Denver, then Los Angeles and across the Pacific. By nine o'clock in the morning she had worked her way back to Europe, calling the newsrooms and agencies in every capital. Only then did she start on London and the rest of Europe. She had taken blow-up stills and had them on the desk of every national newspaper by motorcycle messenger before anyone got in. And through the morning, the story worked its way slowly up from the bottom of the news list. She was lucky. It was a poor news day. There was nothing better, nothing funnier, nothing in all the world that on that day didn't appeal more than Vincent's dramatic débâcle. And Harriet had the footage. With each showing, the reputation of the Circus was enhanced. In the afternoon features departments were starting to ring her to set up backgrounders. What was the Circus? Who was behind it? Who was there? Was the meal really as good as that? Why has London got this reputation for food? What did Josephine do to Vincent to make him so violent? Where is Josephine? Who is this fellow Cartier? We think he looks really good. Could we do a portrait?

No matter that there had only been one Circus. By the time Vincent had run his famous thirty yards into the cake, the idea of the Circus as part of the living fabric of tourist London was firmly embedded in the imagination of the watching millions. Travel agents from Minnesota to Tai Pai wanted to book the Circus.

By five o'clock, *New Yorker* magazine had commissioned Hannibal Tetris to write ten thousand words on the greatest meal that had ever been cooked, for a reputed sum of $40,000, the highest single commission for a magazine article in its history. Ten minutes later he dictated into his machine:

'This was a meal that drove a man mad. You didn't think cooking could do that? You didn't think food could be that powerful? Then you don't think at all. This was a meal that made nuns dance on the tables. This was a meal to which even the greatest of all the French masters, Marcel Martinez, genuflected. Never will people think of circuses as having animals and clowns after this evening.

'I first discovered the brilliance of Miss Jojo Coltrane . . .'

Whatever tensions had driven Vincent to the point of madness had been expunged in his act of exorcism. He had woken quite calm and penitential. The guilt and anger had been appeased by his public embarrassment. He went about his early morning preparations as usual. He tried to phone Cartier but was unable to raise him. Harriet had rung about ten o'clock, had consoled him first then warned him that the papers were on to the story.

'My best advice is to go with it. Play the whole thing up for all it's worth. It's your only choice. Besides, there's more money in being known as a mad chef than a good one . . .'

He took her advice on board. When the photographers camped outside the Montague he snarled for the flashlights. He brandished his now famous cleaver. And when the reporter from the *News of the World* offered him money for his story, he took it. It was all good publicity. Everyone seemed to like him as the mad, bad chef.

Unaware of how Harriet's pictures had cast him as the global buffoon, he was locked into the day-to-day routine of overseeing kitchen and customers. He had no access to Japanese TV, so he did not see how his face had become the logo to a new cult series of videos of people losing their tempers. (Although, a year later, he would notice many fans of the series turning up at the Montague, anxious to acquire the status of having eaten with the maestro kamikaze chef.) Nor did Vincent find out that he was voted Funny Moment of the Year by viewers of a Korean station. He never discovered that Harriet was to receive fifty pence for every copy of the *Let's Get Started in Graphics* CD ROM which featured his whirling dervish act on the front cover, as sold on the Internet.

Customers mentioned, often somewhat nervously, the newsreels, which had flashed his drunken assault on the cake all round the world. But Vincent could play the mean and moody chef so long as people kept coming to his restaurant.

Reservations soared. In that perverse way of London restaurants, the Montague was destined to become an attraction as that-restaurant-where-the-chef-goes-crazy. When, a few days later, Vincent asked a table to leave and tore up their bill because they said they did not like his cooking, he found himself back on the news pages again. The Montague was booked four months ahead.

The only tangibly hurtful upshot for Vincent was being asked to leave the Academie Culinaire of Master Chefs. They judged he had demeaned the profession. But the Montague was full. So why should he care too much?

He took to answering the phone himself in the afternoons so he could vet would-be customers. To his old customers he was unfailingly charming and solicitous. Unfamiliar names he cross-examined.

'Why do you want to eat here? Do I know you? Is it an occasion? Do you want anything special? Are you serious about food?'

At any hint of lack of respect, he would snarl:

'I'm not sure you are the sort of person we like to have at the Montague.'

This usually brought one of two responses.

'Oh, please, Mr Vincent, reconsider . . .'

In which case he relented. Or:

'I've never heard anything so preposterous in all my life . . .'

In which case Vincent would say goodbye and hang up. But his regular customers approved and enjoyed the added cachet of bringing business colleagues and friends to the one restaurant in London where no one could get in and where the patron was so notorious.

By the time Jojo surfaced again at the Vicarage, the Circus was well and truly on the road. She had worked for this. She had imagined this. But not the way Cartier was telling her now.

'The Circus is news. Turn on the TV. It'll be on the six o'clock news.'

'You're ragging me.'

'Go and check your faxes. These are real offers from real companies. I think Paula's got another one coming in now from Italy. We are going to have to do something. And fast.'

'OK, send me up what you have got. I'll sleep on it. You better get up here tomorrow morning.'

Cartier read the next day's papers on the train with some amazement. Even the *Telegraph* had run the photo of Vincent. And the tabloids were full of it. It was just one of those stories. They couldn't seem to get enough of it. Harriet must have been making a mint.

By the time he arrived at the Vicarage, Jojo was riding the storm. Cartier had forgotten to get the decorators to fix his garret. It wasn't going to matter. There would be plenty of time before he used it again. Josephine was about to shoot him into hyperspace.

A small, brown-suited, bespectacled lawyer was ensconced in a chair by the drawing room desk, rummaging through scrolls of faxes. Mr Lee stood patiently to one side. Jojo was pacing. Her red hair was pinned tightly back. She wore no make-up. She was dressed for corporate battle. The iron fist was back in the velvet glove. Even though she had tried to hide it in a grey smock, as if she had deliberately put that side of her life in a cardboard box on a shelf, the animal sensuality of her movements betrayed her. But the discipline was impressive. In most people, Cartier reflected, one side won out, but with Jojo, the warring sides of her character were both privy and obedient to her will. She was no longer cook, nor gardener, nor hostess, and the emotions that she had been prey to that night in Christopher's were all gone.

'Cartier, am I glad to see you.'

'We seem to have caused quite a stir.'

'Yes, we have, haven't we?' Jojo beamed. 'Harriet, bless her, seems to have done very well.'

She was already somewhere else. She had cast him into the future and was mulling over the best way to break the news. It was her best, do-anything-for-me-as-I-would-for-you smile. She looked like a schoolgirl asking for a special favour. He felt like a fighter pilot summoned to Flight Control to receive his orders for his next mission.

'Come over here.' She took his arm and led him over to the window. 'We are going to have to come to some agreement on this. We don't have much time. You are going to have to trust me that I will sort it all out. Do you think you can trust me?'

220

She looked at him with those emerald eyes and he knew that even more than the flirting, even more than asking to sleep with him, even more than the Circus, this was a real question, one that mattered to her, and that ultimately, whatever he answered, it would cast their relationship irrevocably down one path or another. If he said no, they might never see each other again. If he said yes, then he was entrusting her with his life. The spectre of Vincent came back to him. She might have been proposing marriage, only at that moment it was more.

'I want you and and Mr Lee to take the Circus on the road. I can do the deals and the business side but I can't physically leave here. Nor can Pascal. He has to stay and keep the Vicarage's reputation intact. You and Mr Lee are the only people who can do it.'

'What do you mean, on the road?'

'I've booked both of you for New York on the nine o'clock flight.'

'Tonight?'

'Tonight.'

'That sounds more like up in the air. To do what?'

'There's an offer to set up a Circus in a disused car showroom on Broadway. I want you both to get over there and check it out. If it is no good, try and find somewhere else. Let's do New York.'

'What about my other clients?'

'Cartier, you haven't got any clients.'

He flinched at the dig.

She said, smoothing his ego, 'Or not as big as this. I'll have to deal with any you have got. You can fax or phone me with what to do. You can sell JCA into the Circus. I don't know how long this is going to take and I need you. It is a dragon and somebody has got to ride it. You are the only one who knows it well enough . . . and you are the only one I can trust. We can make a lot of money here.'

'How much did you have in mind?'

'I'll give you twenty per cent and a salary and a bonus . . .'

'Twenty per cent doesn't sound very much.'

'It'll be a big cake.'

'Twenty-five per cent.'

She paused and looked across at Mr Lee, and spoke louder so he could hear.

'And Mr Lee gets the same.'

He remembered something she had said the first time they had met about not liking rejection. She was holding his elbow. She was so close he could smell her. The lawyer looked up. Mr Lee was watching too.

And so it came to pass, as Cartier had foreseen, that the Circus took over their lives and became dots on the map. Cartier and Mr Lee embarked on a world tour. Jojo stayed behind at the Vicarage. She became embroiled in rights, in contracts, in licensing, in leases. At times she woke in the middle of the night, frightened of what she was doing. But the legal wrangling was not difficult for her. Winter had taken over the garden. The new fame of the Vicarage ensured those few extra customers that fulfilled the forecast of her business plan. Sometimes she felt twinges of envy that the two men were out in the real world having all the fun, but she could not find it in herself to be that kind of actress. She was at home with the business. She put in two extra phone lines and adopted Cartier's London agency to deal with calls. She talked to Milan. She talked to Las Vegas. She talked to Hong Kong. And each time Cartier and Mr Lee gave a performance, the selling got easier.

Each country had its own ideas. In Hong Kong they wanted to convert the top floor of the Mandarin Hotel to put on a Circus called the Fireworks of Fu Manchu. In Los Angeles, Jojo licensed a run-down theatre that had been used for auditions and comic turns to be transformed into a permanent Circus in the shape of a Cadillac. Then she persuaded the car firm to sponsor it. In Lyons she licensed a restaurant to give performances of the Circus that covered the history of French restaurant cooking.

The menus changed. The wines changed. The scripts changed. The acts changed, but the idea was the same. And for each deal there was a royalty.

Jojo moved Cartier and Mr Lee around the globe like they were pieces on a giant chess board. Cartier had to be flown in to give his approval of each deal. He checked on the kitchen, on the script, on the place itself, while Mr Lee investigated the standing of each new company. Cartier sent back cryptic faxes:

Hong Kong: *Get better elevator access.*
Los Angeles: *Who are these gangsters? Drop them.*
New York City: *Good boys these.*
Rangoon: *Kitchen hopeless.*
Sydney: *Hate script.*
Singapore: *It's fine. Go with it.*

And at the bottom of each fax he would sign it with love, or with a kiss, or regards (she didn't like that) and she would file it away with the contract and demand the edict be followed, or she refused the deal. He was her eyes on a world which otherwise was just so much paper, so many clauses, so much faxing, so many foreign accents. She felt like a crab in her shell, with Cartier out there as her claws. The world was too far away to care about. It was just business. It was just numbers. It didn't matter. It was no longer personal. The Circus was a game.

Before dawn sometimes she would wake beset by her old doubts and memories. Maria had said that she was turning into a nun. Could that be true? Had she taken holy orders in celibacy?

In a moment of weakness she dressed and went down to the office. In the half-light, while no one was there, she scrawled a fax.

Cartier, do you think I am some kind of nun?

She read it again. And tore it up. He would think she had gone crazy. Or was self-obsessed. She picked up the pen again.

What are you doing?

She slipped the paper into the fax and pressed SEND. She went through to the kitchen. It smelled of disinfectant from the cleaners. She made herself a coffee. She heard the machine beep next door. The paper was still whirring out.

I'm in the bath. What's up?

She laughed and quickly scrawled another note.

I wanted to say hello.

Two minutes and the machine answered.

Hello.

She wrote again:

Do you think I'm a nun?

The machine took longer this time.

Nuns can have fun too . . .

11

MARTINEZLAND

IT WAS 3 A.M. in the hold of the SS *Canberra*. Cartier was still resplendent in his ringmaster's kit: long shiny jackboots; tails uncomfortably rumpled underneath him; spongy, sweaty cream jodhpurs; flashing bow tie still twinkling softly as the battery faded; tall top hat on the sofa beside him; long cane over his knee. He had been wearing the uniform for so many weeks now, it had taken him over. It was him. He caught himself, occasionally, slipping into the awful music hall jargon of the script: 'the most, scintillating, serendipitous sensationally sumptuous . . .'

'You want another drink, Mr Ringmaster?' Mr Lee spoke.

Mr Lee fed the fantasy. He was the minder of the dream. He guarded the cases. He carved the vegetables and the ice sculptures. He looked after the explosives. Customs were a nightmare. 'Yes, I have gelignite, chain saw, and a set of murderous ornamental knives.' Jojo usually fixed it before they got there. One night, in Washington, they had missed the show, locked up in the interrogation room at Customs. The story made the *Post*. Hundreds of angry senators and their entourages demanded their money back. The Circus rescheduled for the next week. After all the fuss, they had to do three dates instead of one. Democrats, it turned out, wanted their own special show as well as Republicans.

Cartier and Mr Lee could pitch a Circus almost anywhere now. They had become seasoned troupers. Normality had been discarded, like clothes left on the floor when they jumped on to this great, squashy, crumpled bed of fame.

Mr Lee pressed the spare costumes for tomorrow and polished the second pair of boots. Cartier sprawled on the sofa, exhausted. These days he always seemed exhausted. His energies were reserved for his performances. For all the glamour of the travel, his life was actually monastically focused. These after-the-show sessions, after everyone had gone to bed, were the only moments he had to himself. Plus Mr Lee, of course. He didn't mind that. Mr Lee was good company. The trouble with the cruise ships was there was no escape. People had nowhere to go home to, nothing to do tomorrow. The evenings just went on and on.

'You have to say, Ringmaster, that although this work is very well paid, it is not good work. One is not with one's family and friends. No mother, no sister, no wife, no daughter. Only the whisky. No woman would let you drink as much as I do, Ringmaster. Not even one of those country and western ladies you listen to.'

'I haven't been drinking that much this week,' Cartier protested. 'Besides, we are famous.'

'And what, Ringmaster, does famous mean?'

'Money, wealth, recognition, status, future. When Marcel died look at how the papers carried the story of the great master chef. He even got a mention in the *New York Times*.'

'He had to die for that.'

'That is a proper tribute to a man, an obituary in the *New York Times*.'

'Is that what you want?'

'I'm not ready to die just yet.'

'If I write your obituary, Ringmaster, I would say

226

you were just a symbol of western decline, a last divertissement for those swept up in the sinking era in the decadent west. You have everything, but you have nothing. You are living in neon. You just flash in the night.'

'We give people a little pleasure they would not otherwise have had. We are entertainers. What is wrong with that?'

Mr Lee dreamed that one day he would return to Thailand triumphantly, with money and a bride. He had developed a singular approach that brought him regular conquests with both sexes, sometimes at the same time. Depending on his mood, one night he might cast himself in the female role and seek out a man, where another evening he would dress and behave like a man himself. Either sex seemed to find him attractive. Cartier kept a tally. When he was successful, Mr Lee skipped their late night discussions and the next day was a panic.

'I'm sorry, Cartier. I just got carried away. All that drinking and food, it just makes me so sexy. I can't help myself.'

Of course he could, if he wanted to ... His seductions were cunning. Through the first course, Mr Lee cruised the tables, carving flowers and animals out of vegetables. When he found a beautiful woman or man, the sculptures became more risqué. A couple embracing, a naked torso, an erect penis. As the meal progressed he could give his seducees a whole series of romantic suggestions before finally inviting one of them away from the dining room.

'That beautiful girl on table four tonight,' Mr Lee said. 'Did you see her? The one with the silk blouse, and the suede boots and earrings. She look at me nicely. I try and talk to her tomorrow.'

'I wouldn't fancy your chances. Texas girls on cruises

227

don't often run off with bisexual Thai vegetable carvers. You do not have enough gadgets in your kitchen.'

'Gadgets I can buy. It is electricity that is the problem.'

'Look on it as a flirtation.'

'I am tired of all these strangers. I would like to have someone I do not have to say goodbye to all the time. I feel like a novelty act. It is not very nice.'

'You could always read a book . . .'

'I get bored so easily. Besides, what is the point of being in a Circus if you can't take advantage of the audience? And I need sex. It is natural. It is lovely. You should try it.'

Fame affected the two of them differently. Mr Lee relished it like a schoolboy. It was fun. He tucked up in Cartier's slipstream and enjoyed his new-found status. People were interested in him. He would get moody if he made no friends in a city or a country. He enjoyed the camaraderie of being with Cartier too. It gave him a sense of balance. He didn't want it to stop just yet, not until he had been all round the world, and if he dreamed of going home, it was in some distant future.

Cartier saw fame as a road crash. Others had taken over. Jojo had taken him over. He was trapped in the wreckage, unsure of the damage to limbs and faculties but secure at least in the knowledge that the blood was still pumping round in his veins. The ambulance was coming. He was the centre of attention. Things were going to get better. He was going to get out of this mess and be cosseted on a stretcher. He was going to get morphine. And then he was going to get to hospital where a whole building of people were waiting to look after him.

If it had been a bad smash, a really serious dose of fame, then he was going to read about himself in the papers. And get cards and grapes and well-meaning

visitors. Fame, he concluded, was damage. He dreaded
the moment the doctor would finally come up to him
and say he could go home and lead a normal life again,
because it would inevitably be with impediments.
Besides, he had no home to return to. Soho would have
forgotten him. But while the sirens wailed, he felt
centre-stage, alive.

'What are you going to do with all your money,
Ringmaster?'

This was a favourite line of conversation. Mr Lee
could not go to sleep at night without running the
question past Cartier.

'You don't spend it on nothing. On nobody. What
do you do with it?'

'You know what I do with it.'

'In the bank. In the bank. In the bank. Always in the
bank. But then what? You got to do something else
with it.'

Then Mr Lee would proceed to spend it for him.

'You buy a Maserati. A red one. They good cars.
Women like men in Maseratis. So maybe you cruise
round Monte Carlo and get yourself a pretty woman.
You take her to the casino. You lose a little money.
You buy her some diamonds. You get really good sex
like that – those kind of women really love a man who
can give them things.'

'Women like that are as dry as a five-pound note. Sex
is like going to the lavatory for them. They always take
a box of tissues to bed. I'll save my money if it's all the
same to you.'

'You just an old miser, Ringmaster. But you better
think quick. I get my Texas woman, pretty soon the
Circus is over and I will be on the beach with the
daquiris and my little children around me, teaching
them to read and write in the sun. You be on your
own.'

Cartier had this vision of the two of them getting old like Del Shannon or Chubby Checker, endlessly going round the world to ever smaller dining rooms, trying to sweep up those last few diehards who just might shell out a few pounds to witness an idea they had first heard decades before. How long could the Circus go on at this rate? At first it had been exciting, but the novelty was starting to wear off. What did a former ringmaster of a gastronomic circus go on to do, even if he was rich? Or worse, if Jojo's grand schemes didn't work out, if he was poor?

The Vicarage fax was insistent. Keep going. Keep going. The next stop was New York again in two days. Three nights there. Then another cruise liner. This one to Bermuda. One night for a private party at Necker. Fly to Dallas for a week. Home to Soho for two days to pay the bills. Jojo might be there. He hoped so. He hadn't seen her for six months and had only talked to her long-distance when one of them was invariably half asleep. Their only other contact was by fax or messages on the answerphone from the office agency.

'New York soon. I like New York. Nice boys in New York.'

'The world, I would say,' Cartier pronounced, 'doesn't look a lot different at three a.m. wherever you are. It is just one big Intercontinental.'

'The beach sounds good to me. Jojo she rescue us soon. She come and get us off this treadmill. You see, Ringmaster.'

'I hope so, Mr Lee. The only way I can tell where we are these days is from the whisky – Glenlivetsville, Lagavulin town, Wild Turkey city. I.W. Harper springs, Laphroaig spa, Bushmills village, George Dickel state. I only have to check the label to know where I am. Christ, what's this we are drinking now? Urgh, this is Chivas Regal. I hate Chivas Regal. What has happened to us?'

★

Cartier watched Mr Lee zigzagging towards him along the deck. He was waving a piece of paper. Behind him the Atlantic stretched out, a great empty sheet of blue running imperceptibly into the blue of the horizon.

'She sent for us. She sent for us. We're going home.' Mr Lee beamed.

Jojo had written the fax herself in her loopy, jagged scrawl that ran right across the page.

> *Meet me Hôtel Martinez, Cannes, soonest.*
> *Nashville cancelled. Love J.*

And there was one X on it. For both of them.

'Hurrah! Hurrah!'

Mr Lee was overcome.

'Maybe we give up all this touring and spend some money. About time too.'

'As you say, Mr Lee, about time.'

After the chill of the air-conditioned plane, the heat outside was as thick as molasses. It swamped them as they walked across the runway, making their clothes soupy wet before they reached the shack that passed for Cannes International Airport. A swarthy man in a green uniform was standing on the other side of the barrier with a placard bearing their names. They hung around for what seemed an age for their cases to come through the purgatory of no-man's-land. Finally they were out. They were free and in France.

The limo was cool again. It purred down the short strip of dual carriageway and glided elegantly to a halt at some lights. It seemed an uncommonly big car next to the buzzing scooters and Fiats, and oddly plush next to the tattered, peeling walls of the narrow back streets.

French cities were always like that, Cartier thought. All the glamour was up front. Go back a few blocks and real life began. The limo swung out of the catacombs of tenements down a long chicane where the houses towered eight and nine floors above them, their balconies filled with washing. Then suddenly they were on to the flamboyant palmed square and down the Croisette. The beach on one side. Rolls Royces and Mercedes parked bonnet to boot on the other. A girl on the roadside in a short skirt and a half-buttoned blouse stuck out her thumb.

'*Putain*,' muttered the driver.

The Hôtel Martinez shone like a white palace in the morning sun. A doorman took their bags and pointed them away from the main entrance towards some steps. Jojo was waiting for them by the pool.

Mr Lee waved his bowler hat and bowed so deeply his forehead almost touched the pavement as his arm swept ceremonially in front of him and his bum peaked upwards between the flaps of his jacket.

'Mistress Jojo. How great it is to be home. Is this home? Where is it? Is it famous? It is by the sea. It is wonderful. I love you, Mistress Jojo. You make us very rich and very tired.'

She gave him a large glass of white wine. He swallowed it in one gulp.

'You know, Mistress Jojo, what I am going to do? I'm going to have a swim.'

He jumped fully clothed into the pool.

'Yippee!'

His hat floated on the azure surface as he dived underneath like an oyster-catcher, his baggy black suit billowing around him. Surfacing at the shallow end, he called to the waiter:

'Bring me a bottle of champagne. I want to know all about Martinezland. I want to swim here in the sun and get to know it . . .'

Cartier, rather more reserved, sat down with Jojo under the parasol.

'It must be jet lag,' he said, watching Mr Lee disappear once more beneath the water. 'We haven't slept for three days.'

'It's good to see you.'

'Is it?'

'I wanted to be here when you arrived, to say hello. But I have some things to arrange. Jean has instructions to look after you. Relax, have a swim and get yourself cleaned up. There is much to discuss and to consider. I am glad you look so well. Mr Lee said you had been drinking, but it does not seem to be showing too badly.'

She lifted her glass and toasted him.

'*Santé.*'

There was no touch, no kiss. She gave him a quick smile and then she was gone.

Mr Lee squelched out of the pool and lowered himself on to the white iron chair beside Cartier. Water dripped from his clothes while he drank three glasses of champagne so quickly he sneezed in the middle. Then he turned his head to the sun and closed his eyes.

The hotel manager had a list of instructions.

'Madame Coltrane has left a change of clothes for both of you in the rooms. You have until seven o'clock. A car will pick you up. You will be eating with *madame* tonight but we have a very fine restaurant here. I hope you will dine with us tomorrow or the day after. We will be honoured to have two such famous gastronomes.'

The public areas of the Martinez were a frieze. The marbled woods, the Art Deco clock fascias, the enamelled mirrors, the zigzag pattern of the carpet, even the deep green seemed an old-fashioned choice of colour. A mural spanned one side wall, depicting a kitchen in action, the cook caught in time with her ladle in the pot.

The rooms were large and had been decorated with a minimum of fuss. They were for sleeping, for staying cool. The bathrooms by contrast were opulently fitted with mirrors, bidets, marble, lush towels, oils, perfumes, scissors, tissues. There was everything you needed, to lather, to shave, to wash, to powder, to groom, to manicure, to wipe dry, to paint. How different, Cartier thought, from those myriad hotels they had been living in. There was no in-room pampering. Not even a TV. The bed, if anything, looked hard. For all its elegance it was a room that knew its place. Cartier could see why Jojo admired it so.

On his bed fresh clothes had been neatly laid out – seven shirts in different shades of cotton; designer jeans in beige and blue; socks, boxer shorts. There was a card beside them from the shop. It read: *De la part de Madame Coltrane.* Cartier noticed the Madame. For the maître d'hôtel it was correct. Had she married? Could she have married without him knowing? Or was it just a sign of respect? What had happened while he had been out there in hyperspace? Would Jojo still be the same person? Did he know even who that was? For that matter, was he?

As they drove up into the hills, the damp, sunny breeze of the Croisette became a deep, smoky-dry cauldron on the back streets and along the messy Route Nationale. Gradually, the air became lighter and richer. It swept up the smells of the scrubby herbs on the verges and absorbed the mellowness of the evening. The limo headed through pine trees on to a rougher road. The pot holes became deeper. Dust blew up behind. And way below, the sea appeared, glittering and calm, between a pair of stubbly hillocks.

Jojo's villa was carved into the hillside, a modest four rooms, perhaps, above a cellar, with a terrace that looked out on the bay. It was set in the midst of a vineyard which was encircled by olive groves.

Jojo was standing at the top of the steps below the terrace with a glass of wine in one hand, a book in the other. She was wearing a crimson dress, a silk scarf around her neck and no shoes.

She walked slowly down to meet them.

'Mr Lee, it is very fine to see you. I have missed our little chats in the kitchen. You look well. The clothes I bought, I hope you are pleased with them?'

Cartier was unused to Mr Lee being greeted before him.

'And you, Cartier. Let me look at you properly. Yes, Mr Lee said you were very tired. It shows a little. You must be getting old. But that girl in the shop chose well for you. How does it feel to be out of uniform? Some of the photos actually made you look quite handsome.'

She took him by the elbow, just like she had done once upon a time in the drawing room of the Vicarage. The view from the terrace was spectacular.

The three of them sat down on cane chairs beneath a huge canvas umbrella. A bottle of wine was ready for them in a bucket of ice. There were some saucers filled with tiny black olives and others with salted almonds. Jojo beckoned them.

'You must tell me all about your adventures. I bet you have had some great times. I have followed your exploits in the papers. You are quite stars in Hong Kong. But first of all I want you to taste some of the wine we have been making here. I need your opinions before anything. Then we will do some business and afterwards have a little dinner and chat.'

Jojo poured the wine and presented Cartier with a glass.

'Tell me what you think.'

Cartier sipped. His thoughts were elsewhere. It was

months since he had seen her. She had made him an international hobo, cut him off from his own world. Yes, she had made him famous, but now what? He had thought about her a million times without ever fully trusting his own instincts. Here she was again. He noticed a freckle he had forgotten to the side of her nose.

'Well, what do you think? Don't just nose it, drink it.'

He did as he was told.

'Very good.' He took a second drink, this time letting the warm tannin roll around his teeth before swallowing.

'I'm so glad. It is from these fields over here. We only sell it locally at the moment, but I have been sneaking some into the restaurant at the Martinez. I think it is charming. Your turn, Mr Lee. Come on, you always had such a good tongue, tell me what you think.'

Jojo had picked out a long shirt in emerald silk for Mr Lee, and he sat there on the terrace smiling like a potentate. There was no sign that he shared Cartier's foreboding that they were on the cusp. Perhaps in his mind he was already on a flight to Thailand or to Dallas.

'The colour is lovely,' he declared. 'The flavour is of blackberries rolled in caramel.'

'Bravo, Mr Lee, you have not lost your touch. Now to business. Let us be serious for a moment.'

Jojo leant forward, and then with both hands swept her hair behind her head and held it in a bun with one hand.

'I have sold the Circus . . .'

Cartier sat up. Of all the possible outcomes, that had been the one he had never contemplated.

'Who to?'

'A media and leisure group.'

'For how much?'

'Quite a lot.'

'What does that mean?'

'It means I can write you a cheque.'

'So we don't have to go back on the road?'

'That's up to you . . . but you shouldn't need to. But I should like to ask something first. I promised that I would share the company with you and I keep my word. But I would like to send something to Pascal and Marylese, so that they can buy the Vicarage together.'

'How much are we talking about for us, exactly?'

'I'm not precisely sure, not to the last penny at least, not yet, but it is about four million . . .'

'Francs?'

Jojo shook her head.

'Dollars?'

'Pounds.'

'For all of us?' asked Cartier, trying to seem calm.

'No. For each of you . . . So two hundred thousand for Pascal and Marylese is not such a horrible gesture, and I'll pay most of it.'

'You are one clever woman, Mistress Jojo,' said Mr Lee.

She smiled coyly. Cartier laughed aloud. Mr Lee looked concerned.

'Mistress Jojo, please, can I just ask you that again? Are you saying that you are going to give me four million pounds?

'I'm not, but a company called International Events is. I had to let them have the film rights, which I didn't want to do, but there you go. I thought we'd all prefer to have it now. There was a chance to buy the Martinez after Marcel died, so I went for it. This is his mother's old house. She left it to me in her will. Besides, I didn't want the two of you out there buzzing round and round the world like astronauts for the rest of your days, did I? Not without me anyway. It is not so much money.

Cannes is full of gigolos looking out for rich women. I need some chaperons.'

'You bought the Martinez?' Cartier asked.

'Only a part of it. Marcel left me his share, which was only a small percentage. I can probably get most of the money together. We'll talk about that. I have an envelope here for both of you. They contain the receipts for the money that I have drafted into your accounts. There'll be more but it will do as something to be getting on with. Shall we have dinner and celebrate?'

She passed them each a dirty-yellow Martinez-embossed envelope.

'You trusted me. Here is some of your reward,' she said to Cartier.

'Mistress Jojo,' Mr Lee said after checking the numbers on the cheque advice slip in the envelope, 'you are a genius.'

'What about you, Cartier? Are you going to say thank you?'

'No. I earned it.'

'Charming as ever, I see.'

Jojo had prepared a simple meal. There was no one to help and she brought out the plates herself. They told her about their night in prison in Washington charged with importing explosives. About Hong Kong where the queue was so long that there was nearly a riot when the back end snaked all the way round the building and went in ahead of the front.

'Half of them had no tickets. They just camped in the dining room and starting eating the table decorations. The people outside who had tickets couldn't get in so they stopped the traffic to get the police. Then someone accidentally set off the cannon. The police thought there was a riot so they charged in with batons, cleared the room and destroyed everything.'

'What was that story about you and somebody's husband?' Jojo asked Mr Lee. He looked sheepish.

'It was nothing. I was just being friendly and he was a bit drunk.'

'But you were in the ladies' loo?'

'Yes, with his wife, who was charming. But when he came in, the other women didn't like the idea of a man in there and so they set upon him. It was most unfortunate. We took him to hospital with four broken ribs.'

'And what did the wife make of it all?'

'Oh, she didn't mind too much. She said if the hospital wanted to keep him in, then I could go back to her place.'

'You are a rogue, Mr Lee. Cartier, did you not teach this man any morals?'

He raised one eyebrow.

They ate as the sun went down over the bay. There was a large green salad with leaves that Cartier had not seen before, dressed in thick virgin oil and garlic. The centrepiece was a *pot au feu* of potatoes, cubed and steamed with red wine, bacon, kidneys and black truffles. To follow was a small local goat's cheese, fresh bread and more of her own wine.

They recounted their other adventures to Jojo's promptings. About the doorkeeper in Jamaica who tried to steal the takings. About the private night for the sheikh and his harem. On the road they had all seemed such great tales to fill in the late evenings. But as the sun went down over the bay, Cartier mused that they all seemed a bit parochial now.

The jet lag and the news of their sudden riches were soporific. Jojo let them drink too much. The stars spread out like a glittering blanket in the sky over them. The conversation became more jagged. She had hoped they might want to go on and celebrate, dancing somewhere.

But they were both past it. She watched them bantering boyishly and finally let them stagger off without her into the night.

Lying back on the black leather seats of the limousine, Mr Lee was bullishly happy, in that unwieldy way before sleep finally sets in after many hours awake.

'I am rich, beyond my dreams. Is that possible, Cartier?'

Cartier was cruising in his mind, grateful that someone else was looking after them.

'Apparently.'

'You want that woman, don't you?' Mr Lee said.

'Do I?'

'You want her. You should take her.'

'Just like that?'

'She don't know what she wants. She's asleep. You got to show her what she needs. Be a man. If you don't show her what she wants, she never going to wake up, and she never going to say yes to you, she never going to know . . .'

'Suppose she says no?'

'So what? That's life. That woman, that brilliant woman who made us so rich, she need to be touched. You don't touch her, she never remember what she been missing. How come you being so bashful anyway? You rich now. You used to be a real pain in London, but you mellowed out a bit. You give it a try. But don't go talking about it, just take her in your arms, sweep her up . . .'

Mr Lee was miming as he spoke. His arms were open and he was kissing an imaginary woman who was sitting on his lap.

'I make sure you do it. Kiss her like this?'

Mr Lee pursed his lips and kissed the night, and chuckled as he canoodled his invisible siren. Cartier gazed out of the window. Tiredness had suspended his emotions. Looking out at the great soup of the cosmos it seemed that some unseen hand had been toying with him.

For Jojo, seeing Cartier again came as a shock. Of course he had always been there in her plans, at the end of a phone or a fax, as part of a memo, but there was none of the stubble, the stale breath and those slim hips.

The comfortable purgatory of the Circus and all its business trappings was gone. Perhaps he wouldn't like her any more? Perhaps all that intensity had just been part imagination. Perhaps she had just used him as an excuse to herself not to bother to go out into the real world. But the Circus was over now. He could disappear completely. She had no more power over him.

She touched the tiny scar on her hand again. She wanted to put her foot down on the accelerator and speed everything up. But then she didn't really know him. And without the Circus what would be left?

Standing under the stars she felt in her mind for the curse. Its power seemed to be fading. Could that be true? She pursed her lips together and blew into the night air.

'Go away. Go away,' she repeated.

She listened for an answer. There was a long silence. She tried to sense it. It hadn't gone, but it was very faint, like it was away, busy doing something else.

The heat woke him. It was gone eleven. Cartier decided to go for a swim. The sun was dazzling. He swam ten lengths in the hotel pool, mostly underwater to keep out of its way. Then he positioned himself in the shade of an umbrella, ordered coffee and tried to read *America Today*.

Mr Lee joined him.

'So, you finally decide to get up. I have been shopping. Look at these. Are they not lovely? Martinez-land is a dream.'

He produced a neat package in elegant paper. Inside was a velvet box with a a gold bracelet encrusted with rubies.

'That must have cost you.'

'So? I am not old miser like you. It is lovely. I like it here. Maybe I stay.'

Jojo emerged from the hotel and stood behind Cartier with her hands resting on his shoulders.

'Good morning. Are you feeling better today?'

'I feel great, mistress, absolutely great,' said Mr Lee.

'If you are going swimming, perhaps you'll take your clothes off this time. Jean, the manager, was a little concerned yesterday. He likes everything to be just so.'

'So it shall be,' said Mr Lee, starting to undress.

'You won't read anything into this?' she said to Cartier.

'Into what?'

'If I kiss you. Because it is not that kind of kiss. It is just to say good morning. It is the custom,' she whispered, brushing her lips against his cheek as she sat down beside him. The way she kissed him did not feel like any custom he knew. She ordered a coffee as Mr Lee dived into the pool.

'How is your hand?'

He held up his middle finger. A fat white crinkle split the tip and ran round the side.

'There is one thing about the Martinez deal you should know.'

'What's that?'

The morning sun, the heat, the long sleep, the days of drinking too much, perhaps just not seeing her for so long, his feelings were a jumble. He had forgotten how precise she always was.

'With Marcel's shares and some of my own money I can raise about sixteen million. I am about six million short. I can probably raise the cash somewhere but it would be much better if I could find someone who had some money they needed to invest. I need some help here. And there's the wine. That could be a good business. The hotel has an excellent reputation but it is a bit old-fashioned. It could be lifted a notch or two . . . and besides, these French people always think they know best.'

'Is that a proposition?' he asked. At least when she was talking money there was never any doubt what she meant.

'Something you might think about for a few days. I wouldn't want to put any pressure on you, either of you.'

'I've only got four million. You make me feel poor.'

'Mr Lee might chip in a bit too.'

She looked at Mr Lee in the pool, lying on his back, face up to the sun, hands to the sides just tapping the water to keep him afloat.

'Is that the deal? You make the money and now you want to spend it for me? I was thinking of going to the West Indies and buying a bar and drinking rum all day.'

'There's nothing to do in the West Indies except loaf about and listen to your brain rotting. I thought you had done enough of that.'

'I've always wanted to have my own place.'

'Cartier, don't be so boring. You are respectable now. You could have a place in a town like this where everybody comes when they have made it. Nobody has any history to speak of around here. You don't have to hustle any more. You are not cut out to be a barman. Besides, you couldn't stay in one place for long without getting bored.'

'I was never bored in Soho.'

'You would be now.'

She withdrew, blushing coyly, sitting back and covering her breasts with one arm.

'Well, we can explore all that. That's why you are here. I'm very happy to see you again. Will that do?'

Jojo went to organise lunch. For a moment she stopped in the shade of the marble pillar. It was cool. She was alone. She was completely alone. There was nothing there. She could have been in a tomb. Her naked feet enjoyed the cold of the marble. She leant against the pillar, letting it imprint its coolness on her side. Above her was this mansion. Over there was Cartier. For a second she realised, like that first moment of waking in the morning, that she was just herself. It felt odd and frightening. A porter passed by and disturbed her. She hurried on.

Jojo insisted they eat the shellfish.

'It is a celebration. And Cannes has the best fish market in the world. I think we should have something simple and sensual. And lots of wine and mayonnaise.'

The waiter came back with a silver tray three tiers high, covered with cork matting and piled with clams, winkles, oysters – Pacific and natives – crabs small and large, a huge langouste, two small lobsters, whelks, matted with seaweed and garnished with halves of lemon.

Mr Lee talked endlessly about spending money as he picked over the clams with a pin.

'I want to buy a Mercedes or a Porsche.'

'Porsches are for spivs.'

'I could make good spiv, don't you think? This afternoon I will buy some more clothes and jewellery. And some suitcases. And a painting. I must have something for the house for when I get one. Something from Martinezland . . .'

Jojo broke a lobster open with her hands and let the juices run down her forearms as she sucked the flesh out. Cartier filled their glasses and studiously ate oysters, stacking the shells in a neat pile to the side.

'Cartier, perhaps you should buy a car?' she said.

'Maybe I'll get a driver instead.'

He watched Jojo eating. She had pronged a new potato on her fork and was peeling the skin off with the blade of a knife. She held it uppermost and sliced it into ovals. Then she smeared each slice with mayonnaise.

'Garçon!' she called. A young man in black was by her side in a trice. 'Can you ask the kitchen please to send me out some basil?'

She resumed her tinkering. This time she took a lobster and flicked the body meat out of the shell, then sliced it, like the potato, into discs.

The waiter returned with a bush of basil.

'Thank you.'

She took one fat leaf off the plant, tore it in two and laid it on the mayonnaise. Then she covered it with the lobster.

'Try this,' she said to Cartier.

'A new recipe?'

'No, it's just for you.'

She held the potato and lobster in her fingers and beckoned him towards her with her free hand. He leant forward. She raised the sandwich to his mouth and fed him with her fingers.

The waiter came back with a tray of three chilled glasses.

'Ah, I wanted you both to try this. It is a basil soup. It is just fresh tomatoes, whizzed, and then put in a muslin so the juices drip out cleanly. I chill it and then chop up a little basil at the end . . .'

Jojo attacked her basil bush again, this time shredding three leaves and throwing them in the soup. She picked up a spoon and swirled them round the clear pink liquid. She passed one glass over to each of them.

'Gosh, that is wonderfully pure,' said Mr Lee. 'Quite marvellous.'

Cartier smelled it. It was cold and fragrant, tart from the tomatoes and pungent from the basil, slightly salty and peppery at the same time.

'No stock, no nothing. Brilliant.'

'These days I find that is all I want – just very intense, very pure, very faithful flavours. I can't bear all those stocks of old bones and all that cream and butter. It just gets in the way. I want to taste what I am eating. The boys in the kitchen were horrified at first. I bought them a juicing machine. They took a bit of persuading but now most of our sauces are just that – juiced raw vegetables mixed with a little grapeseed or olive oil. There's no need to do anything else.

'Do you like it, Cartier?'

'It is the best soup I have ever tasted.'

'Don't mock me.'

'It is fresh and pure, what else is there? There is only so much food can be. Perhaps you have found the best way. Frankly,' he looked carefully over his shoulder to check he could not be overheard, 'I'm not sure I can take all those French sauces any more.'

They collapsed in laughter.

'I am much more comfortable with this approach,' declared Mr Lee.

'Have some more wine. Now tell me what would you like to do this afternoon?'

'I know what I want to do,' said Cartier.

'What's that?'

Cartier leaned over the table. She smelled of the sea. Her face was so close to his, not touching, her eyes roving across his face, looking for little details. Her breath fanned his cheek. She whispered softly, nervously:

246

'Don't . . . please don't.'

He was so close. She was going to say something else. Suddenly he knew that all he wanted in the world was to explore her body.

He kissed her on the mouth, tenderly. She drew back and rested her head on his shoulder for a second. He could feel her trembling, breathing slowly and very deeply, almost whistling, as if some spirit was leaving her. He could feel the heat coming off her body.

He lifted her face up to his again. The touch of his flesh seemed to banish the remains of the spell. She closed her eyes and felt as though she was waking up again. She had found something she had lost aeons ago.

He kissed her again. This time her mouth was open. She sucked him in gently and met his tongue with hers. His lips seemed to cauterise the spell. She felt it vanishing from her head.

Someone was shouting in the distance.

'Bravo! Bravo! Bravo!'

Mr Lee was applauding beside them. And so was the waiter.

'*Félicitations, madame.*'

Mr Lee started to clap. So did the waiters. The nearby tables turned and joined in. For a moment it seemed like everyone around them was clapping with happiness. It was so embarrassing. She looked across at Cartier.

'They take love seriously here,' he said gently.

'Is this love?'

He nodded.

She swept the table clean with her hand. The basket of crustacea toppled over, sending shellfish all over Cartier and on to the floor. The bottle of wine flipped over into Mr Lee's lap.

'Now I can see you better.'

Her eyes roamed his face. He could feel tiny frissons

running through her fingers. She was trembling still. She was biting her lip in an effort to hide it. Little darts of smile caught the corners of her mouth. She was engulfed by an awesome tide of emotions and was reaching out to him to join her in it. Tiny beads of sweat dotted her cleavage. Her hand moved from his face to his shoulder. The fingers slipped under his open shirt and grasped his collar to steady herself. He could feel another tremor as she clasped him tighter. A tear broke in her eye. She was crying.

'I must have been asleep for a very long time,' she said.